The Moonstorm Series

Volume One
Land of the Frozen Sun

Volume Two
Book of Dreams

Volume Three
Destiny's Children

Volume Four
Time Weaver

Volume Five
Death is the Door

Volume Six
Aranae in Red

Special Thanks:

Peter Gawtry
Stephanie Gawtry
Ren Johnson
Chris Mayer
Pat Sullivan
Jack Svenningson
Ricki Terry
Tracy van der Leeuw
Christopher West

ARANAE

IN

RED

A. P. Malloy

The Moonstorm Series

Ardilla Blanca

Cover design and artwork: Mari Fridley Larsen
marilarsen.com

Learn more about the series
and order promotional copies:
moonstormseries.com

The author welcomes correspondence:
apmalloy1@gmail.com

CONTENTS

CHAPTER ONE
Teller

IN THE FUTURE, Jeremiah the Storyteller will ask:
"Where were we?"

And he will take a seat on a smooth-faced boulder.

"Lightning went to the past to meet her ami-kan," a girl in a green shirt will volunteer. Her name will be Natalia. "Now they're going to the future to save Aranae."

"Ah, yes," Jeremiah will nod.

"And Submission and the Bristles are in trouble with Whitetails," a boy who sits at the rear of the assembly will say. His name will be Bo Lin, and he will lounge with others in the grass and stare at the dashing clouds.

"And Lightning's oti-kans ran into the rogue kezel," one of the adults in attendance will add.

"What are oti-kans?" Natalia will ask.

"Big brothers," her neighbor will respond. He will be a pale-skinned boy with a green shirt of his own, and his name will be Sammy. "The orange twins, remember? And Stone, too right? The one who attacked Submission and ran off to the Redteeth."

"Oh yeah. But what about that crabby queen?"

"She's off doing Ozag's business," an older girl will reply. Her name will be Ani, and she will have a question of her own. "What I want to know is what Viktor's going to do. I think he's planning something."

"Yuck!" Bo Lin will say. "I'd rather learn about the

Aranae in Red

bombas." This will meet with general approval from his fellow cloud-watchers, as well as from the new arrivals, a pair of adults and a nursing baby, who will meander into the gathering and settle in the grass.

"What about Captain Monroe and *Destiny*?" Sammy will ask. "That's what I'm wondering."

"Only because you're related," Natalia will object. "Tell us about Maya, and Watt, and Sister Janet."

"I can see we have a lot of work ahead of us," Jeremiah will reply in a sober tone.

"Something tells me," one of the adults will say, "that you'll hear about all of those—if you ask nicely."

"Yes!" the children will reply in unison, some rising to their feet to holler, "*Please*?"

"Who could refuse such a request?" Jeremiah will say, and the corners of his eyes will crinkle. "But before we start, it might be a good idea to think about time."

This will receive a mixed reception, with Bo Lin sticking out his tongue and Natalia rolling her eyes. But Sammy and Ani and others will say "hush!" and "shush!" and eventually, everyone will.

+ + +

"Some people," Jeremiah will say, "believe that traveling through time is like walking from one end of a path to the other. You walk forward, and you're in the future, you walk back, and you're in the past."

"But that's not it at all."

"Others believe that to understand time, you must imagine an awl swimming in a fast-moving river, a current so strong and fast there is no going against it and no keeping up with it. No matter what the awl does, water will be flowing over it, eroding it as all things are eroded that are trapped in the temporal stream."

"This is better, a nice model, and simple."

"Then there are other people who suggest that we think about time as if we were burrowing our way through a giant ball of snow, where the ball is rolling down a steep

A.P. Malloy

mountain and getting bigger as it rolls, picking up more and more snow. We're moving, but the snowball is moving faster, and where we started burrowing isn't where it was a minute ago. Not only that, where we think we're going keeps changing too. We can't stop it, and because it's always moving, so are we. Even if we sit entirely still, the ball rolls on and grows over us."

"Now, that is an interesting way to look at it, and one of my personal favorites. But whether we see time as a concrete thing or an abstract dimension, a flowing river or a rolling ball of snow, there is one thing we know: All life, from the very small to the very large, is traveling; motion is a constant of existence. And in the world of time, in the temporal field as we experience it, all moving things change as they move. All mass traveling through space undergoes transformation, so that as time passes, entropy increases, and this is known as—."

"Is this part of the story?" Bo Lin will ask.

"Yes," Natalia will say. "Get to the good part." But then she will catch the eye of a frowning adult and add: "Please? What happens to Lightning and the others?"

"Well," Jeremiah will arch his brow. "I thought it was interesting. How do you expect to understand the story if you don't understand how time works?"

"They went to the future," Sammy will shrug. "That's all that matters. Who cares how it happened?"

"That is not a very scientific attitude."

"What about thought?" Ani will ask. "My Auntie Poo says time is the movement of thought. We remember the past and imagine the future; that's time travel."

"Your auntie," Jeremiah will wag his finger, "is a smart woman. But your friends are correct; the details are less important than what actually happened. All you need to know is this: within the temporal field, there are all the events that have ever been, traveling along points that extend outward from the Primordial Singularity like an infinitely branching tree. And if you were to step out of the field, or shield yourself from its effects, you'd be able to observe time unfolding, watch the awl swim in the

Aranae in Red

river without being in the water yourself."

"Then—and here is where your point comes in, Ani—in that atemporal world, a world outside of time, you could move to any point in the evolving field, even the future, and do so by simply thinking about it. The journey would be instantaneous, for in the atemporal world, you see, space has no meaning. Distances are measured and traveled in thought."

This notion will cause a hush to fall over Jeremiah's audience. Some will grapple with its implications; others will adopt various expressions of sobriety, hoping to appear wise and understanding, though in fact the ideas will mean little to them. But Bo Lin, with no interest in appearances, will lean forward and wave his hand impatiently, saying:

"All that matters to me is what happens next."

This will be a shared opinion.

"So?" Natalia will press. "What does happen?"

This...

+ + + + + +

In the past (our past, to be clear, although it was the present to her) when Lightning felt the sensation of being removed from the field of time, she was aware for a split second of another Lightning and another Joy, to her left, both looking at other Lightnings and Joys to their left, like mirror images of mirror images cast out beyond sight, each a bit farther away than the one before. And so to her right, all the Lightnings and all the Joys, looking to their right at others like them, just as she was.

The ones to her immediate left and right she felt much akin to, for hadn't their lives been nearly identical? They were like perfect twins, but even now, they were drifting, their destinies becoming different from hers with the passage of time and movement through space. And then they were gone, and the squeezing sensation passed. She gasped for a deep, fulfilling inhalation, and as the world solidified, she had no time to wonder about the Left

Lightning or the Right Lightning in their other timelines. Hers promised to be challenging enough.

+ + + + + +

But to Left Lightning, *she* was Right Lightning, and to Right Lightning, she was Left, and to them both, she was a brief amazement, a fascinating thing about which they could give only moments of thought. What would become of her? Had she traveled to her own version of the future for the same reasons they had? Would she find the same things? If not, how would they differ?

They would never know the answers to these questions, and so Left Lightning went about her business, checking on Left Joy and noting that Left Thunder seemed no worse for having again traveled outside of time. And Right Lightning did the same, and she waited for their hosts to make themselves present, as she knew they eventually would. And both Lightnings, Left and Right, sat close to their Joys as they waited, each comforted in these strange circumstances by the familiar feel and scent of the other. Both Joys rested one hand inside their sling, idly caressing the artifact resting inside.

Had they known it, this is just what the other Lightning did as well, the Middle Lightning, *our* Lightning. In fact, early on, their actions seemed to mimic one another precisely. But as time passed, and the waiting went on, little differences began to appear. The first was when Middle Thunder, rising to four legs, yawned gigantically and asked to no one in particular,

How long are we supposed to wait?

But Left Thunder, after yawning, thought,

How long do they expect us to sit here?

While Right Thunder yawned and wondered,

How much longer is this going to take?

And all three, scowling, began to pace through *Destiny's* cargo bay, wild creatures weary of confinement—but each Thunder set off pacing in a slightly different direction.

Aranae in Red

Similarly, all three Joys buzzed quietly as they watched their Thunder, each note a half step from the others, so that had they heard themselves, they would have sensed a pensive, three-part harmony.

But of course, they could not hear one another, and with every passing second, their unfolding paths grew more divergent, until it would have been impossible to catalog all the differences without telling two more stories as long and complex as this one. Maybe someday in our own future someone will discover and share with us what became of them. But for now, the Left World and the Right World drifted away to meet their own fates, and they took up no more time in the thoughts of Middle Lightning.

And so, they can take up no more time in ours.

+ + + + + +

Did it work this time? asks Thunder. *Because I am good and tired of that feeling! Like my eyes are going to pop out.* He glowers at Joy. *So? Did it work or not?*

When Joy repeats this question, the artifact's answer gratifies them all.

Perfectly. We are where we need to be.

That, thinks Lightning, *is the best news I've heard in a while.* But her tone is subdued, her mind returning to the past and her encounter with Crystal. What good had it accomplished? The brief but disquieting sight of so many other Lightnings, countless duplicates of herself, weighs on her. They must also have their own countless Crystals, mustn't they? Her one act had done nothing for them. And who could say if a similar opportunity would present itself to the other Lightnings, or if they would take the chance even if it did? How many Crystals would still risk a third litter? How many would die in the face of pressure from a wheedling, self-absorbed jabi?

It's beyond me, she settles at last. *I'm not in charge of those other Lightnings—who knows if they were even real?* And she sighs, recalling her ami-kan's smell and the feel of her spikes against her snout. Those hadn't been an

A.P. Malloy

illusion! Whatever the future holds, those memories, and the certainty that she has corrected a tragic wrong—even if only one among a multitude—comforts her. So, with Joy at her side, she waits to learn what will happen next. This is exactly the question Joy is asking the artifact.

As I have said, it replies, *I cannot read the future. The only way to know what will happen is to wait.*

But we should be prepared, don't you think? Joy asks. *Can't you guess what's most likely to happen?*

I suspect, the artifact replies, *that the major will be scanning the planetary system to confirm we have indeed arrived where we had hoped. I also suspect that before he finishes, we will receive a message from the planet's surface. I believe it is most likely that the people of this timeline knew we were coming and knew when we would arrive. I suspect they have been waiting for us.*

What will they do? Will they be friendly?

If not, we will need to leave this time.

And go where? We need their help, yes?

The next line over, or perhaps the one beyond that. But you should know: We can't do this indefinitely. Even with the power of the young Petros, who is currently back in his place protecting Maya's unborn child, there is a limit to how many moves outside of time we can make. At some point, we will be unable to return to our home line.

Then we need to find our answers soon.

No response. Joy clicks a quiet, stuttering tempo, and she runs her hand over Lightning's spikes, trying to calm her nerves. Thunder's pacing does not help, but for whatever reason, Lightning's mind is tranquil. Joy takes solace in this as she wonders: what is the major learning?

+ + +

On the bridge, Javon watches the dynamic planet on the monitor before him, but his mind drifts. Clouds blossom and hurricanes spiral, and all the while, he reflects on the disembodying sensation of time travel. Part of him wishes that recent events had been a harmless 3V show, and he a casual spectator. How much easier it would be had the implausible turns occurred not to him, but to some beleaguered character at the caprice of a script writer. Then there would be no need to explain the things that had continued, one after another, to defy likelihood and acceptance.

"Damn you, Willie," he mutters.

Corporal Skola looks up from his station.

"I am sorry, Major, did you say something?"

Javon turns from the monitor and rubs his temples. He has seen enough.

"No, Corporal. Is everyone in position?"

"Aye, Major. Commander Rickles is on his way to the cargo bay with Doctor MacLean and Miss Nandini. Sister MacLean and Deputy Kim are nearing the brig."

"Doc Foster?"

"She is in the infirmary, sir, as you ordered. Chief Abara radioed to say she will be here in five minutes."

"I don't suppose there's any hope the magister also followed orders and stayed put?"

"I am sorry sir. He insisted on being here."

"Which is where he should be," Magister Healey proclaims, blustering onto the bridge with a sandwich in one hand and a cup of something in the other. "You need to keep me in the loop, Monroe."

Javon imagines a loop around the magister's neck—not for hanging, mind you, but control, like a collar. But who would hold the leash?

"Oh, Chuck, you worry too much. If anything exciting happens, you'll be one of the first to know. But you set a bad example when you can't follow simple instructions. And there's no food on the bridge."

The magister takes a giant bite of his sandwich and is about to gulp from his cup, but at a nod from the major, the nearest security guard relieves him of both, sending the items to an unceremonious end in a waste chute. Magister Healey's face goes red.

"What's the plan, Monroe? What is it we're trying to learn, now that we're here?"

A.P. Malloy

"When Shonda joins us, she'll answer that question for both of us."

But Chief Abara doesn't join them. Instead, her three-dimensional image appears to the right of the major's chair. She is leaning over a viewfinder and pressing buttons, and for a time she says nothing.

Javon bites his bottom lip.

"Shonda?"

The hologram looks up.

"I'm sorry, Major." The chief's voice is rough in a way that can't be explained by bad speakers. Javon knows she has slept no more than he in the last forty-eight hours, but beyond that is the newly minted friction between her and Doc Foster, a thing unheard of—until now. The image straightens its rumpled uniform.

"You don't need to apologize, Chief. But I would love some good news if you have it."

"I think I do, Major. I would have delivered it in person, but I'm double-timing it on the inoculations."

"You're fine, Chief. What have you found?"

"Everything she said we would. Based on her star chart progressions, we've moved to a time well over two hundred years into the future."

Magister Healey puffs up to say something, but Javon raises one hand, palm out like a stop sign.

"The moon?" he asks. "Can you see it?"

"Negative, Major. I don't know where it went, but there's no sign of it. If it really was going to be a threat to this planet, the threat has obviously been averted."

"Thank you Chief. Good news indeed. Anything else? Are we in range to detect habitation?"

"We will be soon. Stand by, Major..." The hologram turns to whisper with an assistant who has appeared in the image. Chief Abara nods and dismisses the assistant even as she turns to flip several switches. "Corporal, are you getting this?"

Corporal Skola checks his readings.

"Yes, Chief. I am now." He presses headphones to his ears and squints, concentrating. "It is a weak signal...

Aranae in Red

but Major, we are being hailed."

"Origin?"

"From the planet, sir, via satellite."

"On speakers."

The voice crackling through the bridge is at first warped beyond any understanding. But as *Destiny* maneuvers closer to the planet, digital mush coalesces into a clear voice. Someone is greeting them in System English. The voice strikes Javon as oddly familiar, and this bothers him. He feels he should know the speaker, and the fact that he doesn't causes him to delay. The greeting is repeated, this time with emphasis.

"One-way video," Javon orders, and moments later a flickering hologram joins them on the bridge.

"Major!" thinks Corporal Skola. "It is you!"

+ + +

Except it isn't. That much becomes obvious the moment the image finally stabilizes. Yes, there is a remarkable likeness, but the man in the hologram is younger, bearded, and not in uniform.

"Major Monroe," the image says again. "Are you there? My name is Magister Jeremiah. I represent the System colonists on this planet. If you are receiving this message, please respond. We have urgent business."

"Audio only," Javon motions to the Corporal, who pushes two buttons and nods his cue. "This is Major Monroe," says Javon. "We come in peace, Magister."

"We know why you've come, Major," the hologram replies solemnly. "May we speak in private?"

"Absolutely not," Magister Healey exclaims, huffing and puffing. "Anything you have to say, you can say to me, too—the *real* magister."

The hologram's expression is stern.

"Is that Magister Healey, Major?"

Destiny's magister throws back his shoulders.

"It surely is, *Magister* Jeremiah—if that's who you really are—which means I co-command this mission. You have something to say? Include me!"

Javon hisses like a leaky tire.

"I'm sorry, Magister Jeremiah," he says, and he stares at Charles Healey with smoldering eyes. *"Our* Magister is a little insecure. But he's not wrong. If you really do know why we're here, you know it's best if I include my entire council in our discussions."

"I do, and I do," the hologram assures. "We suspected you would say that. Will you be our guests on the surface during your recovery time? We can explain everything and answer your questions over a meal."

"A generous offer, Magister, but we're still working on inoculations. We're not prepared for contact."

"We may be able to expedite that process, Major. We've had time to perfect our immunities. Won't you shuttle down? Bring your council—and bring the kezel. Are we correct in believing you have two of them in your cargo hold? And a third guest as well?"

Now it is Magister Healey's turn to hiss, unhappy at how much this stranger knows about them.

"You are correct," Javon replies. "That's not all."

"Yes, Major," the hologram makes a chopping wave with his hand, a disconcertingly familiar gesture Javon had thought was unique to him. "We know all about Janet MacLean—the one from the past. And if she isn't already in your brig, she should be."

"Your advice is noted," Javon replies, and he decides at once to abandon the chopping gesture.

"Thank you, Major. Please, make what preparations you must and join us as soon as you're able. There's no time to waste."

+ + +

In the brig, Deputy Kim stands at a distance from the two Janets who face one another on opposite sides of the barred cell. His finger traces the handle of his holstered sidearm, but this is mere habit; he has no plan to shoot anyone. Still, this is by far the oddest experience of his short life, and he is nervous.

"They are not to touch, stand close enough to touch, or exchange wireless signals of any kind, understood?" the major had instructed, and like a good soldier, Deputy Kim had repeated the orders and taken the handheld meter Chief Abara had given him to ensure compliance. "And under no circumstances is Old Janet to be released, allowed to give anything to anyone, or talk to anyone but our Janet or me. If she starts grilling you, Deputy, tell her to save it for the major."

"Is understood, sir," the Deputy had replied, and as always, he meant it. He didn't need the major's stern tone to inspire obedience; he lived to enforce.

But thus far, no enforcement is required. Chief Abara's meter blinks serenely in his left hand, and the two Janets are three meters apart, the Old sitting on her cot, while the New stands and stares. They haven't spoken yet, gauging one another through the lens of silence, perhaps curious who will be first to speak.

In this case, it is Young Janet.

"We believe it worked," she says.

"You will need incontrovertible evidence," Old Janet replies. "Not belief."

Young Janet arches her eyebrow.

"That is our plan."

"I suppose the major intends to meet with the natives? I should be allowed to join them."

"That will not be possible."

"Why did you come here, then?"

"To gather information. Before we meet with the Aranaean colonists in this time, we want to be prepared. What should we be asking them? What should we be aware of? Are there any risks?"

"We are in a time and place foreign to me," Old Janet replies without emotion. "I can't say what you will find, nor what risks there might be. As for what you should ask, you already know. I've given you all the data relevant to the rogue moon, and the questions are simple: at what point in its orbit and at what location on its surface should the detonation take place? What magnitude should the force be? Will any debris from the explosion pose a threat to the planet? What perturbations have been documented in the four other lunar orbits as a result of the rogue moon's absence?"

She stops and looks at the deputy.

"Am I forgetting anything, Mr. Kim?"

"Is to be saved for Major," he replies reflexively.

Old Janet surprises him by closing her eyes and bowing her head, sighing like a person fending off tears. The deputy isn't a soft man, but neither is he heartless, and he is moved by the sorry state of this creature, the chaplain to another Garrett Kim in another timeline. He wonders if she had counseled that deputy out of his grief when his girlfriend had left him for a senior officer on Luna. He wonders if she had been as kind and attentive in her own ministry as the Sister Janet who had pulled him back with her words when he had been one trigger's length from suicide. She is a disheveled wreck, frankly, hair filthy, glasses broken, smock rumpled and stained. But no one has bothered to help her clean up; no offer has been made to see if she needs medical attention or her glasses replaced. He wonders at this, for the major is known to be a gentleman of the highest order.

And yet, dutiful to the core, Deputy Kim cannot himself ask these questions or make these offers, and before he can suggest it to his Janet, Young Janet, he receives a private message from the major, relayed directly to his aural implants. He listens carefully, then signals Young Janet.

"If is nothing else, Chaplain, we're wanted."

"*Is* there anything else?" Young Janet asks Old.

The latter looks up, removing her lensless frames.

"This isn't our future," she says simply. "It's someone else's. You shouldn't assume anything—and you should all be armed."

Young Janet accepts this suggestion with no remark and pauses only a moment before turning to leave the room. Deputy Kim follows close behind, but he turns

Aranae in Red

and nods at Old Janet before doing so. It isn't technically a violation of orders, and it eases his conscience.

+ + +

While Thunder paces the cargo bay and Lightning tries not to dwell on all the possible ways this bizarre circumstance could end badly, Joy sits with her hand in her sling and focuses on Illumination.

Is there another Book here? One like you? she asks. *One that belongs to people in this time?*

Trust me, it is one of the first things we scanned for. But as far as we can tell, there is not, and I can't say why. There are Readers, however.

Will we meet them, then? The other Readers?

Perhaps.

Joy considers the thought of other Readers, and she clicks a quiet but nervous tempo.

How many are there? What are they like?

Four adults, six children that we have identified.

Joy's antennae tingle, and she buzzes.

Any like me? An anom...anoma...a hybrid?

One.

Is she nice? Will she like seeing me?

It is not certain that she will see you at all. Our role in this mission remains to be decided. We may spend the duration just as we are.

Joy whistles. That is entirely unacceptable. If others are going to visit future Aranae, she is determined to join them. They couldn't refuse her! She is their only channel to the power of the artifacts.

They can't do it without me, can they?

If by 'it' you mean travel outside of time, to be technically precise, they need both of us.

Then I'll make them! They can't say no!

The Book may have feelings on this issue, but of course, it offers nothing in reply.

Can they? Keep me here against my will?

You might be surprised at what humans think they

A.P. Malloy

can do—no matter what the evidence suggests. They are a prideful species, singularly egocentric.

Humans! I don't think very much of them.

Lightning stirs at her side as if waking from a nap.

Careful, she thinks. *That one slipped through. If I can sense you, some of these humans you're not so fond of might sense you too.*

Joy's tone is petulant.

You feel the same way; I can tell.

No argument. But have I ever told you what Ancian used to say about prudence?

I don't even know what that word means.

It means there's a time and a place for restraint. "Brave doesn't mean stupid." Those were her words. And right now, we need human allies, not enemies.

Joy's eyes grow dim, and her low buzzing reads like an apology. The Book has never mentioned Prudence, but it has on numerous occasions warned against Pride.

I understand. I just want to go home.

We're doing everything in our power to make that happen, Maya Sharma thinks as she enters the control room on the other side of the grated partition. The one named Watt joins her a moment later. Both are clad as usual in their peculiar orange suits, their faces distorted by the clear surface of their headgear.

Thunder strides forward, curling his lip.

Then let's be about it, he growls. *We're tired of this adventure. Haven't you learned what you need?*

Not yet, Maya acknowledges. *Almost. We're going down to the planet. You're invited if you want to come.*

To which the answer is immediate and unanimous, three thoughts as if from one mind:

Yes!

Chapter Two
Stage

IN THE PRESENT, the bomba brood huddles in and around the Eye Tower. There are chicks grown to full flight, mature, muti-hued adults, and elders faded by time. The first two of these groups have split into six different squadrons, each preparing to take a separate route to Congress, the mighty gathering of broods from every continent. This time-honored tradition is normally a celebration, but it is now a somber affair, absent the usual flapping and squawking that would have filled the maison with revelry. The only thing filling the dome at the moment is the scourge of the white worms, which reports indicate are multiplying as they consume the bomba's precious stores of awl and rixli.

Ansel, Head of the Brood, has not returned.

He will not find them, thinks Ilda. *You sent him on a fool's mission, and we will lose both our sons because of that kezel and its deformed companion.*

Oracio is too tired to disagree. The flight from the maison to the Eye Tower had, for many of the elders, been no flight at all, but a long, arduous walk, followed by a mountainous climb that had claimed the lives of Ector and several others. These losses, following close on the heels of Ari's death—and that of his companions Illari and Arvie during the fight against the worms—suppresses any talk of returning to the dome for revenge. Too many have perished already, and no amount of anger can overcome such an unfathomable enemy. Crewels had been effective, but these are in limited supply—and the worms possess a multiplying power that can't be explained.

He will be back, is all Oracio can think, and he numbly watches the brood form into groups. A leader from each squadron approaches.

We are ready, thinks Onri. The others bob their heads, but the tone of their thoughts is subdued.

Should we wait for Ansel? asks Urbie.

It is Ilda who replies, acerbic and abrupt.

Can you not manage? Should someone else be chosen? Wait any longer and you will miss Congress!

Urbie hisses, but he bows to show deference. A northern brood has never been late to—much less missed—a bomba congress. That he might be the cause of it is unthinkable. And yet...

Surely, he dares, *waiting until after the Contraine would not be so great a delay.*

Ilda sticks out her tongue, but Oracio considers this. His mate is not wrong. Already they have waited out the passage of the orange moon, the Flyer, and Congress will start with or without them. But Ansel deserves to be at the helm of the brood.

After the Contraine, Oracio agrees. *He will return.*

+ + +

Soon enough, red and blustery, the Contraine sweeps its wrong-headed way across the sky. The cowering bombas tremble inside the Eye Tower, waiting for their shelter to be blown away, for the tower sways in time to the storm's furious tempo like a lock-kneed dancer. In the maison, they would have enjoyed the tempest as a spectacle, perhaps even watching from the Window, confident in the dome's protection. But here, they huddle on the ground level and mutter, none able to sleep.

When at last the Contraine has passed and they peek out from the tower, deep snow blankets every valley and peak, but Ansel is nowhere to be seen.

+ + +

And still, they can't make themselves leave.

Three whole sleeps the brood dillies and dallies, inventing reasons to stay and often looking to the sky.

Eventually, Mother Green passes overhead, who bombas know as the Egger, and she is joined by the violet Awler, dumping snow and, far to the south, concealing Lieutenant K's escape from Cyclonia. The moons have long since gone their way when the sad truth becomes obvious to all. They can wait no longer.

You must fly, Oracio thinks wearily.

We must fly, Onri agrees, *and perhaps when we return...* He cannot continue. Some of them will not return, a fact of life for the migratory creatures. And what would they find, those who did? How many of their elders would remain, given their current plight?

With no fanfare or pageantry, three of the squadrons prepare to fly east, three to the west, with Onri leading one, and Ubert, Eron, Azel, Urbie, and Al leading the others. One by one, the squadrons depart, each waiting for the one before to vanish over the horizon before themselves taking to the air.

Soon, only the elders remain.

+ + +

You blame me, thinks Oracio.

I blame the kezel and the aberration, Ilda replies as she searches vainly for rixli and grass.

But you know they would never have come to the maison without my assistance. And Ari would still live.

What do you want me to say? That I forgive you?

Oracio bows his head. How could he expect such a thing when he can't forgive himself? The consequences of his actions have snowballed beyond pardon. Ansel...

He picks listlessly at bitter lichen and watches his

companions quest for food. Finding no solace in company, he rises and begins a solitary climb up the tower's broken stairs. He has not been this way since escorting Ari and Ansel many moons ago, but he does not climb in a spirit of nostalgia. He simply wishes to be as far away from the others as possible, and up is the only option.

Ilda watches him go.

The first flights of stairs have suffered damage, with broken rails and chipped edges. He slips and stumbles and curses himself, but he has climbed many stairs in his life, and eventually, he enters the uppermost level, where, just as he remembers it, the Eye stands waiting. He moves stiffly toward the device but has no heart to look through it. Instead, he hop-flaps onto the window ledge and spies the world below. His feathers bend in the wind, and he must squint his eyes nearly closed. So gusty! So unpleasant! If not to use the Eye, then why had he come here?

To jump, he thinks. *Jump and not fly.*

Yes, that had been the reason. His pain was too great, the guilt he bore too heavy. He had invited disaster into their home; his curiosity had killed Ari and how many others? None would forgive him, and why should they? Then he had sent Ansel, proud and morose, on a mad quest to learn the whereabouts of the masked kezel and her companion. For what reason? How could that knowledge be of use?

Cursed, he thinks, and he sways near the edge. *Every step I have taken since that time on the kish plains, cursed to be the brood's ruin. What point, life?*

Ilda wouldn't miss him. Best to leave now.

He leans forward and closes his eyes.

You are as daft as you are wrong, someone thinks, and he turns to see Ilda, laboring up the final steps. *Do not also reveal yourself as a coward. Step away!*

You should have stayed with the others, he thinks.

You should have given me more credit! Did you think I was unaware of your intention?

All the more reason to let me go.

Aranae in Red

Step away! Would you burden me with this loss as well? Are you so selfish?

I suffer! I can see no future that is not pain. I can see no way past the guilt of what I have done.

Then let me do the seeing. Step down! Or are your feelings all that matter?

Oracio's head droops at the end of his long, crimson neck, and he shudders, though not from the cold. He had come close to making another terrible decision. Would his hubris never end? He steps, feeble and stiff, down from the ledge and slumps to the floor.

Ilda moves toward him and sits, their feathers touching, and they remain like this, sharing no thoughts. For what could they say? Sitting is all that makes sense now, sitting and silence, and after a time, sleep. And that is what they do, until at last, the wind subsides, the sky grows blue, and they are wakened by a raucous cackling.

Ansel has returned.

+ + + + + +

The bomba squadrons, half traveling east, half west, have thousands of kilometers to fly before reaching the continent of Primaqua and the shores of the Ebisu Sea, site of Congress. The journey could have been greatly shortened by flying across the lit face of Aranae, but that would mean crossing the Aeolian Waste, an enormous abiotic zone directly beneath the sun, deadly hot and dry, choking with wind-driven sand.

Instead, they aim for Primaqua by circling the Waste, staying within the habitable ring where water and food are plentiful and the sun rides at thirty degrees above the horizon. Those traveling east will cross Indrani Major, part of Aranae's largest ocean—what scion refer to as the Great Saline. At the midpoint of this maritime voyage, their prize will be the islands of the Allery Chain, home to their favorite foods and few enemies.

And there, briefly, a respite.

Their westbound companions will cross the salty

waves of Indrani Minor, only stopping briefly at The Flemish, a small continent dense with scion. Crossing the Kynd will bring them to Ohodune, the planet's largest habitable continent—though not the oldest. That honor belongs to Primaqua, original home of bombas, site of Ebisu, Sea of Congress, and the ultimate reward for those brave and fortunate enough to complete the journey.

Circling their opposite ways, each of the squadrons will join with bomba broods on the other land masses, from tortured Madragall to the tiny islands of the Khuzamaya. Their numbers will grow, their formations filling the sky with rainbows and emeralds. And when at last they reach the shores of Ebisu and are reunited, none will be able to count the bombas occupying every meter of beach, but none will care, for they will be joined in Congress and will be too busy for counting.

Why does this matter, you ask?

Why does any strand in the web matter?

But to answer your question, there is this:

On their way out from the maison, fanning across the continent known as Ibedos, they see many things. There are kezel in conflict on both sides of the wedge. A company of scion moves far from its usual range. And there, beyond belief, are rumidelchia, engaged in occult business. These things they note but do not pause to investigate. All will be discussed at Congress.

+ + +   + + +

Eron's squadron passes over Whisker Lake and the hotly contested border of Bristle and Whitetail territory, but they go unnoticed by the kezel below.

One of these is Brook. She stands atop the Brills, accrete covered slopes overlooking the lake and the Bristle home caves. She is flanked by two bibija Bristles, Stitch and Pitch, both filled with doubt.

'Too inexperienced,' she thinks to herself. *That's what they believe. 'She doesn't know what to do.'*

And if the first part of that claim is yet to be prov-

Aranae in Red

en, the second is undeniable. For the Whitetails have her in a tough spot, and her next move is unclear.

Tell me again, she asks Stitch.

All I can say's what I saw. A troop of Whitetails moving southwest toward the home caves.

Size?

Big. Real big. Moving slow but right at us.

It's not like them to be so bold. Pitch flexes and relaxes his claws as if yearning for a target.

And why send Piedmont and Fluvial? Brook wonders. *Why the promise to stay off our toes?*

The promise was probably a lie, thinks Stitch. *See if you pulled any fighters away from the Brills to the Skull.*

I didn't.

No, and good thing. But you did let those two Whitetails into the Skull, get a look around, tally fighters…

Yes, thinks Pitch. *Your api wouldn't have—*

Don't think it! Brook bares her teeth. *They came in peace. Squall wouldn't have left them out in the storm.*

Maybe, but it's a fair bet they were spies. Ran back to the Big Fork as soon as possible.

Brook's tail lashes.

It hardly matters now. What do we do?

What else? Stitch asks. *Put out the call! Howl for all we're worth! Everyone who can get here needs to. If they overrun the Brills, they'll dig in, and we'll never get 'em out. We'll all be stuck living in the Skull.*

Yes, thinks Pitch. *Isn't much of a choice. Everyone needs to be called south.*

And the ones who are *at the Skull?*

Them too—the Bristles at least. Don't suppose the Sugarfeet'll move without their chief, and Submission's in no shape to march.

Fine, thinks Stitch. *I'll send the message.*

Brook clashes her jaws.

Hold up! Who gives the orders around here?

Well? thinks Pitch. *What's it going to be, then?*

Howl like a champ, Brook replies. *That's what. Every able-bodied Bristle needs to be here when those rot-*

A.P. Malloy

ten Whitetails show up. But I'm going north.

What? Why?

Call it intuition.

Chief, thinks Stitch. *Folks won't like you not being here when the fight starts. Sends a bad message.*

I'll be back. When Vale gets here, he's in charge.

Chief...

But Brook's mind is set. In moments, she is jogging down out of the Brills, heading north. Behind her, Stitch and Pitch raise the call, and as she jogs on, she passes bristly-tailed clanmates heading in the opposite direction. Some pause as if to inquire about the alarm—or her destination—but she hastens on. 'Intuition,' she had thought, but fear is closer to the mark.

When Brook arrives at the Skull, all that remain are the Sugarfoot contingent and Vale, grizzled and scarred. He bares his teeth at the order to return home, but he doesn't disobey.

Not gonna be much fun at the Brills, he thinks when he learns about the large contingent of Whitetails. *Lot easier staying here.*

We'll see about that, thinks Brook.

+ + + + + +

The bomba squadron led by Urbie stays just south of Ozag's Hold, for a derka soars threatening circles over the dam as if searching for something, and they do not wish it to be them. The rumidelchia they spy far below intrigues them greatly, but no curiosity can halt the squadron once it has taken wing.

The rumidelchia—who is Lieutenant K—notices the bombas, catalogs their appearance in a millisecond, and analyzes its meaning. But he has limited experience with bombas, and as they fly on without pausing, he relegates them to his long list of 'not my problem.'

The derka is a different story.

He brandishes his steel pipe.

"Come get it," he dares, glad when it does not. But

neither does it cease its hovering and circling.

An android appears at the base of the tower, dressed, beyond explanation, like a French maid. What in the world? It waves at him, pointing up at the emerald threat and holding the door open like an invitation.

"Aw, scrap it," the lieutenant grumbles, and as the derka swoops lower, he makes his way back to the tower, senses on high alert. "Hello, friend," he waves.

The fancily dressed android does not respond but moves aside, allowing the lieutenant to enter and letting the door swing shut the moment he is inside.

Clang!

They stand appraising one another in the gloom.

"Nice outfit," the lieutenant says, and his grip tightens around the pipe. "So. What now?"

But the android makes a creaky about face and limps away without response, waving for the lieutenant to follow. Its gait is slow and unsure, and it has only gone a few meters when it trips and falls, clattering awkwardly to the floor like a stack of cartoon dishes.

"Helphelphelphelphelphelphelp," it calls out, tinny and frail, and it transmits a distress signal like an interference cloud. Lieutenant K hurries forward.

"Easy, friend," he says, reaching out a hand.

But the android's distress signal is more than that; it actually *is* an interference cloud. It temporarily stymies the lieutenant's sensors and prevents him from recognizing his danger. Even as he leans over to lend assistance, twelve camouflaged scion approach, stealthy but quick, six of whom carry a woven sheet between them. As he is about to take the android's hand, they leap forward and drape the sheet over him, swaddling him in a stubborn, adhesive cocoon.

"Chyort voz'mi!" he curses, nearly falling. But he is no jabi kezel unable to reach a cutter; he is a synthetic combat unit. Quick as thought his fingers transform to blades. Up he slices, down he slashes, and away he tears the sheet, swearing as if to win a trophy.

The scion remain camouflaged and suppress their

agitated whistling, turning quickly and spraying a black mist that douses the lieutenant. His work suit melts away, and tendrils of flame lick their way from his knees to his shoulders. He drops to the floor and rolls, his steel pipe clanging. A layer of synthetic skin sheds in seconds, the charred cells powdering the floor as he leaps to his feet, naked and bald—but no longer on fire. The scion circle him, and now they chitter anxiously, for this is a new type of enemy, and they worry. Will bites have any effect? Their ally, the android maid, has tottered off toward the stairwell; no help there!

They will strike and bite, their leader thinks.

But with the android safely removed, the lieutenant can now sense perfectly well—not thoughts, but body heat and motion. Camouflage is useless, and he is toasted, not cooked. When the scion attack, he ducks, dodges, and leaps, smacking one adversary with his pipe and kicking another as he hurries to catch the escaping android. Too late. It has disappeared into the stairwell behind a thick door, locked and impenetrable.

"I'm not done with you!" the lieutenant hollers. "Tricky old tin can!" And he hammers at the door with his pipe. But his threats are empty, and the scion, it appears, are not done with *him.* He turns to face them, his expression twisted by rage and charred skin. Two minutes seventeen seconds, he calculates. That is how long it will take him to end this threat. He plots the first five moves, crouching to attack.

And the door opens behind him.

"Drop the weapon," someone says. The voice is high and soft, but oddly forceful. Lieutenant K doesn't need to turn around to know he is the target of a loaded firearm, but he slowly places his pipe on the ground and turns anyway, his hands held up and open.

The scion chitter at his back and inch closer.

There, framed in the doorway, is a boy, no more than ten years old, his pale face pinched and dirty, his red hair wildly disheveled. But his hands are steady. The barrel of the weapon he aims doesn't waver.

Aranae in Red

+ + + + + +

"Destiny," Ensign Morales commands. "Patch your sensors through to the infirmary."

"You're angry at me," the ship replies.

"There's no time for that. The vessel you've detected is an enemy—a very dangerous enemy."

"What do they want?" asks Delta One

"Destiny. They want Destiny. And any resource they can scavenge from the planet."

Captain Morales lies on the exam table, his eyes closed and his head wrapped, He wakes slowly and looks around the room, seeming confused at first.

"I fell asleep again."

"Yes sir. Here, take your meds."

He sits up gingerly and drinks the concoction with an ugly look on his face.

"Worst breakfast ever! How long was I out?"

"Several hours. We're nearly at Dansim."

"Why do they want me?" asks Destiny.

"No good reason," the ensign replies, and she checks the captain's reflexes. "But plenty of bad ones."

"They'd love to get their hands on us too," says the captain. "You know, just for the record."

"They can't have us," Destiny objects. "We have a mission to complete."

The ensign stows the last of the medical supplies and closes the cabinet. The scuters observe carefully, moving to keep her in a tight ring.

"They don't care about your mission, Destiny! And if you can see them, it's only a matter of time before they see you. Please! Send your readings to the infirmary so I know what they're doing."

"Aw, skeebies," the captain says. "We know what they're doing. Once they've scanned the system, they'll plot an approach. I give us less than an hour."

The infirmary's monitor blinks to life, dotted with different-sized points of light.

"Yes sir," the ensign points. "There they are...stationary for the moment. But I agree: once they realize there are no planetary defenses, they will approach. Unless they've already located us, in which case, they'll just come directly here."

"What will they do?" Delta One asks.

"Oh, not much," replies the captain. "Just disable and board Destiny, that's all. Tow her back to one of the Guild shipyards, collect a huge bounty, and be galactic heroes. Once they've pillaged the planet and gotten us out of the way, of course. Probably out the airlock for me. Don't ask what they'll do to Morales."

"But we have a mission," Destiny objects.

"So does everyone, beautiful."

"I have two pulse mines left. Would they help?"

"Sure, those and a pea shooter and we'll be set."

"You are making a joke."

"It's how I handle stress."

"I know about that. It's called a coping mechanism. But it isn't very helpful. Should I move us around to the other side of Dansim?"

"The moon would hide us," agrees the ensign, "but it would also prevent us from seeing them."

"If they approach, I will take us to the surface."

"No!" the ensign calls out. "Destiny! You weren't designed to land. Even if you survive re-entry and land safely, you'll never get off the ground again."

"I don't think she cares," the captain frowns.

"I will land safely, ensign," says the ship. "If I have your help. We've run all the simulations. And I don't need to get off the ground again. If I land in the correct location and overload my drive at the correct time, all the rest will take care of itself."

"If?"

"The optimal location and time for detonation remains unknown. Sister Janet promised to return and give me that information—and I so want her to see me fulfill the mission. But this new ship may mean there is no time to wait. If it approaches, I'll have to estimate and overload where and when I think is best. Say! Maybe if we let them

Aranae in Red

get close enough, we could destroy that other ship, too. Wouldn't Sister Janet be proud?"

"Is there a part of that plan that doesn't involve us being vaporized?" asks the captain.

"Not if we want to succeed."

"Well, shoot," says the captain. "If that's the way it is, I guess I better say my last prayers. There a wheelchair around here, Ensign?"

"Yes sir." And she disappears into the next room followed by half the team of scuters.

"Where are you going?" Delta One asks.

"The chapel, of course," replies the captain. "Destiny's soul might be ready for heaven, and I know Morales is set, but mine needs a polish." He collapses into the chair the ensign wheels into the room.

"Sister Janet would like that," Destiny says. "The chapel was her favorite place, you know. But you mustn't stay long. When I've maneuvered into position, I'll need you both to help us land safely."

"What about me?" Delta One flails his arms.

"Don't worry, Shiny, we'll pray for you too."

And so, followed by half the scuters, Ensign Morales pushes the captain out of the infirmary and down the hall toward the nearby chapel, the one room in this part of the ship with no cameras or microphones.

+ + + + + +

Piedmont and Fluvial are not treated poorly by their Sugarfoot hosts—aside from being kept in a hole. They are given sufficient food and water, a pair of talihew hides to lay on, and Cliff as company. Fluvial stretches out on her hide, eyes closed, though she is not sleeping. Piedmont's discourse makes this impossible.

Ya see now, he thinks, looking up at Cliff, *them gutted plumpies I's been tellin' yous 'bout, they don't care fer the shadows, no-ee! But you's a regglar smarty-like, I reckon, so you's already up on that news, yeah?*

Actually...no, thinks Cliff, who has never heard of

a gutted plumpie and admits as much.

Well-ee! That's a cuz what I's been sayin.' They aint no friend o' the shadows, see? Love them some brightly ol' sun times, layin' on ther backsides 'n' warmin' ther bellies all the chance they can get. You aint never gonna see no gutted plumpies up in these parts, what within all the shade 'n' whatnot—how it usta be, I mean, not now within all the 'cretes burned up black 'n' all, but anahoo, Clawpaw, let's not mistake: they aint gutted plumpies 'til they's been gutted, see? Til then, they's just plumpies. Gotta catch 'em, give 'em a good bitin,' then split 'em down the middle and scoop out the insidey parts— can't eat them, no matter what you's a mighta heard (Cliff has heard nothing)—*and hoo-ee! Then they's proper gutted. You know what next?*

Cliff does not.

Next you stuff 'em! Yeppir, I said it. With whatever you's a happen to have 'round, you know not dirt or scales or nothin.' Ol' Piedmont's a 'talkin' 'bout eatable things, see? Like you maybe got some crushed ol' caepod shells and yer thinkin' 'What 'm I gonna do with these?' Or mebbe thers a patch a them berries yer ami-kan's always goin' on 'bout how they's good fer ya, even though they taste like a tail end, see? But you stuff yerself a gutted plumpie with any o' that like—things you can eat but mebbe don't want to so much—and leave 'em to set out in the sun for one whole cycle and kerploofy! You's got the tastiest thing you ever gobbed inta yer gobbler.

It does sound delicious, thinks Cliff.

Hoo-ee! You can say that four time four and it'll be just as truthy the last time as the first. Ol' Fluvial here's one o' the best at catchin,' guttin, and stuffin' a plumpie, aint it so? Sure-ee! Piedmont answers himself when Fluvial rolls over and pretends to snore. His thoughts grow still as he gazes at her, and he sits on his haunches, his shoulders slumping.

Any news on that ol' Whitetail fuss on the Bristly side, hm, Clawpaw? Any words to share?

No sir. We've heard nothing new.

Aranae in Red

Ya don't blame us now, do ya? Ol' Piedmont 'n' Flu-vial? Don't think we's a part a that fall-dee-rall?

Are you?

Course not! Hoo-ee! We's been over this, Clawpaw.

Then no, sir. I don't blame you.

But we's still landed in this ol' pit, aint we? An' Flu-vial's back don't ker fer such hard 'commodations.

I know, Cliff replies, *and I'm sorry.* For he has grown to like Piedmont, the only bibija who has ever given him so much attention. *I bet once things get settled you'll be let out to go as you please.*

Oh, sure-ee, I spose it's so. Or mebbe things get set-tled the wrong way and we's left to starve 'n this old pit. Oh, buddy! You's not gonna let that happen, yeah? Not gonna let yer ol' pal Piedmont wither 'way in a derned hole, or poor Fluvial here? Never hurt no one, she aint, just as clean as new snow! Not gonna leave her to rot inna hard ol' pit now, is ya ther, buddy? Pal? Clawpaw?

No sir, thinks Cliff uncertainly. *I don't think it'll come to that. I'll...*

What would he do? Go against orders if told to leave the Whitetails to die? Try to stop Curly if she aimed to use her thrower on them? And what certainty did he have that the two of them weren't somehow complicit in the Whitetail attack? Maybe such an ending would befit them both. *But they could have been spies,* he recalls privately, *and they chose not to be.*

I'll make sure nothing like that happens, he thinks at last. *I'll at least try.*

How's about tryin' right now, hm? Why wait? We's been no trouble, just go on our way 'n never look back.

I don't think I can do that.

Sure-ee, ol' Piedmont unnerstands, 'course he does. You'da catch all kindsa heat iffin you's to break or-ders and do us goodly like that. He unnerstands. But we's buddies, now, Clawpaw, so's you gotta look out fer us, see? Aint no honor in keepin' good kezel inna hole.

No sir. I mean, yes sir, I agree.

Well-ee... Piedmont's thoughts fall still for a time.

A.P. Malloy

Then he takes a deep breath and looks up at Cliff. *I reckon iffin we's stuck here, might 's well make somethin' goodly happen, like ol' Piedmont can tell yous 'bout hows he met ol' Fluvial here and she got to fancyin' him right 'way, seed how he was a brainy type and reliarble.*

You fancied me, thinks Fluvial, not rolling over.

Well-ee! thinks Piedmont. *And who coulda blamed me, I wonder? Not no one! Cuz Fluvial here, back in the history days, she was a sight, sure-ee! Let's say—*

But what Piedmont is planning to say they never learn, for Serenity ducks her head in the cave.

Someone's firing a thrower, she thinks. *Down by the Butte.* And she hurries away without offering more.

+ + + + + +

Shimmer rides atop the alp, her basket nestled between its plates like a houdah. The ride is singularly uncomfortable, but they make good time, and soon enough, she and her escort arrive at the vumierre compound known as the ag facility. Her alp thumps across the retractable bridge and approaches the compound slowly, grazing as it goes. Shimmer sees neither the machine posing as a vumierre nor the orange sharksha.

There are no weapons.

Halt the beast! Conduct a search. But take care! Ozag has decreed peace between scion and sharksha, but who can say if all sharksha have learned the news? And the pale-skinned vumierre is not to be trusted. If found, it will be subdued and brought to her.

Viktor whistles, and his soldiers clamber from the alp and spread out across the compound, some daring to enter the underground facility and search the darkness inside. Shimmer remains aboard the alp with her pluripotents; her eyes grow dim.

'The test,' Ozag had said, *'is just beginning.'* But she had said it with such an encouraging tone its successful completion had seemed a certainty. If the Quintessential and Mesmerizing believed she could do it,

Aranae in Red

who was she to doubt? But what had seemed straightforward had turned out to have many moving parts, each
with its own occult motivation.

Viktor limps toward the alp.

They have located the sharksha's trail, he thinks.
*It goes toward the land of cold. But there is no sign of the
machine-vumierre, though its scent is everywhere inside.*

The transporting device? inquires Shimmer.

Sealed. But Queen knows how to open, yes?

Shimmer buzzes short, angry bursts.

*Queen does, yes! But if the disgusting creature left
by this means, there is no telling where it may have gone.
Oh, worry and woe! How is she to pass the test?*

If, thinks her prime, *the sharksha and machine-
vumierre are in league, perhaps the latter rode the former
as the Oddity was wont to do. Its scent would be hidden
thus. Or perhaps the sharksha have eaten it?*

Shimmer considers this, wings agitating.

It seems only natural.

What does Queen wish? Viktor asks.

She wishes to think! He will be still!

The seed derka lies motionless before her, to all
the world dead. She runs her pincers across its scales.
She has reached a crossroads, squeezed into a tight corner. Surely Ozag would be displeased to learn she had
known of the machine-vumierre's survival and done nothing about it. But what could she do? If it had used the
transporting device, guessing where it went could be a
disastrous waste of time. And the weapons! Had they gone
with the sharksha? She must be sure. But who knows
where the hideous brutes are going?

Up, she orders. *They will carry her to the sky.*

And her pluripotents do just that, lifting her and
the derka within the basket, rising from the alp's plated
back as the soldiers and handlers watch.

Up, up, they go, the basket pushed and bullied by
the wind. But all Shimmer sees is flat upon flat, the plains
stretching out as limitless as the Undying herself. The
Doorn behind them is the only break in the yellow, banks

A.P. Malloy

of thorns easy to see.

Higher! she commands.

And up the pluripotents go, their wings droning a furious pitch. The basket rises, the wind jostles, and the chittering of soldiers below can no longer be heard, tiny like bits of fallen scales in the hateful realm of sharksha. Still they rise, and still Shimmer demands more, until the air grows thin. And there, at her pluripotents' limit, Shimmer stretches her wings and leaves the basket, the derka motionless inside. Her wings have little to lift against, but she manages another fifty meters, her pluripotents worried and whistling.

Aranae lies spread out around her.

Hers, she thinks. *From the Saline to the Hold, Ozag's realm is hers to claim—if she passes the test.*

And she turns in the air, her sharp eyes glittering, and though her lungs burn and her wings sputter, all three hearts take courage from what she sees. Far to the northwest, directly in line with the trail left by the sharksha, lies a butte, lonely but high, the tail end of a jagged massif. It calls to her like a lost friend, and at the sight of it, she settles slowly back into the basket. The pluripotents gratefully descend, returning her to the back of the restive alp and the awe-struck gaze of the assembled company. Viktor bows low.

What, he thinks, *did she see?*

Her destiny, Shimmer replies in a lofty tone. *Take their positions. They will follow the sharksha!*

Handlers, soldiers, Twenty-Seven, and Viktor: all do as they are told and board the alp. But as it hammers away, they exchange subtle, fractious thoughts, and Shimmer, too exalted, does not notice.

+ + +

Another seventy thousand kezel strides pass, and not even torpor can entirely shelter the company from the battering they take from riding the alp.

But then it slows and stops.

Aranae in Red

It senses something, thinks Viktor.

Investigate! Shimmer commands, and the soldiers dismount, disappearing into the grass.

Moments later, a shrill, whistling call rises above the wind. A pair of soldiers skitters forward, natives of Cyclonia, buzzing and bowing.

They have found something, the one thinks.

Yes. Found. But not easy. Hidden well.

No. Not easy. But found. Cyclonian soldiers clever.

Yes. The cleverest. Searched end to end.

Yes. Stamina and diligence. Serving Queen.

Yes. Serving!

Shimmer clicks harshly.

Then divulge, sluggards! What have they found?

Digging, thinks the one.

Yes, thinks the other. *Digging and burying.*

Yes. Burying and hiding. Sharksha are good diggers. Good buryers.

Yes. Good at hiding. But not good enough.

No. Not good enough for Cyclonian soldiers. They found. They discovered

Yes. Discovered.

Discovered what, dolts? Out with it!

But her answer arrives in the form of another half dozen soldiers, buzzing and chittering as they labor to drag a filthy, woven parcel across the ground, loaded with something lumpy, jutting, and heavy.

Shimmer's prime whistles her surprise.

The vumierre weapons, oh Queen!

And so it is, for when Shimmer orders the parcel opened, there lie the numerous devices, sheathed and holstered, as well as their attendant boxes and bandoliers of ammunition. The soldiers step away, forming an uneasy circle, but Shimmer leans forward hungrily.

Is this the full measure? she asks her prime.

Most. But there appear to be three missing.

Becursed! Shimmer clicks sharply. *Entanglements and mysteries! Who has them? And why bury these? No matter. It is a sign from Ozag. Load the weapons on the alp and be off! The trail grows fresher...*

But Viktor hesitates.

Should they not be burned, here and now? he asks. *For they are the tools of slavers. It would be best not to let them fall into vumierre hands—or return them to the vumierre-worshipping sharksha.*

This inspires general, buzzing agreement.

She shall decide what is best! Shimmer whistles. *Have they not attended? It is Ozag's will that they should be returned to the sharksha and that there should be peace between scion and vumierre.*

Peace! thinks Viktor. *With slavers? Forfend!*

Yes, thinks Twenty-Seven. *Forfend!*

But Shimmer's pluripotents agitate their wings like a threat, and this minor insurrection is stifled.

Onward! Shimmer commands.

+ + + + + +

The rogue kezel grips one of the long throwers between his massive jaws, but the other he keeps pointed at Rock and Crag, for Stone is clearly no threat. The stunner he has strapped around his forearm. He forces the twins to carry the fallen Redtooth and orders them back to the Tavaline Massif. Even marching bipedal, they set a pace Stone can barely maintain, and the rogue, walking at the tail, prods her with the thrower.

Move, he thinks. *Or we'll have two bodies to carry.*

Rock looks back at their captor.

What's the plan here, boss?

For you to march and not ask questions!

Sure, boss, thinks Crag. *We're marching. But then what? Redteeth'll be back soon enough. Lots of 'em.*

Then I guess you'd better pick it up! They won't have spit to say once we're back at the Tavaline.

Sure, thinks Rock. *Until you run out of ammunition.*

Or food, thinks Crag.

Don't worry, the rogue snarls. *You're carrying my dinner. And you'll do it faster, or you'll be joining him.*

Aranae in Red

Yeah? thinks Rock. *Then who'll do your carrying?*

Enough! thinks the rogue, and he whacks Stone with the butt of the thrower. She yelps and stumbles.

OK, OK, boss, thinks Crag. *We're moving.*

And for a time, they march on, leaving the cloven pass and stepping up and out onto the edge of the grassy plains. From there, they re-trace their steps to the west, the scent of Stone's dried blood marking the way like a prohibition—one the rogue stubbornly disregards.

Don't mean to be contrary, thinks Rock. *But there may be a better way, boss.*

This is the fastest way. Keep moving.

Sure, boss, thinks Crag. *But what he means is there may be a better way than holing up in that old massif. Cuz that's what you've been doing right? Can't be much of a life, all alone, no friends, no clan, no accrete, always hiding and sneaking…*

Who's hiding? Who's sneaking? And I don't need friends. A kezel's just another meal.

OK, boss, thinks Rock. *But what if we turned this party around and headed north? Soon enough we'd be at the Sugarfoot caves, and you'd be a hero. Returned three missing ibiwas, some throwers. A champ, you'd be.*

Yeah, boss, thinks Crag. *Sugarfeet got no grudge with you. What's past is between you and the Bristles, the way I heard it. You could have a whole new life, and talihew, and babelrack, and folks coming to visit—or not, if you want to keep to yourself.*

The rogue thinks nothing for a time. The twins glance back. The aimed thrower never wavers, but the bibija's eyes have drifted out of focus, as if he is imagining the world they describe. Rock wonders to what depths he has descended to stay alive, what depravity has become normal for him. Crag tries to picture what sickness must eat at his mind with cycle after cycle of only boulders and wind for company. Neither have time for sympathy, but both recognize for fleeting moments a kezel that had once been like them, not despised, not fodder for tales to scare a wabi, but a real, breathing member of a clan, with fears

A.P. Malloy

and hopes of his own.

Then he growls and glares at them.

Nice try, he thinks, and he whacks Stone again.

The oti-mus exchange glances but march on. Ahead of them, Rite Butte rises above the horizon.

CHAPTER THREE
Hero

IN THE FUTURE, once Javon has accepted the invitation to visit the surface, the landing party must be chosen. Joy and the kezel will travel in the rear of the shuttle, leaving only four seats in the forward compartments. Javon plans to pilot the mission, and no one wastes breath arguing.

"At least take Kim," Commander Rickles pleads. "And one of his Enforcers."

"This is a diplomatic mission, Terry."

"As far as we know. But we don't know much! They might be up to no good, Major." He pronounces the word 'May Jor,' which endears him to Javon but doesn't change his mind.

"I think Maya, Janet, and Healey."

And with that, the shuttle is boarded and they begin their descent. The ride is largely made in silence, for which Maya is grateful. The person she really wants to communicate with is harnessed in the back along with her two alien companions. On one of the cabin's monitors, she sees the spiky creatures strapped into their modified seats, and she yearns to be with them. In fact, she had requested as much and had been flatly denied. Now, as the others observe the planet's approach, she watches Joy and the kezel.

Can you sense me? she asks, careful to keep her lips from moving. She has little hope; she and Watt could

A.P. Malloy

not sense each other through a simple closed door, and the bulkhead is much thicker than that. And yet:

This is Joy; yes, I can sense you.

Nice. Very nice. Are you OK back there?

Kezel don't like to fly, but we're OK.

We'll be there soon. Javon's a very good pilot. Maya stifles her childhood recollection of the shuttle explosion on Luna. It hadn't been her personal reality but had been such a powerful part of her mother's that its influence could be felt every time she flew. Not the kind of thing their guests needed to know.

What do your guests not need to know? Joy asks.

Maya puckers her lips.

Nothing, she thinks. *Just my own worries.* She redirects the conversation to the meeting ahead. *I'm not sure I want to learn too much about my future.*

It's not our future; that's important to remember.

No, but it will be close in a lot of ways, and I have a feeling we might see some things that—

A red blinking light on the major's console and the sound of Javon's voice interrupts her.

"We're about to enter atmosphere," he says calmly. "Things are apt to get a little bumpy."

+ + +

They descend near the mining compound, the dome-like structure bombas, in another timeline, refer to as the maison. Except that in this timeline, the module is situated in the middle of Allery Isle, the largest island in the Allery Chain, as big as California and a third of the way across Indrani Major. Lightning, Thunder, and Joy peer through their windows.

Is it supposed to look bumpy like that? Joy asks, for the entire island is a hilly expanse, covered in knobby, gray stone growing out from under a coast-to-coast blanket of heathery green.

No idea, thinks Lightning.

Don't know, don't care, thinks Thunder. *Suppose*

Aranae in Red

there's anything edible down there?

Whether there is or not, the island is part of Aranae, and seems better by far than being stuck aboard this cramped vessel. They squirm in their harnesses, impatient to be on solid ground, and as they approach the complex, Lightning and Joy note the differences from their memories. First is the traffic going in and out—both terrestrial and motorized. But beyond that, this dome is in markedly better shape than the maison. Joy can't make sense of it, and she refers her questions to the artifact she hugs close.

Shouldn't it look older? Isn't this the future?

It is, the Book replies. *But it is possible these colonists did what we have done.*

You mean they came here from the past?

It seems from our earlier scans of the planet, theirs is the second Destiny *to visit this Aranae. If we were to travel to the mainland of Ibedos, I suspect we would find a mining module that is older and in worse condition.*

When Joy explains this to Lightning, she wrinkles her snout and looks away.

Seems like we're caught in a loop, just going 'round and 'round. They did what we're doing? And what? They came from a past where some others were also doing what they're doing? When does it end?

Hopefully soon, thinks Thunder.

When at last they set down, Joy and the kezel must wait, looking out the windows as the humans step from the shuttle and are greeted by a contingent from the mine. Joy tries reading their thoughts, but they are too far away or have no thoughts to read. One of them looks like a relative of the major, younger and bearded.

The natives' attire means nothing to Joy or the kezel, but Maya perceives them as recently come from or preparing to attend a formal celebration. Javon notes the fancy dress but is more interested in the two armed guards flanking what he hopes is a welcoming party.

He approaches the one bearing his likeness.

"Magister Jeremiah, yes? We come in peace, Magister. I hope we can expect the same."

The bearded man extends his hand, which Javon clasps as well as his flight suit allows.

"You can," Magister Jeremiah assures. "But you can also expect we know how to defend ourselves."

"We never doubted it, Magister."

"Please. Call me Jeremiah. We know you have lots of questions, Major, and hopefully we'll have answers. But first—should we let your passengers out to explore? There's a crab-like animal that lives in the pools. Kezel think they're very tasty. Plus, we have guests arriving soon I think they'll want to meet."

When the shuttle's rear hatch is opened and Lightning, Thunder, and Joy step out into the light, they receive a most unexpected response from the natives. Some cheer, others clap, beaming as if they've received a fine gift. Jeremiah steps forward, his smile wide. He takes Joy's hand and shakes it formally, and to the kezel he offers a low bow.

"I've waited my whole life for this," he says to them, and the Book translates.

Sorry, thinks Lightning, *we can't say the same. But anyway, if you can help us with our questions, we'll say it's been nice to meet you.*

When Maya translates this, Jeremiah laughs and bows again, surprising Thunder by offering him the longest and lowest.

"Everything we can give," he says, "we will."

"You mentioned other guests," says Javon. "Do I dare ask who they are? And when they'll arrive?"

"Will you indulge a surprise?" asks Jeremiah. "It will be more fun that way. It's the kezel they really want to meet. And it shouldn't be long. While they're exploring and waiting, we can do business. We have inoculations for you inside. The protection is almost immediate. By the time our other guests have joined us, you'll be able to remove your suits and be more comfortable."

To this, Javon is amenable—Lightning as well.

We've had plenty of being cooped up. We'll wait for

Aranae in Red

your guests--and sniff out those tasties you mentioned.

And with this, the natives turn and lead the way to the mining compound, with Javon, Maya, Magister Healey, and Sister Janet following close.

Whoa, hey wait! thinks Lightning, and Maya turns. *What about derkas?*

Upon hearing this translated, Jeremiah's smile grows, lighting his face. He winks at Thunder and spreads his arms to the sky.

"Not a worry in the world," he says. "You'll see."

+ + +

Despite Jeremiah's reassurance, they explore cautiously, staying close to the shuttle and often glancing to the sky. Not a single derka do they see. They come to a pool, broad but shallow, blue as the sky and temperate. It appears empty, but as they have many thoughts to mull and nowhere to go, they sit on the heathered turf and wade into the shallows.

Lightning sniffs the water and takes a drink.

Ahh, she thinks, and her ears relax. *Now that's the way water is supposed to taste.*

Hey! thinks Thunder, and he leans back and points. *There is something in there.*

When the ripples settle, Lightning and Joy peer closely. At the bottom of the pool, camouflaged to look like a rock, a creature the size of a well-fed virble walks on eight jointed legs. It picks its way deliberately with no apparent destination or fear.

Joy whistles softly.

There's another one! And two more over there!

That's enough for Thunder. He wades stealthily, approaching the largest of the walking rocks, and he dives with no warning, breaking the surface snout first.

Splash!

The creatures can move quickly at need, propelling themselves with jets of water. But Thunder snares the one he was aiming for, crawling out of the pool with a

A.P. Malloy

treasure clutched in his jaws, its jointed legs flailing. One good crunch and the flailing ceases.

Joy's eyes sparkle.

Is it good? What does it taste like?

Thunder runs his tongue over his teeth.

Potential, he replies. *It tastes like potential.* And he tosses his catch to Lightning, who agrees.

Smells amazing, actually, she thinks, not knowing that, in another timeline, Rock and Crag had, not long before, thought the same thing near Cyclonia.

Go ahead, Thunder offers, but Lightning is too preoccupied for food. She watches her oti-mu break the stony shell and devour the flesh inside, legs and all, but her mind is on difficult questions and an abiding sense that something important is about to happen.

Joy moves close and sits beside her.

I feel it too. Big decisions are coming.

Lightning curls her lip.

Let me guess; it involves humans somehow.

Joy's buzzing is subdued.

Probably. I don't think we can avoid it. She wiggles her fingers and pats her legs as if they are their own answer. *They're everywhere we look.*

Yeah, Lightning growls. *But I wouldn't hesitate— not for a breath—if I knew we could chase every last one of them off Aranae. Gami-kan! Always going on about how they'd come back some day...made it seem like that was a good thing, but I'm not seeing it.*

Me either, thinks Thunder, and he washes down his meal with a drink from the pool. The other walking rocks have either taken shelter in submerged crevices or are so still their camouflage renders them invisible. Thunder gives up his search, occasionally casting his gaze skyward. *I will say this, though: at least this batch had the wits not to settle in kish or derka territory—or anywhere near the accrete.*

As far as we know, Lightning points out. *Anyway, it's not these stinkers I'm worried about. It's the ones we're traveling with. Sure, they say the right things, but what do*

Aranae in Red

you suppose they're going to do when they get back to our time? Stay out of the way? Not cause trouble? Makes me think the Redtooth rumor about Moondwellers using throwers on kezel might be true. Grr... If we didn't need them to get back ourselves, I'd leave 'em here like that! And she snaps her jaws like an exclamation.

That makes two of us, thinks Thunder, and he wanders away from the pool to explore.

But of course, Joy's perspective is different.

There may be one thing they're good for, she thinks to Lightning, imagining the artifact's singular hunger. *More Readers means easier to find the Way.*

Lightning wrinkles her snout.

Readers? What do you mean? But then she raises a clawed hand. *No,* she thinks. *Don't tell me. It's...Readers are...Yes! They're part of that rock thing.* She pauses and scowls. *It's happening, isn't it?* she asks. *I'm forgetting.*

Joy sighs

It can't be helped. That's how he works. Her eyes lose some of their glitter. *You'll remember longer than most—but not forever.*

Something about this sits uneasily with Lightning—but only if she struggles with it. Her memories of the artifact are wind-borne smoke, impossible to hang on to, and when she tries, intense frustration is the result. What did the thing used to look like? It had a name, didn't it? And a human form? But maybe she was confusing that with someone from the ship. So she relaxes and lets it go, and the relief is immediate. Joy will tell her what she needs to know. Who cares about the rest?

Well, she thinks after a time. *It isn't your fault. And Readers or no, there's no point in my wishful thinking. Whether we like it or not, our only ride home is with humans who apparently plan to stay. The only thing to do is keep them in line once that happens.*

Good luck with that, thinks Thunder, who has returned from his exploration and is now staring to the western sky. There, in the distance, a vessel has appeared, identical to the one they arrived in.

A.P. Malloy

He growls.
Looks like their guests have arrived.

+ + +

The new shuttle lands near theirs, and as it does, a second greeting party exits the dome, this one smaller, comprised only of Magister Jeremiah, two attendants—neither armed—and Maya. Her helmet is removed, and she waves for Lightning and the others to join them. This they do, as the shuttle crew (a pair of unknowns in flight suits) moves to open the cargo bay hatch. Before getting wind of what lies inside, Lightning had assumed it was another group of humans—*Because why not? It's not like a few more are going to make things worse!*—so she can't hide her surprise when what steps forth from the rear of the shuttle are three grown kezel and a quartet of spiky, rambunctious wabis.

Spitting yits! Thunder exclaims. *If that isn't you, Lightning, I'm blind as a sneer.*

Lightning's eyes grow narrow, and her ears pin back. The oldest of the three kezel has as many white spikes as copper. She steps away from the shuttle and into the sunlight, bowing to each of them in turn.

I told them not to make it a surprise, the Elder Lightning thinks solemnly, *but some people can't resist.*

Maya translates this, and Jeremiah beams.

"Guilty as charged."

Lightning can think of nothing to say. The kezel before her is somewhere between the age of Submission and Ancian, sober but not bent, deliberate, but not feeble. Her vest and mask are sleek and black, but interestingly, she wears no boots or gloves—much as Ancian—though the others wear the trappings of the Sugarfoot clan, clean and white. The two kezel with her are ibiwas in their prime, an ah-lah gray and a brindled ah-tah, both in tawny talihew vests. The wabis, too young for such gear, are spiky balls of copper, black, orange, and cream. They charge toward Thunder, who stands frozen while they run

Aranae in Red

circles around him and snap their tiny jaws.

Is this him? they ask.

It is, thinks the Elder Lightning.

I'm named after you! the cream-spiked wabi proclaims. *But everyone calls me Rumble! You like?*

Um, sure, thinks Thunder, alarmed when one of the wabis grabs his forelimb in its jaws and another does the same with his tail.

You're supposed to be the toughest, one of them thinks. *Show us your moves!*

Bubbles! Scrap! the gray ibiwa scolds. *Step back and show some respect.* The wabis do so reluctantly, watching as the two unnamed adults add to Lightning's amazement by standing two-legged before Thunder and bowing to him. He ducks his head, his eyes wide, and Joy's buzzing gives voice to his surprise. He looks to Lightning for help, but the situation exceeds her.

I think you might have the wrong kezel, Thunder offers, and his tone is apologetic.

No, thinks the Elder Lightning. *There's no mistaking my pain-in-the-tail oti-mu.* And she steps forward in a dignified fashion, leaning in to touch his nose with hers. He accepts the gesture, if only because all eyes are on him and he feels compelled by a lifetime of deference to adults. But he can scarcely get past the smell; it's Lightning, all right, a Lightning with many moons of experience under her vest, and—if he's not mistaken—at least one litter of wabis to her credit.

Her eyes meet his and he can't look away.

You have been in my mind a lot lately, she thinks.

I... Thunder hesitates. *I don't know...*

It's OK, thinks the brindled ibiwa. *We knew this would be confusing. We'll get you all caught up...but for now!* He snaps his jaws at the wabis, who have once again begun scaling Thunder's legs and jousting with his tail. *These four need to run off some energy. Would you mind? They won't go anywhere unless you do. Maybe explore for a while then head to the feast? It would mean a lot to them. I'll go with you and make sure they behave.*

Um, OK. Thunder looks at Lightning as if asking for her approval, but what can she say?

Go ahead, I guess. She looks at Maya. *We're staying for a feast? I thought we were in a hurry.*

Yes, but there's a lot of information being shared, and since we have to rest before our next trip, the major thinks it's OK. They've invited, and we're accepting.

Your major, thinks the Elder Lightning, *sounds as smart as ours. Inside! I was promised talihew.*

As the brindled ah-tah leads Thunder and his adoring crew of wabis away from the shuttle, Lightning senses the ibiwa, twice Thunder's size, introducing himself as Bluff and then adding, so implausibly she wonders if she mistakes the idea:

I'm your oliwot, you know, your nephew.

Then Jeremiah, nodding happily, turns and leads them all toward the dome, and she can only guess what Thunder's reply might be. As they walk, Joy stays close, and she peppers the Book with questions.

Is that future Lightning? And her grown woli?

It certainly appears to be.

And is the big brindled one her woti?

I can only presume.

And those four are her wabigaps and gams?

If forced to guess, I would say so.

Why are they fussing over Thunder so much?

I suspect we are going to be told.

Don't you know? I thought you knew everything.

I do not.

The walk to the dome is not far, but the weight of the remarkable situation rests heavily on Lightning, and she feels she must say something, must with words somehow make credible the mindboggling events.

I'm sorry, she begins. *I don't mean to be rude, but...*

The Elder Lightning doesn't break stride or turn back to look when she intuits and replies.

You don't have to apologize. Just let me get some talihew in my belly and I'll answer every question I can.

Aranae in Red

+ + +

They do not enter through an icy, submerged opening along the base of the dome, for there are none of these. No cracks or flaws mar the building's exterior. Nor do they enter through the Window. Instead, the path, which is smooth and hard like the road to Ozag's Hold, leads straight to a wide entrance on ground level, no climbing or swimming necessary.

Joy's eyes glitter, antennae bending to and fro.

It's cleaner, shinier, isn't it? Smells different too.

It doesn't smell like a bomba brood, thinks Lightning as they pass through the entrance. *That's for sure. And—wow...look at that!*

For the place is lit and busy, brighter than the maison ever was, and just as crowded. But the two-legged creatures walking its passages and congregating in its galleries are humans, more of them than Lightning at her gloomiest ever imagined. The humans themselves aren't gloomy at all. They fill the space with mingled voices, sometimes in raucous groups, sometimes in embracing pairs, their voices low and conspiratorial. And yet, if there is a conspiracy, it appears benign, for upon seeing them, every human stops what it is doing (eating and drinking are obvious, but what kezel has ever heard of dancing?) and they bow. Some offer gifts to Lightning and Joy, garlands of flowers they place around their necks.

Jeremiah smiles.

"Come," he says, and he waves.

They follow on, making their gradual way to the center of the dome, being bowed at and rung with flowers.

What is that sound? Lightning asks.

The music? Maya smiles. *Do you like it?*

Lightning reserves judgement, but Joy claps her hands, keeping time, and as they move toward the heart of the dome, the sound grows, until they step into the wide space, pillared, tiered, and open to the sky above, just as they remember it.

But oh, the differences!

A.P. Malloy

Humans, humans, everywhere. And not just full grown ones, but miniature versions, half the size with twice the energy. They approach in eager groups, putting Maya's translating skills to the test.

"I'm Natalia," says one.

"I'm Bo Lin, says another. "You're Lightning!"

"And you're Joy," says a third, who introduces himself as Sammy. And there, too, are Ani and James and many others, and they chatter and ask questions and say mystifying things like, "It's even better in real life!"

Together they move on, and Lightning looks wide-eyed at the wonders around her. Yes, there are the stairs, just where they should be, spiraling around the open center of every tier, but there are also four separate chambers on vertical rails, translucent and illuminated, conveying groups of people up and down without taking a single step. And the nacht! No longer a yawning chasm, it has been capped with a festooned platform, and on this gathers the ensemble responsible for the thing called music. They make it using devices of all shapes and sizes, some strung and plucked, some hammered rhythmically, some blown into with astounding results.

Joy whistles and buzzes like a living instrument.

It's the most beautiful thing I've ever heard.

But when the performers become aware of their arrival, they stop and rise to their feet. The people on every tier put aside their food and drinks, break off from their dancing, and from ground level to the aperture far above, the murmuring of voices grows still. Lightning recalls their first encounter with a bomba brood, and she half expects someone to call out for 'proof!'

Joy moves close and clutches her spikes.

Jeremiah steps onto the platform.

"Citizens of Aranae!" he says, and his voice is deep and clear, but also amplified and audible throughout the dome. "On this day, we celebrate not some abstract principle, like independence or gratitude, not some event from a distant past like the Lunar colony or the first System Charter. No! On this day, we celebrate something far better. We celebrate a life! The life of one who will be joining us soon. But first, I present to you two who have journeyed far with him and know him well. I present to you Lightning Sugarfoot and Joy!"

Now throughout this speech, the Book has been translating through Joy, and the thoughts Lightning senses leave her bewildered and vaguely disturbed. But she has no time to plead for clarity, for there arises on every tier such a clamor of cheering and clapping that she feels sure no bomba brood, regardless its size, could have done better.

Then Jeremiah steps down and rejoins them.

The music begins again.

The cheering rings in Lightning's ears.

+ + +

"Come," Jeremiah says, and they follow him to one of the conveyors, whose clear door slides open, allowing a group of partiers to step out just as Maya and their host step in. Joy does so without hesitation, swept along by the buoyant spirit, but Lightning hesitates.

It's OK, thinks Maya. *It's called an elevator. You'll like it. It's fun!*

Joy grasps one of the garlands around Lightning's neck, pulling her gently inside.

We'll wait for Thunder, thinks the Elder Lightning, and she and the ah-lah gray sit with the air of creatures who have seen plenty of humans and are neither afraid nor overly impressed.

The elevator door slides shut.

"Top floor," says Jeremiah, and just like that, up they go, smooth and quiet, the tiers sliding past, each with twinkling lights, dancing bodies, and glowing faces turned to watch them pass. Many people wave, and Joy delights in waving back.

Then they have reached the Window.

Ami-kan, look. All the nets are in place.

They are indeed, drawn across the circular opening at the center of each tier, not a single one torn or frayed. And the safety railing around each is lit, though it is unnecessary here, for the sun does all the work, shining through the clear walls on a room arrayed quite differently than in the maison. There are tables and chairs (or so Joy learns to name them, for they are things kezel have no use for) and seated on the latter are Major Javon and his crewmates. They are eating and drinking, joined in conversation with three strangers.

"Our guest of honor," says Jeremiah, "is currently being mobbed by fans, but here are Lightning and Joy."

The strangers rise in turn, bowing as they introduce themselves.

"Doctor Clarence," the one says, a small man with a fine, ashen beard. "Very glad to meet you."

"Chief Verde," says the other, popping a berry into her mouth. "But you can call me Chica."

"Delta One," says the third, most remarkable of the bunch, for it is a labor android, shiny and metallic. "Honored beyond measure."

This is all very proper and meets with Lightning's approval, but she can't focus on a suitable reply, for a pair of humans have climbed into the Window bearing stone bowls filled with a most delicious smelling bone stew. And this is just the beginning. More people come and go, each bearing dishes of various delicacies which they place on the tables or on the floor near the stew. There are filets of awl, fresh and clean, thick slabs of sneer, sliced just as they should be, and not a pesky leg in sight. Nearby is a giant plate of fungus, berries, tubers, and more. But the best is saved for last, when humans, perspiring from all the bustle, bear into the room the finest cuts of talihew, some cooked and placed on the table, most raw and slightly bloody, served on a broad salver. Lightning stares, hypnotized. Where the humans drink from mugs, glasses, and cups, the kezel are given large bowls of clean water, and she drinks some of this, trying to ease the growling of her stomach.

"You needn't be shy," Jeremiah assures, gesturing

at the bounty. "There's enough for twice as many hungry kezel. Please, enjoy!"

Thank you, thinks Lightning. *It's amazing. But I'll wait for the others.*

She doesn't have to wait long. In the tiers below, the music changes tune. The whole of the dome joins in singing words which mean nothing to Lightning but which she finds stirring, nonetheless.

Up rises a great cheer!

When at last it has subsided and the dance music resumed, an elevator reaches the Window and out steps Thunder, four wabis clinging to him like a living vest.

The others are walking up, thinks Thunder.
Creepin' cremlins! Did you hear all that ruckus? His eyes are wide, his ears set high and swiveling, and his nose twitches with a mind of its own. He doesn't seem to know whether to bow to the strangers who are standing and clapping, drool at the food, corral the wabis who have begun shamelessly lapping bone stew, or simply sit and shake his head. He chooses the latter.

Don't look at me, thinks Lightning. *When I imagined the future, it wasn't like this.*

When translated, this receives a hearty laugh from the natives. Jeremiah takes a seat.

"In my experience," he says, "the future rarely matches our imagination. Sometimes it's worse, but this is one time when I say it's better. Better by far!"

"Hear hear!," his companions exclaim, and, "You can say that again." Then the Elder Lightning arrives, making her stately way up the final stairs, followed by Bluff and the ah-lah gray.

All the food and beverages have been delivered.

The servants leave the space.

"That's it, then," smiles Jeremiah. "Our own private party while the others celebrate. I thought it would be easier to communicate this way—and better for the success of your mission, Major. But before we get to serious business, please, become acquainted and share the little time we have in peace and camaraderie. After all, we are creating precious memories, and before long our guests will need to be on their way. So, feast, I say, and enjoy! The troubles of the world can wait for a while."

+ + +

And feast they do. Lightning and Thunder join the other kezel and are delighted when there is none of the typical age-hierarchy fuss. In fact, Thunder is given first go at the food—once Elder Lightning has offered a proper invocation. He is suspicious in the beginning of being the butt of a joke. But assured this is not the case, he shamelessly snatches up the finest cut of talihew he has ever sunk teeth into, and the wabis, inspired to emulate, play tug o' war with their own portions.

It's OK, Lightning motions for the others to proceed. *I'm used to waiting.*

But they will hear nothing of it, encouraging her to help herself even as they do. It is an awkward feeling, sitting so close and feasting so freely with adults, but refusing would be seen as an insult, so she selects a humble slab of sneer, chewing politely.

Joy delights in lova juice like nothing she's ever tasted, but even more interesting are the two Lightnings. Her eyes move from Elder to Younger, cataloging the differences and buzzing to herself.

Well, thinks Elder Lightning. *Don't just sit there staring. You have questions. Ask.*

Joy looks to her own Lightning for approval.

As long as they don't mind, she thinks. *I have questions too. Maybe we'll both learn something.*

Joy clicks a sprightly tempo.

My first question is what is everyone's name?

The gray ah-lah looks up from the berries she's picking through, her snout stained pink and violet.

You maybe sensed, but that's Bluff, she thinks, aiming a glance at the brindled ah-tah who meticulously tears apart strips of fresh awl. *And I'm Gem. You already know Rumble; that's Scrap, Bubbles, and Selenophile. But you can call her Moony.*

Thank you! It's nice to meet you all.

The brindle named Bluff nods absently, more concerned with his meal, and the wabis pay no attention at all. They have eyes for Thunder only, and they copy his every move, berry for berry, egg for egg. When their appetites are sated, they climb him while he eats, testing their strength by trying to push him over. He tolerates this without complaint, sampling his way through the feast, careful to give every item a tasting.

Elder Lightning watches all of this, gnawing casually on a large talihew bone.

Next question?

Joy has her choice ready.

If these are your...who is your fancy?

But Lightning interjects.

No, she thinks. *Don't tell me. I don't want to know.*

Good choice, Elder Lightning replies. *Because I wasn't going to.*

There are lots of things we're not supposed to tell you, Gem admits. *It was the humans' idea, but we agreed.*

Joy's buzzing is low and grumpy.

That's not very fun. What is the point?

The point, Bluff replies, *is to let you live your life without undue influence. Let's be clear: this isn't your future. It's our present. Yours is likely to be similar, that's pretty sure. But different or same, it has to come about because of your choices, your free will—not because you're trying to copy or avoid what you see here. That's not you living your life, that's you trying to live ours.*

But we came here for help and advice.

And you'll get it.

The two Lightnings look deep into one another's eyes, but neither shares what they are thinking.

How about why everyone's acting so strange to me? Thunder asks. *Can you at least tell me that?*

Elder Lightning takes this question, but even as she replies, she continues to hold Lightning's gaze.

When I was your age, we did...what you three are

A.P. Malloy

doing right now. Or something very similar. What you're experiencing at this moment for the first time feels like déjà vu to me. I was you, and another me sat where I'm sitting and said what I'm saying. And our Thunder, when we finally returned to our own time...well, he did something pretty amazing, something I wouldn't have thought he was capable of, and a lot of good came from it.

Gem nods, and she gestures at the feasting humans and the celebrators on the tiers below.

All this, she thinks, *kezel and humans working together, no derkas messing up the party—*

No scion to bite or be bitten! Bluff adds.

Humans in their place, Elder Lightning thinks, *and Rock and Crag alive to tell the tale.*

It's all true, thinks Gem. *And it's all because of what our Thunder did when we got home.*

Rock and Crag are alive? thinks Lightning.

They are in this time, Elder Lightning assures.

Geez, thinks Thunder, his ears laid back. *What did I do? Dazzle everyone with my intellect?*

I'll tell you what you did, thinks one of the wabis. *When you get back, you—*

Moony! Gem bares her teeth and snarls, and the wabis cower in unison, quivering.

Again, thinks Bluff. *Let's be clear! It isn't what you did. It's what our Thunder did, before I was even born. Who knows what you'll do? Who knows if you'll face the same opportunity or even get off this planet alive?*

Joy's antennae lean forward.

Whatever it was, your Thunder sounds very nice.

No nicer than yours, I suspect, Elder Lightning replies. *But 'character is revealed in action.'* She again locks eyes with Lightning. *You remember the saying?*

You know I do. Ancian said it all the time.

For good reason. We are what we do.

Yeah, I get it. But can you at least tell us how you got these Moondwellers, these humans, to 'stay in their place,' as you call it? It doesn't seem to be something they're very good at.

Aranae in Red

Terrible, in fact, Gem agrees. *The worst.*

So? Lightning prompts. *What's your secret?*

Even if I hadn't promised not to tell, thinks Elder Lightning, *I wouldn't. All you need to know is this: cooperation is possible. And when the time comes, you'll know it.* She looks at Thunder. *Don't hesitate. Act!*

But also, Gem adds, *don't turn your back or fall asleep on duty. I like to stay positive, but humans are an odd bunch, and they're more apt to behave if they know they're being watched. Which reminds me of some kezel I know.* And with a snap-snap! of her jaws she summons the four wabis from their adoration.

Can we come back after the meeting? Rumble wants to know. *Please?*

Either you'll come back, or Thunder will come to you, Gem promises. *But now the adults have business.* She leads the wabis to a circular door along the outer wall, and Joy whistles happily.

The slide! she thinks.

And Gem turns a latch, opening the door. The wabis scramble inside, howling to hear their voices echo, One by one, away they go, Moony, Bubbles, Rumble, and Scrap, spiraling down and away. Before she takes her turn, Gem faces Thunder and bows.

Things will be what they will be, but I wish you the best in your own time. It was an honor to meet you.

Well, thinks Thunder, so flummoxed he forgets all about his food. *Thanks.*

And Joy watches Gem slide away, all the while caressing Lightning's spikes.

I want to join the humans a bit, she thinks. *It's OK; you can stay with the kezel.*

+ + +

Which is what Lightning wants to do in any case. The future kezel may be secretive, but they are also fascinating. She nods Joy on her way, watching only long enough to see her request and then be granted a seat between Maya and the major. The seat is too low for her, so she must kneel on it to see properly. But to Lightning's surprise, Chica Verde hurries from the room, returning with an armful of cushions to raise her up. Lightning watches Joy among the humans, observes the way they look at her, her slender legs swinging back and forth. She wishes she could sense their thoughts, but only Doctor Clarence has that kind of brain, and it is tightly closed.

Elder Lightning looks at Younger.

It's pointless to tell you not to worry, she thinks. *I used to do it all the time.*

Used to?

OK. Still do. I'm not sure that ever ends.

So? Where is she?

My Joy? Elder Lightning's tone is evasive. *You may get that answer. We'll see.*

Lightning wrinkles her snout. She wonders for the first time what Joy's nakedness might mean to the humans whose form she shares but who are wrapped from head to toe in garments of one type or another. She imagines herself vestless in the company of her peers and knows she would feel shame—not for being exposed, but for not having the means or wits to be otherwise.

Hey! thinks Bluff. *We've only got each other for a little while. Let's not waste it daydreaming, yeah?*

Lightning turns from Joy and the humans at their table. Thunder, it seems, had also been lost in thoughts of his own, and now they both attend to their hosts.

Agreed, thinks Lightning. *This is amazing, for sure, and I don't want to take it for granted. But...it seems like all the things I want to ask, you can't answer.*

Surely not everything, thinks Elder Lightning. *And if you can't ask, maybe you can answer. We have questions of our own—or at least Bluff does. He's heard a lot about my—our—adventures, and I think there are times when he thinks I'm exaggerating.*

Then let's take turns, Thunder proposes. *We ask, you ask. But if we ask one you're not allowed to answer, we get a second chance. Agreed?*

Aranae in Red

It is. And for the duration of the feast, they spend their time this way, trading questions. Thunder continues to test the limits of the prohibition, and his questions are often rejected—though with eminent courtesy. Lightning chooses hers more carefully, moving back and forth between Bluff and her elder self.

What are the latter's best attributes as an ami-kan?

What, according to the former, are the qualities of a good fancy? The merits of one litter over two?

As promised, Bluff is most interested in stories of Lightning's adventures, and he seems to relish the chance to hear old tales from this new perspective.

But Elder Lightning reserves most of her questions for Thunder. She moves to sit beside her younger self and asks him many things. She is kind and solicitous, but Thunder can't help feeling he is being tested in some way. He and Bluff move their gazes from one Lightning to the other, cataloging similarities and differences for their own unique reasons but similarly awash in the sense that they are living two lives at the same time.

+ + +

Lightning's worry is unfounded, for the humans are in deep and sober converse when Joy is finally seated comfortably, and most pay her arrival little attention. But Maya leaves off from exchanging thoughts with Doctor Clarence and turns to her with a welcoming smile.

Anything look good? she asks, gesturing at the bounty spread before them.

Joy peers closely at the plates and bowls and terraced serving dishes, some steaming, some chilling in beds of ice, and all in their own way a delight to the eye. But her training is kezel, and what matters is not appearance, but scent. She points at a nearby plate on which are arranged neat, spiraling rows of something orange, sliced into small, thin squares.

What is that? It smells strange but amazing.

Maya removes a slice and hands it to Joy.

Some type of cheese, she thinks and takes a slice for herself. *Baleb...rabel...what did they call it?*

Babelrack?

That's it. I don't know, Maya thinks, biting off one corner of the square. *It's not as good as feta, but still...*

And she downs the remainder, smiling.

Joy sniffs and nibbles her own.

Cheese. That's a funny word. Mm! That's good!

Delight glitters across the facets of her eyes, and she leans forward to sniff at other nearby offerings. She turns up her nose at a plate of green leafies and is confused by the crystal salver of salted fish, which both attracts and repels her. But on one of the shiny, multi-tiered stands are arrayed a variety of triangular slabs, ornately decorated, and by far the sweetest smelling, most enticing items within reach. She looks at Maya, then back at Lightning, occupied with her elder self.

It's cake, thinks Maya. *You've never had?*

Joy clicks a thoughtful cadence.

Cake. No. Can I? I mean, should I?

But this last is directed at the Book, not Maya.

A little won't hurt, it thinks. *Your body is evolving. No more steady diet of awl for you. That started the moment you first tasted lova in Albion. But slowly!*

And yet, when Maya serves her a slice of the brown and white marbled glory known as cake, going slowly is one of the hardest things Joy has ever done. What a taste! How had she ever lived without it? Fluffy in parts, creamy and sweet in others, it mixes perfectly with the red berries Maya ladles over the top.

A little ice cream, too, she thinks, plopping a scoop of something white and chilled onto the plate. *That's how my daada used to like it. What do you think? Here, wait. Use this instead.* And she hands Joy a metallic utensil with a quadrant of tines at the end, for of course she is sampling with her fingers. She accepts the utensil but doesn't use it, licking her fingers hungrily.

I could eat this forever. Cake! So good...

And yet, no one else at the table is using their fingers—or displaying nearly so much enthusiasm. So, she demonstrates the utmost restraint, grasping the utensil as Maya shows her and trying to bend it to her will. Her lovely cake gets hacked and poked into a creamy mess, and none of it reaches her mouth as quickly as she would like. Thinking no harm can come of it, she abandons that plan and leans forward, her proboscis emerging and sweeping over the plate. With a slurp-slurp and a suck-suck, the whole thing is cleaned in moments, and she releases a deep, satisfied sigh.

But now everyone at the table is looking at her.

"Hooray!" Jeremiah exclaims, and Chica Verde claps. Maya smiles kindly and passes Joy a rectangle of cloth with which to wipe her hands, and Major Javon nods as if approving.

"Now that's the way to eat cake," he says.

But the red-faced Magister Healey scowls.

"Can we get on with business?"

"Indeed," Jeremiah agrees. "It is time." He waves at one of the servers who bows and exits the room.

Moments later, the music changes tone, becoming quieter and less bouncy. The celebrating voices on the lower tiers follow this cue, and laughing and singing turn to whispers and silence.

"Friends, guests," Jeremiah rises and motions to humans and kezel alike. "Join me, won't you?" And he moves to stand near the central barricade, looking down into the heart of the dome.

He points.

"Your patience is rewarded. Ozag arrives."

Chapter Four
Undying

THE FUTURE KEZEL are unaffected by the announce-ment; they remain seated near the feast, Bluff gnawing on a bone and Elder Lightning watching Younger as she moves to stand next to Joy at the barricade. At the men-tion of that portentous name, both had risen to their feet without question, sure that whatever was about to hap-pen couldn't be missed.

Thunder follows, gulping down the last of his stew.

S'pose this is the same Ozag we heard so much about? he asks. *What's it doing here?*

Good questions, Lightning replies. *Let's hope we get some good answers.*

Joy buzzes her agreement.

But Ozag is a she, not an it, she reminds.

The humans make room for them—courteously for most, fearfully for Magister Healey—and they look down over the barricade. The nets on each tier retract smoothly, giving them a clear view to where the music stage has begun to split into two perfect halves, one slid-ing to the right, the other to the left, the performers calmly riding along. The nacht is exposed, but the bottomless shaft is not dark as Lightning recalls, but is instead lit with bronze and gold.

And there, in the depths, something stirs.

Joy's clicking is quiet like a whisper.

Do you see that? Do you hear that?

Lightning does. Rising from what Oracio had called the Root of the Maison comes the unmistakable sound of wings, a chorus in metallic harmony. A moment later, a dozen gleaming scion, bronze-skinned and black-eyed, spiral up out of the nacht, followed by six companions of sterling silver. They hover in tight formation, waiting as one last figure rises from the depths, radiant gold and the object of everyone's attention. Humans on every tier and kezel alike stand with breath held as the golden creature rises like the sun, circled and trailed by bronze and silver. Up through the dome they fly, and many they pass bow or bend to one knee. Joy feels a pressure growing inside her as the winged company draws near, and she makes no sound, but she imagines music swelling in her mind.

Hold on, thinks Lightning, and the spikes rise along the length of her spine. *Wait just a beat now...*

But there is no pause to the ascent. The flyers reach the Window and pass seamlessly up into the sunlit space, arraying themselves in a glittering circle around the room. The final member, gold and shimmering, remains aloft, casting reflected sunlight and the song of its wings throughout the space, and not one person speaks, though several bow nearly to the floor.

"Greetings, esteemed guests," the creature says, and it spreads its arms like the invitation to an embrace. For this is no ordinary scion. Lightning stands frozen, her eyes locked to the form, humanoid but winged, bipedal but gold from its antennae to its ten fingers and toes. It turns its large, sparkling eyes her direction, and its mind reaches out to her like a balm—and it smiles.

Hello Lightning...ami-kan from another time. I'm so happy to see you. Do you like my new look?

And it twirls in the air, dancing with the sun so that its gold-hued garments shimmy and gleam.

But Lightning can think of no reply.

+ + +

A.P. Malloy

Below them, the music resumes, as the partiers return to their celebration.

In the Window, all eyes are on the new arrival.

"I present to you Ozag," thinks Jeremiah, and though the Book translates through Joy, sensing the words hardly makes them less mystifying. "Scion Queen, Graceful and Righteous, Head of the New Gaian Council, and heir to the legacy of two species, worlds apart."

"Oh, thank you, Jeremiah," thinks the golden creature, laughing, and she lands easily near Elder Lightning, wings settling at her back. "But that's silly. Just call me Joy." She wraps her arms around the gigika kezel, and they exchange warm, sheltered thoughts.

"What is this 'Head of the Council' business?" Magister Healey frowns. "And what is an Ozag?"

"I hope you don't mind," thinks the Joy in gold. But she addresses Major Javon, not *Destiny's* magister. "I guess there was a vote or something. It was nothing really, just a formality, you know. People like their traditions, don't they?"

"So, I take it," says Javon, "that the future me is...dead? Or was I disgraced and run out of town?"

"Oh, no! Nothing like that. But you'll see, in your own time. Who knows? Maybe things will be different for you. But there was a need, and people thought I could do the job. I don't know. It seems kind of silly."

She hugs Elder Lightning once again and leans in to touch noses with Bluff. He accepts the gesture with easy familiarity, but when the Joy in gold turns to Thunder, his ears lie flat, and his eyes are wide.

It's so nice to see you, the Joy in gold thinks. *I was going to say 'again,' but of course, it's the first time for us, isn't it? How are you enjoying your party? Isn't it fine?*

Oh, swell, Thunder replies. *Just grand.*

The Joy in gold buzzes a happy melody, but then she tilts her antennae forward and offers a thought so subdued Thunder barely senses it—though it echoes in his mind long after.

Your secret, she thinks, *is safe with me.* And then

Aranae in Red

she rests her hand briefly on his shoulder.

Turning away, she approaches the humans, raising the hem of her dress and curtsying for Maya.

Thank you, she thinks, *For all you did—and all you will do. Never doubt it was for a good cause—and will be again!* And she takes Maya's hand and kisses it.

Maya stands speechless.

And me, all blue, the Joy in gold exclaims, and she turns to face her younger self, wingless and a head shorter. *This might sound strange,* she thinks, *but I am very proud of you. No one knows what you've been through better than I. But none of that fancy Queen talk for us, yes? Proud, but not prideful.*

Joy's buzzing quavers.

How did I...how did you get wings?

I stayed alive, that's all! And the Joy in gold laughs. Many in the room brighten at the sound of her voice, clear and musical, though only Joy senses the message. She coils her hair around her fingers.

And you can speak the human language now.

That took a lot of practice. But it's been useful!

And...Ozag? The Undying? How did that happen?

Oh, thinks the Joy in gold. *That was nothing. It just sort of came about naturally, you know. I didn't ask for it. But it's turned out pretty well, I think, all things considered. But!* she adds. *I wouldn't take that 'Undying' thing too seriously. It's just part of the title. I say people should let it go, but they're so traditional, you know. It's silly.* She reaches out and gently disengages Joy's hands from their nervous hair curling, clasping them and smiling softly. *Choose your habits wisely,* she thinks and releases Joy's hands, allowing them to settle at her sides. There they rest, for the moment at peace.

The Joy in gold now faces Janet. She solemnly extends a hand, and the two exchange a formal handshake. Golden eyes glitter fiercely, but if she intends to say something, she isn't given the chance.

Magister Healey raps on the metal barricade.

"Moving on, then! We've eaten, we've drank, we've

listened to music and given out lots of hugs and happy handshakes. But we haven't gotten one scrap of useful information—which is the only reason we came here."

Major Javon grimaces.

"You'll have to forgive my companion," he says. "He can be disagreeable when he's awake."

The magister's cheeks puff up, but the Joy in gold raises a hand, whistling a low, even note, and whatever retort he had been planning falls silent.

"Your ideas," she says to the magister, "are too often motivated by an...undue attention to your own well-being. But that does not automatically make them wrong. You did come here for information. But you also came here for rest and healing." She gestures to the slender, bearded man beside Maya. "Dr. Clarence tells me a full night's sleep is necessary after using an astral drive, and if you will honor us, I believe we have quarters ready for you once our business is finished." She turns to Jeremiah and tilts her head.

"We do indeed," he says. "As comfortable and to everyone's liking as possible—if our guests will stay."

Javon's glance touches each of the *Destiny* members, and he nods.

"Twenty-four hours is protocol. And if we have to rest and recover, I suppose we're better doing it here than on a ship's bunk with cold rations."

"Hooray!" the Joy in gold claps her hands. "That will allow us time to share the information you need, give a tour to those who want one, and enjoy a fast breaking in the morning. Well, you know, there won't be a sunrise or anything, but once you've slept, you'll be hungry! And now I understand there are wabis waiting for their hero. Have you been down the slide yet, Master Thunder? No? Oh, it's great fun. Joy! Lightning! Would you care to show him how? We have business to discuss that will only bore you, and I know you prefer being outside."

Truer words have rarely been spoken. And so, taking their temporary leave from the others, Lightning and Joy walk Thunder to the slide and demonstrate the proper

Aranae in Red

technique. He wrinkles his snout but watches as they zoom out of sight.

Wait 'til they're all the way down, Elder Lightning advises. *You'll know when you hear them.*

And eventually he does, a jubilant howling call echoed by the piping voices of impatient wabis.

Hero shmero, he thinks, and he quickly counts to sixteen, his luckiest number. *Here goes nothing...*

But 'nothing' turns out to be one of the most exhilarating experiences he can recall, and he, the wabis, and several of the human children take trip after trip, up the elevators (to cheers from the reveling humans) and back down the slide, howling delight.

+ + +

In between slides, Lightning and Joy guide Thunder on a tour of the dome, while Gem and four abundantly energetic wabis take their turn showing the visitors around the island. They are far inland, but when they climb the highest of the lumpy tors, they see the Great Saline in the distance, wreathing them in blue.

Ancian never said anything about that, Thunder marvels at the endless water. *Or any of this! I'm not sure she'd like it if she saw it, but I don't hate the place.*

Indoors and out, up the dome and down, with breaks for snacking and brief exchanges with adoring humans, they occupy their time as happily as possible, all four wabis often riding Thunder's back at once and he never complaining. Each return to the Window finds the small group of humans and scion still working through their conversation, and they try to remain patient.

In fact, the meeting is almost at its conclusion.

Magister Healey has continued to press the natives for answers about the future.

"What do I do when...?"

"How do we respond after...?"

"What should we be looking for during...?"

But Jeremiah and his companions—as well as the

Joy in gold—are polite and resolute.

"There are things we think you need to know," the winged creature commiserates. "And things we think you shouldn't. The area in between is gray, but generally, we believe it is best if you are allowed to find your way with minimal influence from us."

This does nothing to placate *Destiny's* magister, but his bluster is useless, so he broods over his wine and glares around the table.

Major Javon raises a hand.

"Does that rogue moon qualify as one of the things we should know about?"

"In that matter," Jeremiah replies, "all we can say is what worked for us. We can't guarantee it will be so successful for you. But this..." and he reaches into his pocket, pulling out a small data stick. "This is audio, video, co-ordinates, everything—what we did, how we did it, and what the results were." He hands it to the major, who tucks it in a zippered pocket near his heart.

"Since you're still here," he notes, "the results must have been good."

"There were what they were," Jeremiah replies, a cryptic response but as good as they can expect. Javon considers other questions—*Are you my son? How could you not be?*—but he checks himself. What good is groping for answers like a hungry man in a dark kitchen?

"How about we make things easy?" he suggests. "Maybe you could just tell us what you think we need to know, and we'll trust it will be enough."

"Ooh," the Joy in gold claps. "Well said!"

Jeremiah nods at Doctor Clarence, his lithe form and ashen beard making him seem calmed by age but not weakened by it. His gray eyes twinkle. His accent, indeterminate non-English, adds depth to his message, even when the words are difficult to understand.

"Eet eesa my pleasure," he says. "My friendsa haff geefen me the honor anda the ease of bearing the besta, mosta concrete information. You are alla, by your own unefentful exposure to our...enfironment, proof of theece.

Aranae in Red

Our eenoculations haff been refined to nearly one a hundred percent efficacy. Vee haff hada only one allergic reaction and no complete failures." The doctor smiles, his teeth, Maya thinks, charmingly disarrayed. "I am pleasedd to say thata before you leaf, your shuttle veel be loaded veece enough eenoculant meest for all of *Destiny*. You veel safe months of seentheseece anda..."

He stops himself and glances at the Joy in gold.

"Let me leaf eet ata that," he concludes.

Eyes are turned to Maya, who, as the only scientist among their contingent, is expected to respond in some way. She has been silent for most of the meal, using her mind but rarely her voice, and she feels the need to cough or clear her throat.

"We're...very grateful. Thank you."

And then, to prove she isn't a complete loss as an ambassador, she adds for the doctor only:

I'll make sure everyone learns what you've done for us. If lives are saved because of you—or time—that alone will be worth our trip here. Your name will be known.

And Doctor Clarence raises his glass to her and takes a polite sip.

Jeremiah now motions to the android. It replies as it has all meal long, simply and without emotion.

"I am a labor android. I am not a slave. Remember that when you reach your Aranae."

And that is all it will say. Not even Magister Healey dares a response.

They turn their attention to Chica Verde next, full-figured and singing along with the music.

"Oh! Is it my turn?" she asks.

"It is," Jeremiah waves.

"OK. Check it out." Chica turns her mind from the music to the people at the table. "That moon you're worried about? That's a real thing for sure. Worry about that. But there's something else, and almost as bad."

She glances at the Joy in gold.

"How'm I doing?"

"Splendid! But you've only just begun..."

A.P. Malloy

"Right! OK. So, you know, we did what you all are doing now. Something like it. The details were different here and there, but for the most part, yeah, the same. But it took us two tries to get it proper. The first one we overshot the mark and ended up in a future too far out there...and it was no good. I mean wiped out, no good. And not from any moon. The planet was a dustbowl on one side and a helluva tundra on the other. Dead as dead." She looks around the table to ensure everyone's attention. She has it. "Humans were behind it, of course— or their tools. *Destiny* had been stripped to her frame, the colony pillaged, the whole place... I really hate the word 'rape,' but it's what keeps coming to mind."

"We may have heard about these humans," Major Javon bites his lip. "One of them has my name."

"Oh, gee, no, Major," Chica flutters her hands. "I'm not being clear, I guess. It wasn't them. We dug through the wreckage on the surface and pieced it together: someone followed your very great grand-nephew to Aranae—it was them who did it. They tore the place up and left it that way."

"Hold on!" Magister Healey slaps the table. "Are you saying that happened here, too? And you were able to...what? Prevent it somehow?"

"Yes sir," Chica arches a brow. "That's exactly it."

"But you're not going to tell us how."

"No sir. I don't think we are."

"Oh, for God's sake..."

"Now hold on there, Mister Magister," Chica wags a finger at him. "Don't lose your cool. We gave you the heads up! That's a whole lot better than nothing. And check it out. Whatever you decide to do, you can't let them escape. They, or someone like them, will just keep coming back until there's nothing left to come to, you get it? The only way to stop them from planting flags on the place or wiping it out is if they don't know it exists."

"Yeah? So? What's your point?"

"So, think it through and you'll get there."

"But only," Jeremiah is quick to add, "if you return

in time to address the danger. So now, I think it is best if we show you to your quarters. We've arranged adjacent rooms away from the noise of the party. You'll want to be together and discuss what you've learned. But I encourage you, please: do get some rest. When you return to *Destiny,* you'll need to depart at once—and assuming you reach your goal, you will likely be kept very busy for what could be a long time."

This somber note furrows brows and sours faces around the table. Maya struggles to find her earlier equanimity, lacing her hands over her belly. So much trouble ahead. What would they do?

But the Joy in gold whistles a subtle harmony with her silver attendants, who join her in a gleaming ring. Her eyes sparkle, and she smiles like a blessing.

"Don't lose hope, dear friends! We made it through. That means you can too. Come! I hate to see frowny faces. That's better now. Jeremiah will show you to your rooms. I'm going to find our kezel and have them join you. So silly! I hate to see you leave, but there you have it. Time moves on..."

And she rises to flight, the four native Aranaen humans standing to bow as she does. Whistling a concerto with her attendants, silver and bronze, she ascends through the aperture and is followed, one by glittering one, until all that remains is their delicate, allusive scent and the memory of music.

+ + +

Lightning, Thunder, and Joy are given a room made appropriately comfortable to kezel standards. They are shown how to seal the windows against the perpetual sunlight and the door against the sounds of revelry that show no signs of stopping. They do not drift off to sleep at once, but share thoughts about their recent experiences, having many questions but not as many answers. The wabis had begged to join them, howling and yipping, but this had not been allowed.

A.P. Malloy

They need their rest, Gem had explained. *We all do. But you will see them again before they leave.*

When at last their conversation has circled back to its starting point and Joy's eyes have grown dim, they each fall into sleep. The room is lightless and quiet but for their breathing, and it stays so for a long time.

But Joy's sleep is disturbed.

She thinks at first it is the result of cake, cheese, and ice cream, but her stomach gurgles in a way quite distinct from indigestion. This is a fluttering sense of imminence. She sits up. The Joy in gold stands before her, still and silent, but wreathed in a ghostly light.

Joy buzzes softly.

Hello, there! How did you get in here? For the door remains closed, and not a sound had she heard. Lightning and Thunder snore on, unaware.

The Joy in gold turns and moves to the door.

She motions for Joy to follow.

OK. A good walk might help my stomach.

And she rises, shouldering her sling. Except it seems also that she sleeps on, for she can clearly see her body lying curled within Lightning's embrace.

What is this, now? Some kind of trick?

The Joy in gold motions again and passes through the closed door without touching it, her ghostly light disappearing. If a trick, it is a mighty fine one, Joy thinks, and without question, she walks at the door as if it were no more solid than the moon cave's water curtain. Through it she passes, easy as thought—and on the other side stands the Joy in gold, joined by Maya, herself shrouded in a wavering light.

Oh! I didn't expect to see you here.

I'm sleeping, thinks Maya. *I'm sure of it.*

Maybe, but look! We're glowy. Both of us.

The Joy in gold leads them down a passage, and they follow, as if nothing could be more natural. The passage seems to be in the mining compound—where else could it be?—but it reminds Joy of walking in place, for her legs move, yet the walls remain still and unchanging.

Aranae in Red

And just like that, they are in another room.

Look at that, now! And who are you?

This Joy asks to the shadowy figures—nine of them, humans all—sitting in a circle on the bare floor in the middle of the room. The space is unadorned and dark as night, but each of the figures, some adults, some children, shines its own ghostly light. One of them is Doctor Clarence; Joy doesn't recognize the others. They make no gesture or reply. The Joy in gold moves to join them around the circle, and she points to its center.

Joy and Maya clasp hands.

They walk into the center of the circle.

It seems then that the figures become faint, even the Joy in gold, their wavering light made dim, for the moment Joy and Maya step into their midst, a greater, brighter force leaps up like a wakened flame, starting in Joy's sling and Maya's womb and combining to engulf them in a heatless blaze. They stand like a beacon, and from the shadows comes a single thought.

Thank you, it says, and it is the Joy in gold.

Thank you, the other figures echo.

And Joy knows at once that Petros had told the truth. The people of this time have no Book of their own, have only ever heard of it from stories told by the Joy in gold, stories of her youth. She cannot discern the reason for this, how the artifact should have come to be lost when so much else about this time seems idyllic, but there it is. Only the Joy in gold remembers time as a Reader; the others are experiencing it for the first time. Some weep, others grin sheepishly. But all say:

Thank you.

And then their questions come like tentative rain, a drip here and a drop there, and the combined energy of the two Books answers them all, even when the rain steadies and becomes a torrent. Joy feels she is at yet another feast, only now she is the host, and the shadowy figures are hungry souls, and it is her great pleasure to see them fed, though they are never full.

A.P. Malloy

+ + +

Who can say how much time passes?

Very sleepy, thinks Joy, and Maya nods.

The Joy in gold rises to her feet, and the other Readers still their questions as she raises her golden hands, gloved in shimmering light.

And blink! Without warning or sound, the Readers are gone, replaced by Lightning and Thunder, looking fresh as if from a deep sleep, but also filled, like Joy and Maya, with a ghostly light and a distant expression.

Hello, thinks Joy. *I am very glad to see you both.*

I'm sleeping, thinks Lightning. *We both are.*

And there, at the far end of the room, four doorways appear, bordered in light.

There is no doubt what they will do, no uncertainty about which door belongs to whom. Maya moves to stand before the leftmost door, Thunder before the one to the far right, and Joy and Lightning before the two in the middle. The Books' glow increases, the four doors open, and without question or worry, they each step across the threshold of their own door and into the dreams that await on the other side.

+ + + + + +

Except that as they occur, to each of them they seem not like dreams at all; nor do they have the feel of memories. They are, in every detail, a lived experience, immediate and concrete, as real as their next breath.

For her part, Maya sees her own daughter, watches Grace and the New Gaian colony grow together, celebrating their first birthday. Her favorite stuffed animal is Maya's raggedy old tiger, Morris. At the age of three years old, her favorite game is asking it questions and—seemingly—inventing its replies.

Can I play? Maya asks, but Grace patiently explains that Morris only answers for her—and also, she is the only one who can understand him.

Aranae in Red

I used to be able to, thinks Maya.

Not anymore, thinks Grace. *He's changed. His name is Petros now.* And she reaches out, extending the love-worn creature to give her mother a kiss...

...and then the dream moves on and Grace is five. She totes her tiger around in her backpack and reads him stories. Petros, she maintains, is real.

You believe me, don't you? she asks, and Maya, of course, says yes. But she harbors concern.

"Imaginary friends are common for children," Janet assures her. "Two-thirds of parents report at least one such incident in their pre-teen children. Interestingly, that number increases to nearly eighty percent among children with no siblings."

"Now I feel guilty," Maya frowns.

"Oh, no reason for that," Janet folds her hands. "Unless you think this game of hers is a problem?"

"No. If that's all it is. A game..."

...and again time unspools and Grace is a fifteen year-old, and the game changes form, for she has become very interested in her mother's research.

Can I come to the lab? she asks, which she had done in the past. But that was the play of a curious child. Now, she is focused and persistent, fascinated by each piece of equipment and step in the process. After that, she never has to ask again, because she is always invited.

You're a model scientist, thinks Maya, and she never comments on the propriety of a teenager carrying a stuffed tiger in her backpack.

They study the scion, friendly and fearless. But also orphaned keel, curious bombas, and one injured babelrack, pregnant and trapped in a ravine. Brains are scanned, physiologies analyzed. They spend many long hours in this endeavor, sometimes sharing their results with Watt and the Council, and sometimes with members of the private group Grace has started among the most precocious children. She calls it a book club.

Don't be too exclusive, thinks Maya. *No one likes a snob, and cliques can be dangerous.*

A.P. Malloy

I only invite people who will enjoy it.
And how do you know who they are?
Grace shrugs, reminding Maya of herself...

...and Maya watches as time flies ahead, and for Grace, fifteen turns to twenty-five, and they prepare a presentation to the Council to object what is being called the Fabyldyr Reduction. Maya is more nervous than Grace, who approaches the presentation with her typical cool and her glowing aura.

"We believe," Grace says to the Council, "there is a better way to modify fabyldyr behavior than to trigger cannibalism. We fear unintended consequences."

But when asked what her alternative is, Grace is forced to admit:

"We don't have one yet. But the proper course of action is often not the easiest."

It is one of the few arguments she loses...

...and as the dream progresses, Maya watches her daughter win many more, sees her go from tutor to teacher to leader of the entire Academy. And the number of telepaths in the colony? Growing like leaves on a well-fed tree, one rooted in charmed soil.

And she sees—no she senses, with her mind!— small breakthroughs in their attempts to communicate with the native fauna. Scion, bombas, and keel, even the thick-headed babelracks are changing, and their change is faster than anything Maya could have anticipated, and Grace is the reason.

...and Maya's life continues to unfold.

Her daughter ages, but slowly, apt to live to a hundred and fifty, and New Gaia grows, too, a generation of grandchildren becoming adults. Watt, Javon, and all her friends, including Janet, weather the vagaries of time, respected and admired in the twilight of their lives.

Watt passes first, living long enough to witness the birth of his great-grandson, who is named George.

Heck, he says, looking at the chubby fingers and wiping his eyes. *He's got more hair than I do.*

Javon follows not long after, leaving behind several offspring, a wife who is revered by all, and a legacy greater in the eyes of the colonists than Washington, Tubman, or Raahithya Sharma himself. Charles Healey, doing everyone a favor, had led the way years earlier...

...and then the end is near, and Maya's hair is white, her face deeply creased, her eyes wise but tired, and she is confined for a time to her bed.

Grace comes to visit.

I want to show you something.

And, with more than one white hair of her own, she tells Maya about the Book, about the wonders it has revealed, surprised to learn that Maya is not.

I knew you were keeping something from me, she says, and she pats her daughter's knee. *But I never worried. Here.* She takes two silver chains from around her neck and presses them into Grace's hand. Grace knows what the titanium vial contains, knows also the purpose of the key. She accepts both, placing the chains around her neck, and she is sad but does not cry.

I can't introduce you to Petros, thinks Grace. *You'd just forget; that how he works. But if you like, I'll sleep with you, and he can visit us in our dreams. I've been thinking a lot about our future, and I want you to see. One day, because of your research, we'll communicate with the non-humans like good friends.*

In my dreams?

Mine, actually, but we'll share. I can't say what they'll be, but the word 'possibilities' keeps coming up. Petros promised something good. He likes you.

And in the dream, that is how the Maya of that timeline leaves her life, sleeping peacefully next to her daughter, her mind moving through visions of what might be. She sees many things, but none please her more than a copper-spiked creature, small but fierce, ridden by what seems to be a girl wearing blue. And these two characters communicate, but they use no words.

When Janet arrives in the early morning, they are still sleeping, and she finds them both smiling.

An hour later, Grace wakes, but Maya is gone.

A.P. Malloy

+ + + + + +

For her part, Lightning finds, upon walking through her own door, that she is a wabi again, and it is story time. Many kezel are gathered, and Ancian has the stage. It is a story she has heard before, and she itches to go outside and play, for she is a rowdy thing, full of big ideas but not much patience.

Still your boots, Little Spark, thinks Ancian. *This is the story of where I was born, the land of Redteeth, and that makes it your land, too.*

And she tells of the keel time and the Wall, a time of darkness and ignorance. But she also tells of the escape to the land of light.

Was that the end of their troubles? Ancian asks. *Were the keel safe on this side of the Wall?*

I dunno, wabi Lightning replies, because she and wabi Thunder are pulling one another's ears.

The answer turns out to be *No,* from Ancian, thanks to the scourge of derka and kish—and the scarcity of accrete. It also turns out to be *Settle down, or you'll get a real ear pulling,* from Submission.

Ancian tells of the Moondwellers, who teach the keel to think, spawning the First Kezel, and who help grow the accrete. By their magic, the foothills of Ibedos are covered in living stalagmites and filled with prey.

For what other word fits? Ancian wonders. *Magic!*

But then she tells of the Change, when kezel west of the wedge began spreading rumors that all was not well with the bipeds. They told of a skirmish, a noisy battle, where awful weapons had been used and some Moondwellers had been killed.

And the rumors didn't end there.

Renders far to the northwest, thinks Ancian, *swore that Moondwellers had come with noisy machines to clear the accrete, driving them from their caves. More than one kezel had perished—or so it was claimed. And hearing this, all Renders and many Redteeth threw away their vests and burned their gloves and boots...and they cursed*

Aranae in Red

the Moondwellers.

But some were incredulous.

They were what? asks wabi Lightning.

They couldn't believe it! Moondwellers? Betrayers? Never! And these Redteeth who refused to believe the rumors are your ancestors, Little Spark. Generation after generation, they moved farther east to find a place they could wear their gear without being harassed, walk two-legged and practice the Way without scorn and abuse. 'A clan that doesn't love Moondwellers is no clan for us,' they thought. And eventually, when I was a jabi and the Moondwellers had long since disappeared, over the wedge we came! And the Sugarfeet welcomed us. They never once believed the rumors. Just stories to scare folks off and gain territory, they said. Sacrilege...

...wabi Lightning doesn't know that word, but it doesn't matter, for in the dream, she is no longer a wabi. Many moons have passed, and now she is a jabi, and she is staring down at a fallen bibija kezel, naked, white, and bloodstained, his eyes still and sightless, and she is carrying a Moondweller cutter...

...and now she is older still, a young ibiwa, and much of the Sugarfoot accrete has been burned, and the wedge is crossable at one point only, and she crosses this, again and again, visiting a family of api-less wabis bringing gifts of food. And when the bereaved fancy asks why, Lightning thinks, *Restitution, overdue...*

...and still time passes, and now she has become a bibija herself, and look! She wears no boots or gloves, and the wedge is not to the west but to the east, and the Redteeth that pass do not call her murderer but Chief, and her wabis they call family...

...until at the end, her spikes gray and her tail bent, Lightning gazes out and sees more fallen accrete bridging the wedge than ever before, and kezel from every clan crossing freely, some vested, some not, and none judged either way. And Joy is at her side, miraculously gold and winged. And when, in the dream, Lightning draws her last breath, she smells every kezel she has ever

A.P. Malloy

loved, and as she exhales, she feels Crystal gripping her by the nape, lifting her like a wabi from her worn out frame and carrying her off to something better.

+ + + + + +

But Joy's dream is shorter, and in it, she is no longer blue or gold, but dusky gray, and she has wings, but they no longer work.

It's OK, she thinks to her companion.

Because it is. She has lived to see humans spread across the Allery Chain and yet remain at peace with the native Aranaens. And scion! They flourish but do not encroach. And she has her dearest possession riding in a refurbished sling at her side. And she has...

Who does she have? Who is this person?

He is a human, at least as old as she, his red hair long ago turned white, and he loves her beyond doubt.

Who are you? she asks.

Dumdum, he smiles, and he adjusts her chair so she can see better. And there, through the window of her imagination, she watches little red-haired children at play, and some with curly black hair, a few with blue skin, some with antennae, and many with her companion's bright eyes. And look how many of them there are! And how happy! That's all she needs.

It's OK, she thinks to him again.

And he kisses her.

I know, he thinks. And she dreams she passes from this life with his taste on her lips.

CHAPTER FIVE
First

JEREMIAH WILL PAUSE in his storytelling, and his audience will be uncharacteristically quiet. Outside of their cozy room, filled with chairs, and sleeping bags, and pillows, they will hear a party that has gone on long past their bedtime. Natalia will roll a single kezel spike between her fingers, admiring its creamy white. Sammy will stir sleepy embers in the fireplace and Ani will lie back, letting the last of the flames play with her imagination. Even Bo Lin will have nothing to say, and Jeremiah will worry.

"Have I bored you?" he will ask.

'No," Ani will reply. "It's not that."

"Then what?"

One of the adults will clear his throat.

"If I may?" he will ask.

"Of course."

Sammy and the others will listen close to see if the adult can express what many of them are thinking.

"I feel," the adult will say, "I feel like we're drawing near the end of things. Our favorite characters are spread all over the world—and time—but I feel like things are going to come to a crashing end sometime soon."

Bo Lin will nod.

"Yep," he will say. "It's not far off. Look!" and he will point to the book from which Jeremiah reads. "How many pages are left? How many chapters? Not many."

"What do you want me to do?" Jeremiah will ask.

Again, the children will struggle silently to make their feelings and desires concrete. A second adult will put voice to their ideas.

"For me," she will say, "I don't want to get to that ending until I've had more of the middle. Or maybe I should say more of the past. I know Maya's original time-line had trouble, but there was good, too, yes? New discoveries, amazing adventures. Say what you want, but I can't imagine a world without kezel."

"Or thinking bombas," Natalia will add.

"Or any of the telepaths," Sammy will agree. "Even scion are amazing. That's what I say."

Jeremiah will nod.

"You want more of the original timeline."

"Yes," many voices will reply as one.

"Yes, please," the first adult will say. "We have so much to learn. Not about the Rift or the Exile. That's depressing. But things that came before. Good things."

"Not just good things," Bo Lin will object. "But more. More about the first time, and how it went."

"The original timeline," Jeremiah will nod and bite his lip. "Good things but not just good. Things to learn." He will smile at them and adjust his seat.

"I think I can do that."

And he will turn a page.

+ + +   + + +

In the original timeline, it was decided after much study that the best place to establish the colony—the best place, mind you, not the perfect place, for such did not exist—was the continent they named Ibedos.

"Go over it again," Javon ordered. "Why Ibedos?"

"Yes sir," said Chief Abara, and she opened up the three-dimensional map, newly and neatly labeled. "The other options are untenable for many reasons. The continent we're calling Primaqua is situated over not one but two super volcanoes. Madragall is hellishly volatile, and Ohodune and the Flemish are crawling with sextans. The

Aranae in Red

Allery Chain is our second-best option; it's temperate and relatively calm, with no scion or keel on any of its three major islands. But the chain has fewer of the raw resources needed to re-build *Destiny's* astral drive, provide for colony needs, or, as Magister Healey is fond of reminding us, make the mission a financial success. Bottom line, Major, everything on the Chain would be harder and take a lot more time."

"I like Chuck's optimism," said Javon. "I really do. But the odds of us returning home—with or without a hold filled with riches—are not great, you know."

"Yes," Shonda said. "I know."

But they rarely talked of this. No one did. There was too much to do, no time for nostalgia, regret, or wishful thinking. Nor had they time for much sleep—not even Maya, who was growing along with the child inside her, and who felt a burning desire to be useful, even when her back ached and her feet complained.

Good Lord, she thought, eyeing herself in the mirror. *I look like a parade balloon.*

But something about her evolving form inspired a feeling in Watt that he could only describe as *ardence.* He loved the way she looked, was fascinated by the hormonal whirlwind that one month caused her to sprout a pencil-thin mustache and the next, acne like a teenager. He couldn't keep his hands off her, and she, bemused but grateful, didn't ask him to.

I have to tell you something, he confided one day. They had not yet established quarters on the surface, and were still living aboard *Destiny.* Janet, who had been formally reprimanded but otherwise exonerated in the Willie affair, had been cleared for duty, and was now counseling patients, the list of whom was long and diverse. Drama in space took a toll on the psyche.

Are you going to ask me to marry you?

Heck yes, I am. But not here. Not now. All sweaty from hauling lab equipment. You deserve...

And he leaned down to where she sat at the workstation, manipulating three dimensional models. He tickled her face with his scruffy beard as he kissed her, leaving her to imagine what she deserved.

No, he said, *It's something else.*

His tone was unexpectedly serious.

I don't want any bad news, right now, Watt.

It's not bad news. But... It's been on my mind a lot lately, and I think you need to know. It's about Janet.

Don't dither, Watt. You like that word? Dither? Well, you're doing it. It makes me nervous.

Aye. Watt tugged at his beard. *Sorry. Better to just say it and be done.*

Yes, please.

Janet has an emergency power-down protocol she doesn't know exists—and I don't want her to know.

He sat down and began unlacing his boots. But he kept his eyes on her the entire time, gauging her response. For a time, there wasn't one. Maya moved slowly from the workstation to the floor, hands and knees on a yoga mat, doing her best cat-cow stretch, her eyes closed in concentration.

Did you sense me? Watt asked, and he placed his boots in their locker.

Yes, I'm thinking. Tell me why this is a secret.

Maya. Maya, look.

She turned her head and opened her eyes. Watt held up a key for her to see, an old-fashioned style like the ones shown tied to Ben Franklin's kite.

The key to my heart? she asked.

He pursed his lips.

Please don't joke. If she knew this existed... Think about it, Maya. The person you trust and love most of all has secretly created a way to shut you down without your knowledge or permission. How would you feel?

Maya left off with the cat-cow and switched to the sitting butterfly so she could look squarely at Watt. She considered the implications of this news.

I would feel betrayed, and I would want every copy of that key destroyed.

Watt nodded. He reached out, attempting to hand

Aranae in Red

her the key, but she refused.

I have one of my own, he said. *I wasn't going to tell you. But when Willie...* He ran his hand through his unruly hair, which returned to its usual state the very next moment. *This one's a copy. Made it here on* Destiny, *just last week. Please take it.*

She did not.

I don't like this, Watt. What are you thinking? That she's going to... You think she'll end up like one of those on Mars? After all your speech making and high talk, this is the bottom line? That she's a thing? That if we don't like something she's doing we flip a switch and problem solved? Who am I even talking to here?

Argh. I know. It's terrible. And yes, there was a time... Watt's eyes lost their focus, and he leaned back in his chair, the key still in his hand. *I was an idealist when I designed her, an idealist when I cultivated her sentience. Every time I transferred her programming from one synthetic body to the next, from infant to child to adolescent to adult: an idealist all along!*

But those people on Mars...

I don't want to talk about this, Watt.

Please, Maya, please. If something happened to you or the baby because of her...

Watt Everett MacLean! That idealism is why I fell in love with you. It's why I trust Janet in spite of what happened to my parents. And now you want to hedge your bet? How is it possible you trust her less than I do?

It's not her I don't trust, Maya. Heck! Dang it and heck! Don't you get it? It's me I don't trust. She'll do the best she can, but the best she can is always going to be defined by my limitations as a designer. And every day I'm with you, every time that baby kicks, or some new threat pops up, those limitations become more obvious. Aye, sure, we can call it idealism, but more and more, I'm starting to see it as arrogance. I thought I could do it better, I thought the Martian designers were idiots. I thought I had all the answers, and she would be different.

She is.

A.P. Malloy

At the moment. But I worry...
Maya reached out, placing her hand on his knee.
Fear is not a good motivation for decision making.
He took her hand and pressed the key in her palm, closing her fingers around the cold silver and looking at her with singular intensity.
Sometimes it is.

+ + +

At three months, the unborn baby that Maya and Watt had not expected but never once regretted was deemed by Doc Foster to be "the picture of health." That it was a girl was no surprise to Maya, but she kept the name she had chosen to herself, as well as the odd series of events that had led to its choice.

Too weird, she thought, *too much on top of everything else.* And not even with Javon did she raise the topic, he who had also been on the bridge when the indescribable presence had appeared, and who had felt it himself. For reasons of his own, Charlotte was the only one Javon told, and she only once.

At the three-month mark, though the site had been selected, the colony was still just a holographic plan. The 'picture of health' was all it was, nothing more tangible than schematics and hope. But several important benchmarks had been attained. Site selection was chief among these, no easy task with all that was at stake and the magister breathing down Javon's neck. He had insisted on being consulted on each point, from satellite and drone deployment to the actual site surveys themselves, which, though he hated atmospheric flight, he had refused to be excluded from.

Air, soil, and water samples had been collected and analyzed, and between Doc Foster, Chief Abara, and their teams, potential pathogens had been identified and inoculations synthesized. That the two department heads were also dear friends on the threshold of romance complicated the project, and when, on the rare occasion personal issues spilled over into the workplace, Javon was hard-pressed to keep the peace.

"I will if she will," was a common response to his many pleas for civility.

"Tell the doctor that…" was often met with, "Tell her yourself," or, "If the chief wants it done that way, one of her flunkies can do it."

But by the three-month mark, the job was well underway. In fact, it was considered the easier of the two primary compatibility protocols. Allowing humans to live and work safely on a foreign body was something the System had gotten good at. Keeping the body itself healthy—specifically anything that lived there—was a challenge of a different magnitude. The careless introduction of a foreign ("invasive" was the word Chief Abara used) species such as humans had been shown in other cases to have disastrous results. Javon was resolutely patient making sure that would not be the case here, and though Magister Healey was keen to begin mining, Javon would hear nothing of it until all the necessary precautions had been taken and the process followed to the letter.

Sterilize.

Limit and diffuse.

Mitigate.

These were the words attached to the planetary conservation protocol, and Maya's job during this time was analysis of the native fauna with those words in mind. How best to eliminate the human-source microbes that might damage this new environment? How to minimize contact and concentration so that indigenous populations had time to develop the necessary immunities? How to lessen the damage done should something go awry and a pathogen wreak havoc?

Janet came to visit her while she was working at one of the modeling stations.

"Can you take a break?" she asked.

Maya could do better than that; she logged off her workstation and quit for the day.

At first, they meandered *Destiny's* corridors hand-

in-hand like dear sisters. Janet had been counting carefully; in all their time together, Maya had given her an
average of one word per minute. Keeping this in mind, she
gauged her questions carefully, conscious of those whose
answers could be open, closed, or non-verbal. She found
Maya's face deliciously expressive, but not always ade-
quate for the information she sought. So she wasted no
energy on "How are you?" "Is everything OK?" or "What's
the news?" choosing instead a question that mattered to
her much more.

"Do you forgive me for stranding us?"

"I never blamed you."

"I calculate myself bearing at least forty-nine percent of the responsibility for our current situation."

"Which may turn out great."

And that, plus a smile, was enough to satisfy Janet as they moved past workshops and laboratories like a
couple in a museum, enjoying the exhibits silently. Then
they arrived at a conveyor, and Janet revealed her purpose in seeking Maya's company.

"Would you accompany me to my office?" she
asked. "I've been meaning to interview you for my personnel files, but there haven't been any openings."

Maya recalled her first encounter with Janet's
files, the first time she had seen Charlotte DuBois.

"One hundred questions?" she asked, her tone
doubtful. "And a camera?"

"That is the template. I synthesized the opinions
of fifty-seven experts in the field to arrive at the list, but
of course you can pass on any of the questions."

"And the camera?"

"Yes, but I hope you won't."

"Has anyone?"

"No."

Maya made no commitment, but she stepped onto
the conveyor, still holding Janet's hand. Together, they let
the tread do the work as they moved down the corridor
toward one of the lifts. They passed some people, baggy-
eyed, with shoulders hunched, and were passed by others

Aranae in Red

bustling and stern. Casual conversation among them was rare; the whole ship had an air of tension and fatigue. But Maya sensed Javon's influence in each face—and her father's. Every person on this expedition, with the exception of Magister Healey, had either been hand-selected by one of the two or accepted by them based on the other's recommendation. This was not a group prone to negativity or resignation.

And this awareness, that she too, had been selected, deemed worthy in the realest of senses by these two giant figures in her life, straightened her shoulders and lifted her gaze. She was meant to be here, as clearly as the child inside her. If the ship's chaplain had decided this was what she needed to serve the crew—and not a single member had refused—who was she to hide behind trauma or family connections to buy an indulgence? No. For good or bad, *Destiny* was her family now. She would pour herself into that relationship.

"One hundred questions and a camera," she agreed at last when they reached the lift, and Janet smiled gratefully. But then a question of her own rose in Maya's mind, and she felt powerless to suppress it, conscious all the while of the silver key hanging around her neck on its own chain, just below Shantikar's vial. She had made sure the chain was long enough so the two would never touch.

"Do you have your own file?" she asked.

"Of course. I answered every question."

"Can I see it?"

"I would be honored! When we're done with yours? And maybe something to eat?"

"You read my mind," thought Maya, glad that it was not so.

+ + +

Janet's office was located near *Destiny*'s hub, just beneath the bridge. Modest but comfortable, designed to put people at ease, it had three video walls with animated nature scenes and the most soothing ambient music Maya had ever heard. Janet's assistant, Corporal Ladera, was putting the final touches on a client visit report when they arrived. She didn't exactly frown when she saw Maya, but her pretty smile hardened, and her mood was easy to read. She had already put in a long day dealing with the mental health of others and was eager to tend to her own. Was Maya another patient?

Janet anticipated the question.

"I'll take it from here, Brandi. But be a dear, won't you, and boot up the camera."

The Corporal was and did, wasting no time on introductions. The moment she had been given clearance, she waved and was gone, leaving Maya and Janet alone.

"Where do we start?"

"Just stand here. Perfect. You don't have to smile. Relax; just be yourself. We'll do the basic intro first and then you can sit. OK... We're set. State your full name, age, and your role on this expedition."

"Maya Nandini, twenty-seven, civilian scientist."

Janet didn't object to her using the pseudonym. She checked the 3V image on her monitor and nodded.

"You're very photogenic, you know."

"You should have your vision checked." But that felt like a waste of words, a self-indulgent habit of denigration, and thinking of Tony, she corrected herself. "I'm sorry. Thank you is what I meant."

Janet motioned to one of the chairs.

"Make yourself comfortable. Would you like some hot chocolate? Or something to nibble on?"

"Both please."

In minutes, Maya sat with her feet elevated, cup and saucer to her side and Janet across from her, glasses in place and notepad on her lap.

"I know this can be tiring," she said. "You can quit any time. Will Watt be expecting you?"

"Not until late."

"Then let's begin." And Janet took a deep, very unnecessary but natural-looking breath.

Aranae in Red

Her first questions were simple enough, but they grew progressively more difficult. Maya didn't quit, but when the session was over and Janet hugged her good-bye, she felt exhausted as if she'd been digging for hidden treasure or been wrung out like a dishrag.

"If you still want to see my file," Janet squeezed her hand, "I can send it to you."

"I do, thanks."

"Oh, that's a lovely chain. Did Watt get it for you?"

Maya's hand moved reflexively to her throat.

"Yes. One for each of us."

"My brother the romantic!" Janet kissed Maya on the cheek. "I'm working late. I'll see you tomorrow..."

+ + +

At the six-month mark, though Maya already felt she could stretch no farther, she knew there would be no rushing this child. It felt happily ensconced inside her as if intending to enjoy every moment of its allotted two hundred and eighty days. Even its kicks and jabs weren't impatient so much as exploratory: How does this arm work? What is this leg good for?

Watt peeked into the bathroom.

Ready? he asked.

She looked away from the mirror and eyed him from head to toe, rebuttoning his crooked lab coat and taming the worst of his rebellious locks with the palm of her hand. He chewed his lip anxiously.

Relax, she thought. *I'm the one presenting.*

Sympathy nerves, he shrugged.

That's sweet, she smiled and kissed him. *But not necessary. I'm fine.* Which was true, of course, but she couldn't say why. At any other time, the thought of presenting to the Council would have made her ill. Now, she merely linked arms with Watt and walked calmly with him to the nearest lift.

Want to rehearse? he asked.

Not really.

A.P. Malloy

If anyone gives you any grief...

They won't.

But if they do...

Why would they? I'm only presenting on the fauna, not offering advice on how we should interact with it.

But you know they'll ask your opinion.

I'm pretty sure they'll leave that for Shonda.

Aye, she'll get her say. But Healey's a slippery devil, always looking for an advantage. You can count on it: he's going to try to catch you off-guard, see if he can expose something useful for his, you know, plans for world domination...heck! What a booger.

Let him. It's OK, Watt. They passed a team of technicians and stilled their thoughts by habit. Once out of sight, Maya took Watt's hand and placed it on her belly.

What am I feeling? he asked.

You tell me.

They stepped inside the lift, and the door slid closed. But they gave no command, instead standing face-to-face, one's hand resting on the other's distended abdomen. Watt's beard scrunched and his eyelids lowered. Maya could read his tension, so common it seemed like a birthright, like skin color or intelligence. It was its own kind of lab coat, and he wore it so often she had begun to think he either enjoyed it, needed it, or was unaware that it existed.

I feel...is it supposed to feel warm like that?

She smiled.

What else do you feel?

That we're going to be late for the presentation.

Watt...

He sighed.

Heck. OK. I feel... he lowered his defenses—just a bit—and she held her hand over his, pressing it closer. *I feel...* He was silent for a time, and his breathing relaxed. He stopped chewing at his beard. To her surprise, a tear formed at the corner of one eye and ran to his mustache. When he looked up, his gaze was calm but wondering.

"She's very happy, isn't she?" he whispered.

Aranae in Red

Maya nodded.

His tears began in earnest.

"I don't think I've ever been that happy."

Maya kissed the tears from his face, carefully choosing five words.

"She wants you to be."

+ + +

Three months later, the first group of colonists settled at the location selected for the agriculture facility, north of what became known as the Doorn River. It was a relatively temperate zone, but short-lived snow was common, and in months of study, no sextan had ever been observed traveling at that latitude.

They appear to despise the cold, Maya had reported, and this was confirmed via satellite. On every landmass but the Allery Chain—where there were no sextans at all—the six-legged creatures, the closest thing Aranae had to a civilization, confined themselves to the warmest fringes of the habitable zone.

Scientists, mechanics, construction workers, and teams of labor androids were among this first wave of colonists. Their mission: to complete the underground facility, some of which had arrived pre-fabricated, and, in the case of the scientists, maintenance crews, and their respective families, inhabit the space and provide the real-world data that no models, surveys, or satellite images could. If all went well for one Earth month, construction would begin on the mining compound and refinery. The pace was maddening to some—life on a crowded spaceship had grown tiresome in many ways— but a misstep at this critical point could jeopardize the entire expedition, and aside from the understandable and expected frayed nerves and occasional angry outbursts, the crew maintained an air of professionalism that made Javon proud. He said as much to Charlotte as they shared a rare moment alone in their quarters.

"One colonist in particular?" she asked, arching a

manicured brow.

"Of course," he replied, and he paused the holographic presentation he had been reviewing to take her hand and kiss it, guessing what she would say.

"Quelle horreur," she frowned. "I'm filthy."

"Never," he murmured.

She tolerated her hand in his but turned her gaze to the hologram. Various Aranaean lifeforms were represented in three dimensions next to the silhouette of an average human to show scale. She pointed to one of the largest, and it came to life, the nightmarish offspring of a pterodactyl and a drunkard's rendering of a dragon, green, toothy, and barbed. The high-resolution images, gathered by one of the colony's earliest satellites, were accompanied by narration. Maya's voice, which Charlotte had only rarely heard before her recent presentation, was velveteen and alluring, somehow making the dry information it conveyed rich and sensual.

"Viridius fabeldyr," Maya spoke. "Carnivorous. Estimated mass range twenty-five kilograms to three hundred and fifty. Wingspan one meter to eleven. Lifespan: unknown. Reproduction: unknown. Population density: high. Threat level: unknown but hypothesized to be high with largest specimens. No observed terrestrial behavior. Attain flight by perch-dropping. Natural enemies: none observed."

"Que c'est laid," Charlotte stuck out her tongue. "But that voice! She makes them sound like elegant pastries. Why does she hardly ever speak? She could read my own obituary and I would listen."

"She's complicated," Javon replied absently. He shooed the fabeldyr image away and selected another, a giant, tusky octopod, yellow and white. Exceeding his wildest childhood fantasies, the beast had two enormous heads, one on each end of a massive carapace.

"Will you look at that," he said. "Like someone glued together a pair of mammoth warthogs—and gave 'em a tortoise shell for fun. And what elementary art student painted these fellas?"

Aranae in Red

He motioned with a finger and the creature began to move, one head down and grazing on blades of yellow grass, one head up and observant. Almost perfectly camouflaged in the snow, two miniature replicas of the creature frolicked nearby, tuskless.

"Ancipitis octopoda," Maya's voice reported, her tone matter-of-fact. "Omnivorous. Eats grass, flowers, small invertebrates, and select carrion. Adult mass over five hundred kilograms. Mass at birth, fifty kilograms. Lifespan: unknown. Reproduction: uncertain. May be hermaphroditic. Habitat: temperate plains. Population density: medium. Threat level: low unless with young."

Charlotte waved the image to stillness and Maya's voice to silence. She moved around and sat in front of Javon, commanding his attention.

"You've seen all of these before."

He took a deep breath and stretched as if waking from hypnosis. With a snap of his fingers the image disappeared altogether.

"I'm sorry," he said. "I was daydreaming."

"I noticed. But about what, I wonder? Old loves?"

"Nah, c'mon, now. None of that."

"It's OK. I would like her too. She's magnetic."

Javon reached out and pulled her chair closer.

"You're the only magnet for me."

"N'importe quoi," Charlotte dismissed. "But I wonder if you would be so quick to allow me to go to the surface if I was as pregnant and inexperienced as she."

"So, you heard."

"Of course, I heard. A quoi tu pensais?"

"What was I thinking? I don't know. She asked and I said yes. Honestly, Char, you would have too. She's changed, you know, since our little dinner party."

"Who hasn't, Javon? But changed how?"

"It's complicated."

"She gets that word a lot."

"Yes, I suppose she does. But haven't you noticed it too? It isn't Watt, it's not even the pregnancy. If she had grown morose or anxious or even short-tempered, I would attribute it to what happened with Janet. But that's how other people responded. She's gone the other way. She's... How do I say this? She's gotten more calm, not less, more confident and outgoing. But never manic, never hopped up on fear. She's just so..."

"Javon! She is nine months pregnant. If something bad happens down there, she is in no shape to deal with it—and she could be a liability for others. Bon sang! What would happen to the baby?"

"I know." Javon held up his hands, defenseless. "You're right on every count. And Chuck gave me The Speech when he heard. 'Violating protocol' and all that. But..." He searched for the proper way to express his thoughts. "Let me say this before you condemn me. She stood there, in front of my station, and as calmly as you please said that not only did she intend to be part of the first group on the surface, it was her intention to have the baby on the planet—at the ag facility. Doc Foster would deliver, and Shonda would be her coach—she said it like it had already happened! I swear, Char, I was very good and ready to say no in at least four different languages, but then she said, 'I need to be off this ship just as bad as this baby needs to be out of me.' And then she smiled, and I forgot all my reasons for saying no. I don't even remember signing the permission to allow her to go."

"Well, you did. She's packing."

Javon chuckled.

"You care for her, I know. And I love you as the mother of my firstborn child—yes, I mean this damn ship!—so I say this with my whole heart: when she smiled at me, I knew she would be OK. I knew what she said would happen exactly as she described it. I can't tell you why, or what excuse a military man has to trust warm, fuzzy feelings. But Char! They were very warm, and very fuzzy, and even now, I don't doubt my decision."

Her eyes met his for long seconds. Then she took both of his hands and held them to her heart.

"If you are going to have an affair, Javon..."

"Char! Don't, please."

"It would kill me, you know that?"

He leaned in close, so their foreheads touched. "Yes, Charlotte, I know."

"But I would kill you first, Javon."

And she smiled, but in a way which convinced him she was serious.

"Yes, Charlotte," he closed his eyes. "I know."

"Now," she said, and rose to her feet. "You will accompany your Chief Engineer to the shower and help her wash the grease off. Your 'baby' is a dirty beast."

Javon stood as well.

"Does that mean I'm forgiven? You approve?"

"Approve may be too strong. But I trust my husband. There is nothing to forgive."

+ + +

Janet's caseload on *Destiny* was such that she was not allowed to join Maya and Watt with the others establishing the ag facility. She pled her case with Javon, but his refusal had been as decisive as it was sympathetic. He shared her desire and guessed at part of her unhappiness now that her roommates had gone.

"I hereby order you to join me and Charlotte for dinner at least twice a week," he said. "If you don't mind watching us eat. We would love your company—and it would be good for you to socialize, I think, talk about something other than work for a while."

When Maya heard this, already on the surface and getting situated in their spartan quarters, she was glad at the news and replied that Janet must accept the invitation and report everything that happened.

She works too much, she thought, and Watt, who knew Janet best, couldn't disagree as much as explain. He unpacked his bag as he did so.

She doesn't see it like that. Her...ethos is rooted in service. She gains fulfillment from being useful.

By choice or programming?

By the temperament and conscious choices that re-

A.P. Malloy

sulted from her base program. I didn't write a code saying, 'you will serve.' She evolved into that type of person. That same base programming exposed to a different set of environmental stimuli would have evolved in a different way. She could have become a hedonist, or her spiritual tendencies could have driven her to reclusion. Heck! She could have spent her life holed up in a cave.

Someday, thought Maya. *I would like to learn more about that 'base programming.' But for now, if you don't mind, I think I would like to have this baby.*

Watt looked up from his shirt folding.

Are you...?

Serious? she winced. *Yep. Pretty sure*

And so, off they went to the infirmary, which was little more than a prefabricated, pre-stocked concrete box buried in the ground, well-lit and ventilated, but windowless and utterly devoid of character. That didn't bother Maya. Nor did the contractions, which were textbook in their regularity and severity, and were thus in their own way a great comfort.

With Watt holding her right hand, Shonda holding her left, and Doc Foster attending, the labor went as smoothly as if scripted for 3V. From full cervical dilation to birth no more than an hour elapsed, and when the baby slipped free of its confines, it was sucking its thumb. It required little persuasion to begin breathing, never complained when being cleaned, and blinked its eyes at each new face. Shonda began weeping at first sight; Doc Foster's usually stern face creased in an unexpected way, revealing a hidden beauty, and she began laughing, a sound Maya had never heard from her. As they watched Maya cradle the child and Watt's face streaming tears, the Chief and Doctor clasped hands, their petty feud forgotten. They would forever mark that as the date they decided on children of their own, though they had never, up to that point, discussed the topic.

"Grace," Maya answered when Shonda wondered about the name, the easiest word she had ever spoken.

+ + +

The baby grew like the colony itself, not without occasional stumbles, but largely according to plan, each benchmark arriving on time and duly celebrated.

The ag facility, once complete and fully operational, provided all the evidence Javon needed to approve the next phase of the expedition: construction of the mining complex and refinery. They were to be built just south of the mountains, and yet far enough apart to prevent a refinery disaster—"heaven forbid," Javon had said—from compromising the mining operation.

All the activity kept the colonists busy, none more than Janet, whose dual role as spiritual advisor and secular counsel kept her in demand by believers and atheists alike. But the moment she had gotten settled on the surface, for the time making her home in the residential quarters of the ag facility, she sought out and spent every spare moment in Maya's company. Her fascination with the colony's youngest member couldn't be measured—it even surprised her.

When weather and fabyldyrs allowed, they spent much of their time outdoors, studying life on Aranae. And when it didn't, they were often found in one of the portable observatories, small but durable geodesics whose composite surfaces were formed like one-way mirrors, camouflaged when viewed from the outside but perfectly transparent to those inside.

"Fish houses," Watt called them, which made no sense to most people, Maya included.

"Sorry," she said as she opened the observatory hatch to allow Janet inside. "It's kinda cramped." She balanced Grace on her hip as Janet ducked her head and stepped inside, sealing the hatch behind her. Grace immediately reached for her.

"Onnie," she gurgled, as close to 'auntie' as she could get, and she entertained herself by squeezing and tugging at Janet's nose, ears, tunic, and anything else she could reach with her fat fingers.

Janet's smile, infrequent since Willie's passing, had found its way back, and she was now rarely without it. She cooed nonsense to the baby while Maya booted up cameras, microphones, and other sensors.

"Research indicates," said Janet as she sat on one of the stools and bounced Grace on her lap, "that it's not just the parents who experience stimulation to the pleasure centers of the brain in the presence of a baby. The effect has been demonstrated in close relatives and good friends—but also in complete strangers. The effect on a synthetic mind is less well documented, so I can't say if my experience is normal, but I must admit, Maya, that you have changed my life with this little one." Grace took a handful of Janet's hair and promptly stuck it in her mouth. Taking this cue, Maya prepped a bottle, which Grace much preferred over hair.

"I think," said Maya to Janet, "you might like this." And she pointed out the observatory, northeast, to the sea of yellow grass on which they seemed to be afloat. Her mouth occupied, Grace couldn't exclaim at what they saw outside, but her eyes grew wide and her head bobbed as if she approved.

For in the distance, a living rainbow approached, falling from the sky in a stately, arcing descent. And as it drew near, it rippled and shook, and it disintegrated into individual units of red, green, violet, and gold. And still they grew closer, until the observers made out many large creatures, hundreds of broad wings flapping, hundreds of bright, green eyes, long, crimson necks, and even longer crimson legs, their three toes splayed.

"Avis arcus pluvis," Maya said, her voice hushed.

"Abasarcaspooba," Grace agreed, and she returned the bottle to her mouth.

"Oh my," Janet exclaimed, as the creatures were now within a hundred meters and had begun to land, confident and strong. Not a one was under a meter tall; most were at least two. To a person with a less analytical mind, they might have appeared to be a fanciful cross between some prehistoric reptile and a most flamboyant os-

Aranae in Red

trich. But they were Janet's first encounter with alien life, and she couldn't help but analyze them. Once landed (she counted one hundred and seventy-four) the creatures fanned out in long, stilted strides. They plucked at the ends of the yellow grass and occasionally jabbed their spear-like beaks into the snowy ground, emerging with something—or some things—so small and quickly devoured she couldn't identify them.

"Here," Maya offered, pushing a button and turning a dial. The creatures became audible, muttering, hissing, and squawking, and Grace cast away her empty bottle, clapping her hands and laughing.

"Do they know we're here?" asked Janet.

"I think so."

"But they're not scared."

"I think they're curious."

And indeed, the creatures never looked directly at the geodesic, but as they plucked and jabbed, they also sidled deliberately closer, until Maya could make out the glint in their green eyes and the spurs jutting from the back of their legs. The nearest ones bobbed their heads and craned their necks, and while they never drew close enough to touch the observatory, Maya sensed from them a burning desire to do so.

"In your report, you mentioned flaming darts," Janet recalled. "Should we be concerned?"

"No observed offensive usage," Maya shrugged.

"If Watt was here," Janet guessed, "he would say we've only been observing for a few months."

Maya nodded, but her feelings for these creatures were impervious to Watt's imagined concerns. They were very much *un*like the fabeldyr or the lapis glaebosis. The latter, clawed and lumpy, had been encountered on the violet havens south and east of the mining compound and had proven exceedingly hostile, attacking the recon rover on sight. They had been unable to do any serious damage to the self-driven machine, but when returned to the compound, the rover was found scored with claw marks, each bearing a trace of deadly poison.

A.P. Malloy

No, these gorgeous beasts were nothing like that.

"They're my favorite," Maya beamed at the creatures bobbing and craning only meters away.

And so she continued to believe until she visited the refinery on the shore of Lake Zelano. There, she and a team studying the planet's hydrologic cycle were observing pistis unoculus, the great seeders of the water. When full grown, they spit forth fountains of eggs, some of which made their slow way to the ocean, where the warm, salty water catalyzed a transformation. From these eggs hatched finger-length creatures who then turned around and swam upstream out of Indrani, seeking fresh water and ultimately the frigid sanctuary of the far northern lakes. Along the way, they grew—those who weren't culled for food. For unoculus, itself a carnivore, was also one of the most common food sources for species all around the hydrologic cycle.

"Fascinating," Shonda said.

"Creepy and terrifying," said Luka the Russian, who cared not a bit for unoculus' lone eye stalk, deadly mouth, and lashing tongue. "But prekrasnyy, too, in a way—beautiful." And he held up his sampling jar, admiring the emerald eggs they had collected like jewels.

On their way back to the mine, Shonda was at the wheel, Maya in the navigator's seat, and Luka in back chatting with Sue Chang, a fellow hydrologist with whom he had a cordial rivalry. None of them were as attentive as they should have been, or perhaps there were just too many new things to look at during the drive. Either way, when Shonda suddenly swerved, Luka shouted, Sue screamed, and Maya wheeled about to see the creature they had almost hit—one so reclusive it had not to that point been documented.

"Shonda, stop!" she said, aiming her camera.

Shonda did, and they all got one long look at the beast. At first, Maya assumed the toothy ball of spikes was an adult, for it looked at her with a discerning gaze and was nearly as large as she.

But a moment later, she realized her mistake, for

Aranae in Red

another of its kind appeared, larger than any grizzly bear and gloriously spiked from prodigious snout to deadly tail. As Shonda re-engaged the rover and motored away, her teammates cursed in terror and gathered data at the same time. The creature rose to its hind legs and roared like a pack of lions, its teeth all the warning they needed. They fled at the rover's top speed, but it never pursued them. Instead, it dropped to four legs and gently used its mouth to pick its miniature counterpart from the ground before shuffling back into the shadows of the nearby accretion stand, one of the few in this region.

They surveyed that area for the next month and never saw either of the creatures again. But Maya was smitten and would not give up the search.

I know what Shonda says about hexapod coeruleus, she thought as she and Watt prepared Grace for bed. *But I don't care. Sextans might be the most social creatures on this planet, the most advanced, by some measures, but they're not the smartest.*

How do you know? Maybe these new ones are just really good hiders. Watt lifted Grace into her crib, handed her Morris, the scruffy plush tiger, and pulled up a chair so he could read the nightly story to her.

I don't, Maya admitted. *But I plan to find out.*

CHAPTER SIX
Breech

THUNDER WAKES LATE. The others have already left the room. He almost immediately feels his dream slipping away. There had been a door, yes? And the Tavaline Massif? And hadn't there been scion? Or were there kezel? It seems perhaps there had been both. And a derka.

For sure a derka.

Stupid, he thinks. *Perfect way to ruin a good sleep.*

And yet, the impressions linger even as the images fade. Soon, he can recall nothing of the dream but feelings. He remembers fear, grim determination, a fleeting moment of doubt, and then glorious, buoyant freedom, the ballast of guilt and shame cut loose.

He strives for a few moments more to recapture the details of the dream, stretching, and yawning, and flexing his claws. The harder he seeks, the more elusive his quarry becomes, until, rising to two legs and reaching for the sky, he snaps his jaws a couple times and lets the last faint image slip away. What difference does it make? Sun shining through the doorway and the smell of food is all that matters.

It's time to rejoin the others.

+ + +

The dome sleeps, or so it seems, for when Thunder

exits the room, he finds evidence of the celebration, but none of the celebrators. Most of the lights have been extinguished, many windows are closed against the sun, and empty cups and scattered tinsel outnumber humans, of which Thunder spies only a few, sweeping up the mess on the lower tiers.

In the Window, he finds leftovers from the previous feast, laid out neatly and in generous amounts. He wastes no time, making toothy acquaintance with a cold shank of talihew. The smell of it at first prevents him from realizing he is not alone. Dropping the food, he squints his eyes and turns.

How long were you going to stand there? He growls. *Did you think I wouldn't notice?*

Harmonized buzzing, high and melodious, comes from the far wall, and a moment later, the Joy in gold appears. She stands with her back to him, surrounded by her six silver escorts, staring out across the island.

Eat up, she thinks. *You haven't much time. Your major is counting every second—that's like a heartbeat, you know. Your oli, too.*

Yeah? They're not alone.

Oh? You haven't liked it here?

You know I have...in its own way. But it's not home, is it? And I have a feeling...it's time to go back.

Yes.

The Joy in gold shelters her thoughts while Thunder lays waste to the remainder of the talihew, a bowl of berries—red and green—the last of the fungus, and a deep basin of clean water. It doesn't take him long.

Appreciated, he thinks. *I don't like...you know, I don't enjoy the feeling of hunger.*

I know.

I don't suppose you're going to tell me what you meant by 'your secret is safe?'

No, I'm sorry.

The Joy in gold turns to face him, her eyes grand and sparkling, and he finds it difficult to hold her gaze.

Well. Guess I should go, he thinks.

A.P. Malloy

Your visit will be remembered for generations, she replies, and she approaches close enough to touch. *I'm very grateful to have met you. I have powerful memories of our Thunder at your age, from many moons ago, but I was young, and the older the memory, the less reliable. Seeing you here, now, in the flesh—what a delight!*

Sure. Like I said. Grand. I'm starting to get a bad feeling, though... Everyone thinks 'our Thunder' this and 'our Thunder' that, but I can't help noticing it's always in the past tense. Should that bother me?

Not in the least. Here...

The Joy in gold leans forward, her antennae tilting as if to touch him. Thunder shies away at first, but then feels foolish for doing so and stills himself. The golden filaments make contact, one above each of his eyes, their tips icy and tingling. A moment later, an unfamiliar portrait fills his mind, the image of a derka, black and red and implausibly tiny, motionless in a woven basket.

You know this creature? asks the Joy in gold.

Sure don't. Looks like some kind of derka. But that basket; guess it belongs to Lightning's crazy queen. I can't tell if the derka's sleeping or dead.

It is neither, actually. It is a hibernating seed derka. And Shimmer is not as crazy as she seems. I hope you will be able to give her a message. Can you do that?

Yeah, I guess, but who knows if I'll ever see her?

No one! But I have a feeling you will. Near the Tavaline Massif if my guess is correct. On Rite Butte.

Why me?

Silly! Haven't you figured it out yet? Because you're the most qualified, of course.

Yeah? So what's the message?

It's already in you.

Where? I don't feel anything.

When the time comes, you will.

And the Joy in gold steps back, her antennae relaxed, and the light in her eyes subdued. As if they had been waiting for this moment, four spiky balls come barreling up the stairs and into the Window.

Aranae in Red

There you are! thinks Selenophile.

I told you! thinks Rumble. *Moony thought you'd be sleeping, but I knew better.*

Scrap and Bubbles grab Thunder by his forelimbs.

C'mon, they think. *Everyone's waiting.*

And they drag him toward the slide.

Oh, thinks the Joy in gold. *Silly! I almost forgot.* And she takes from one of her attendants a large obsidian vial, which she grasps carefully. *You'll need this. The data stick Magister Jeremiah gave the major has the directions for making copies, but this one is especially for you.*

What is it?

Two parts genetic activator, one part catalytic enzyme, one part hormonal supplement, two parts nutrient base, and three parts dihydrogen monoxide.

Wow.

I know! Isn't it amazing? Her melodious buzzing is rich and appreciative. *That's science at its best.*

Sure. Good old Science. Whoever he is.

And the Joy in gold laughs like the unfettering of chains. She hands the vial to Thunder, pressing it into his open palm and clasping it there.

Protect it well; your life depends on it.

What am I supposed to do with it? he asks as he tucks the vial carefully in an inner pocket.

Give it to the seed derka; just unscrew the vial in the middle and pour it in its mouth.

And how will this seed derka feel about that?

Delighted! It has waited its whole life for this.

OK, well, I'll do my best. Is that all?

It is, the Joy in gold bows. *For now, at least. But who can see the future?* She fans her wings, and the space is filled with chimes and a flowery scent. *However things turn out, my amoti from another time, you have the blessing of Ozag, Humble and Grateful, and that is not a small gift. It will go with you wherever you travel.*

Swell, thinks Thunder. Courtesy demands a more formal reply, but the wabis have reached the limit of their patience. They push and tug until he is seated in the slide and ready to go. They howl in frightful unison, and when they feel sure the way is clear, they urge him forward. He looks one last time at the Joy in gold. Her attendants have gathered close in a glittering, silver knot, but she fixes him with a final glance and waves before he slides down and away, her eyes catching the sun and scattering fire.

+ + +

Lightning and Joy wait near the shuttle. Neither they nor Maya have discussed their dreams, for they have largely slipped beyond conscious memory. The humans are saying their last goodbyes, the one named Healey taking every chance to complain about something. Joy sits cross-legged on the ground, attending a plate of cake and ice-cream. Etiquette has no place here; proboscis and fingers are the rule. She proudly wears the going away gift Chica Verde had presented her: practical overalls, modest olive, with pockets and adjustable straps. But she refuses the shoes she is offered, disliking the sense of confinement and the clumsy feel.

"Check it out. You can roll up the sleeves and legs," Chica demonstrates. "Until you grow into it. And see? These are zippers. Up and down, yeah?"

As the others board the shuttle, Lightning sits with her elder self, waiting for Thunder and watching as Joy licks her plate clean.

When you traveled to the future, she asks Elder Lightning, *and you met yourself, but older, what was the most important thing she told you? She had to have given you some good advice. You're here, after all, you're alive. And your Joy, too.*

Advice is only as good as the person acting on it, the Elder Lightning replies, sounding very much like Ancian. *But yes, she told me what I'll tell you: have fun.*

Have fun?

That's it.

Seriously?

As serious as fun can be. She said I was too uptight

Aranae in Red

and worried, too preoccupied.

Easy for her to say.

You asked.

Lightning wrinkles her snout. High above, Thunder squeezes into the slide and howls.

Did it help? she asks.

Her elder self surprises her by reaching out and smoothing the spikes along her neck.

Sometimes, she thinks. *But it wasn't always easy. And sometimes it was impossible. But I'll say this, and then we'll leave it: when I look back now, I see parts of my life that seemed miserable at the time, but which seem like grand adventures now, wonderful stories to be shared with wabis. They sure didn't seem that way when I was in the middle of them. Everything was life and death—no time for reflection, no time for happiness.*

She pauses, and they watch Thunder begin his spiraling descent, speeding around the dome in widening loops, his ears laid back.

There's no guarantee any of you are going to make it through this, the Elder Lightning continues. *But remember: you're in the middle of a story you might get to tell when you're my age. If it's miserable to live, it'll be just as miserable to tell.*

Thunder slides out of the clear tube and gets to his feet, shaking himself mightily and howling like a champion. The wabis come spiraling down next, and Elder Lightning rises to four legs. Bluff and Gem have already approached Thunder to offer their final farewells. Once the wabis have exited the slide, they immediately begin climbing their hero or swinging from his tail.

I'm going to help the others rescue your oti, the Elder Lightning thinks, and she leans in to rub noses with Lightning one last time. *I know you'll do your best. We'll be sending every good thought.*

Thank you, Lightning bows. *We can use it.*

And she enters the shuttle along with Joy, waving goodbye to Jeremiah, the human children, and all their hosts. When Thunder finally joins them, she senses Major

Javon's impatience—senses her own—but she recalls recent advice, and before the shuttle hatch closes, she takes one of the garlands still around her neck and hurries out, draping it over Selenophile.

Otis are a lot of work, she thinks. *We olis need to stick together.* And little Moony's spikes flare with pride. Then Lightning is back on the shuttle, the hatch closes, and their hosts, human and kezel, step off to a safe distance, watching and waving as they take off.

+ + +

The human shuttle passengers are subdued on the voyage back to *Destiny*, Maya and Janet because they are deep in thought, Magister Healey because Javon has ordered him to silence. The major has plenty on his mind and would have loved a good de-briefing, but that will have to wait. He is full to the brim of refereeing Healey's nonsense and would rather stew in silence than try to have a decent conversation with him around.

Secured in the rear compartment, Joy and the kezel continue a discussion whose outcome grows more pressing with each passing kilometer. They are split on what to do when finally returned to their own time.

Joy's thoughts are certain and inflexible.

The bombas. We've already waited far too long.

But Submission's out there somewhere, Lightning frets. *As far as he knows, we were all killed, or taken prisoner. He needs to learn the truth—and if there's trouble in the accrete, he might need our help.*

For its part, the Book continues to believe finding its lost Reader of utmost importance, but it can offer little in the way of suggestions for where he might be found—or even certainty that he is alive.

When Lightning asks his feelings on the matter, Thunder's reply is slow in coming. He gazes out the portside window at the planet falling away beneath them, and he keeps his thoughts sheltered. But images of Rite Butte and a seed derka fill his mind.

Aranae in Red

I'll handle Bruiser, he thinks at last. *You deal with the bombas—or whatever you think is best. I'll let him know you're OK, and if he needs help, I'll do what I can. You can join the fun when your other business is finished.* He returns to looking out the window.

OK, thinks Lightning, greatly relieved. *That's good. Thank you. But,* she asks Joy, *what about...* She points at the sling, though she can't recall what's inside. *Will it let you go to the bombas, or is it going to be difficult?*

Joy whistles a series of quiet notes. This is a question easily asked and promptly answered.

But the artifact's tone is ambivalent.

I'm sure I don't know what you mean by 'difficult.' If I thought you were deviating from the Way, I would say as much. But it is not clear to me which is the path of wisdom. We may waste precious time searching for a Reader who may no longer be alive—or we may waste precious time with bombas who don't need our help and thus be the very reason the Reader perishes. Then again, aiding the bombas may earn us valuable allies with wings—never a bad thing when conducting a search!

Joy's antennae dip, her thoughts forlorn.

You mean to say it's up to me.

No reply.

Will you hate me if I choose wrong?

Of course not. Your choice will have been sincere.

Then there's only one option I can see, Joy thinks, taking a deep breath. *I just hope we get there in time.*

+ + + + + +

Submission sits with Brook and the Brigadier Bone below the mouth of the Skull, near the falling River Tongue. When the wind is favorable, they hear rumors of combat from the Brills, so faint it has the feeling of a dream. Brook drinks from the river, bubbly and talkative as ever, going blithely on its way oblivious to the distant violence that lays Bone's ears flat and curls his lip.

I'm not worried, thinks Submission, trying to ease

his companions' mood. *The Brills are no easy target, and Whitetails are a soft-bellied bunch. Won't take 'em long to see they've made a bad mistake.*

That's what bothers me, thinks Brook, sniffing at the variable wind. *A full frontal assault on a complex as well-defended as the Brills? Whoever heard of Whitetails making a move like that? Even if they gain access, they'll suffer plenty of losses.*

Desperation? Bone guesses. *Stupidity?*

Maybe the first, thinks Brook. *But not the second. Whitetails might be lazy cowards, but they're no fools.* She clashes her jaws. *Something's not right! I can feel it!*

Suddenly, from atop the domed crown of the Skull, comes the howling voice of the ibiwa Digger.

We got trouble, he thinks, peering down at Submission and the others. *Looks like a troop of Whitetails, sneaking up downwind. There's a bunch!*

The Brigadier bares his teeth.

There's your answer, he thinks. *They're not trying to get* in *the Brills. They're trying to prevent anyone from getting out! It's the Skull they want!* And he hurries to climb back into the cave, his spikes flared.

You were right, thinks Submission. *Not fools, after all. And just like them: pick at the easiest target.*

Brook stands and roars defiantly.

It won't be as easy as they hope!

But her heart has begun to race and her mind is clouded with uncertainty. Digger's howling grows more strident; their enemies are near.

We need to pull up the ladder, she thinks, which Submission reads as code for *You need to get inside.*

He snarls. Before captivity, privation, and battle-field woes, he would have scorned the ladder and climbed into the mouth by scaling the Skull's craggy chin—just to prove he could. Or, when Crystal had been alive and his zeal not sapped by awl glands, he would have dared one of the weathered cheeks, making his way to the jutting upper lip, and then into the nose, or higher yet, up into one of the ghoulish eyes. All these and more he had done, but those were different moons.

He rises to four legs but does not immediately move to the ladder. Brook chafes at his side, her nerves taut. She has never faced what is coming her way, and he hopes to set an example of calm in the face of the storm.

Defenses? he asks.

One at each eye and one at the nose, thinks Brook. *The rest at the mouth. That's where they'll go first.*

And how many Whitetails, do you guess? Considering the ones occupied at the Brills?

Too many, Bruiser! They're a big, clan! C'mon, please? Get inside...

Getting, he replies, but even now, he refuses to be rushed. Too many feuds have played out in his life, too much blood spilled to let fear dictate the terms. He limps toward to cave, a thought occurring to him.

The sharpest claw, he thinks.

What about it? Brook wonders, though she hardly seems interested. She often looks back, her nose twitching, and Submission senses that if she could have pushed him to hurry him along, she would have.

It's what Crystal called you.

Hmm...she never told me that.

Well, you knew her before I did. You know how she was. They reach the rope ladder, dangling out of the crooked mouth to the right of the Tongue, as if the Skull were using an awl bone to pick its stony teeth. *She liked the balance of power in her favor.*

If you mean she was only happy when she was the biggest moon in the sky, yes, I do. But she was always sweet about it, so no one ever complained.

Sweet, but not quick with a compliment.

No.

So, you should take this one seriously. Submission grasps the rope ladder and begins to climb. *She felt naked when you weren't around.*

Brook at last turns her full attention to the ideas being shared. As Submission works his slow way up the ladder, she watches him closely, noting his injuries—and trying to banish thoughts of what is to come.

The sharpest claw?

Several times. And she meant it. Submission at last reaches the top of the ladder, grimacing as he hauls himself up over the lower lip and into the mouth.

Let's hope she knew what she was talking about, thinks Brook, and she begins to climb, trying to avoid unseemly haste. She has just crawled inside and begun to reel up the ladder when a Whitetail bursts out of the accrete and leaps for its trailing end. A sharp rock and a bloodied snout is what he gets for his trouble, for Measure, stationed at the nose, is ready.

But the one frustrated Whitetail is soon joined by many others, and as the ladder disappears inside the mouth, they begin their assault on the cave.

+ + + + + +

When they have once again boarded *Destiny* and all is made ready to return to their own Aranae, Lightning and Joy prepare to focus as they have never done before. There will be no mistakes this time.

But even as they make this vow, they are both sorely preoccupied by thoughts of the bombas. Now that it has come to it, they realize desire to lend assistance is just that—desire, unsupported by any plan.

The brood will be gone by now, thinks Lightning. *Oracio and the others will be stranded at the Eye Tower.*

What can we do? How do we help? Joy worries.

But they have arrived at no answer when Major Javon's voice becomes audible, informing them that ship-wide preparations are complete. The time has come.

Hang on, thinks Joy, leaning close to Lightning and gripping a handful of Thunder's spikes.

Darkness, a wall of sound, and squeezing.

Then POP! Out they come on the other side, and the relief is like clamping jaws released from their throats, a boulder lifted from their chests, and they can breathe.

Last time, Lightning grits her teeth. *Last!*

Aranae in Red

You hope, thinks Thunder. *Who knows where we ended up? We could be anywhere...*

But the Book is convinced. They have returned.

I guess we'll see, Lightning scowls. *But if it's true, we're still no closer to having a plan. We don't even know what those things were.*

What did they look like? Thunder asks.

Like nothing I've ever seen before. Not big, but nasty quick...white, blobby, and suckers with teeth.

Never heard of anything like that.

Which prompts Joy to ask the Book:

Have you?

For she knows it has access to her memories and can construct an accurate picture of the creatures.

The device considers.

I am unaware of any such beings inhabiting Aranae. But it is a large planet, and the colonists never claimed to have identified every species.

That's not helpful. Do you know or not?

I do not.

Can you help us get rid of them?

That depends on what you have in mind.

I don't know! Kill them or something.

No response.

Well? What do you think we should do?

Get more information, the artifact replies. *Your memories are incomplete. According to them, the creatures were susceptible to bomba crewels and to a lesser degree the firearm used against them. But they also appeared to possess some multiplying properties so that weapon fire killed some but created more.*

Yes, so? What do we do about it?

As I said, get more information.

Oh please! thinks Lightning when this is translated. *What are we supposed to do? Go down there and bring one back to examine it?*

That would be unadvisable, the artifact replies when Joy repeats the question.

Then what? Please! We're running out of time!

I don't mean to rush you, thinks Maya when she comes to check on them, *but Major Javon wants to know if you're ready.*

They're not, thinks Thunder. *But I am.*

Just give us a breath, Lightning snaps.

Maya puckers her lips.

I'll try to stall, she thinks, and she turns to leave. *But everyone has limits, and I think the major is getting close to his. The sooner you have a plan, the better.*

+ + +

Old Sister Janet sits slumped and motionless on the cot that is her cell's only furniture. She reads *Destiny's* return from distorted space-time via fine vibrations moving through the walls. Three times they have been engulfed in *Valiant's* astral drive field, but where have they gone? To what time and place? Why three attempts when two should have sufficed? The guards refuse to answer any of her questions.

But now perhaps, answers will be forthcoming, for the nearby lift is operating. Its door slides open and speaking passengers step out. They exchange words with the guards and one of them unlocks the door. Janet knows by their voices who the visitors are before they enter: Major Javon and Deputy Kim.

"You lied to us," the major says as he approaches her cell. A thunderstorm gathers on his furrowed brow.

"No, Major, never."

"Really?" Javon clenches his jaws and activates the small 3V mounted to the visitor's room wall. "Then please tell me what this is."

A three-dimensional hologram appears, an image of Aranae, her terminator line running vertical, splitting the planet in half. At this scale, Janet can see nothing out of the ordinary, nor can she tell if the planet she sees is the one from her time or some other.

"I'm sorry Major; what should I be looking at?"

Javon motions, zooming in closer. Mountain rang-

Aranae in Red

es and bodies of water become visible. Zooming closer still, he brings the details of rivers and accrete into view. One more enhancement and there, near the dark side of the terminator line, something moves on the ground. Small, white, numerous and fast, they shoot along the shadowy border with the property of living water, pooling, expanding, squirting forward and pooling again—but rarely crossing into the sunlit face.

"The planet we found and scanned before you arrived from the future and interrupted us," Javon glares, "had none of these creatures. Now, taking your word and coming here with you, we find them encroaching along the terminator line. Did you simply forget to mention them? Or was it an inconvenience?"

"Why do you believe this is my Aranae, Major?" Janet sits up and smooths her tunic. "Am I wrong in concluding you made one previous attempt that failed to reach its destination? How do you know this is not just another missed target?"

Javon looks ready to open the cell and bite her.

"You be the judge."

And he rotates the image, zooming in to various locations. There is the weather-beaten mining compound and the monumental obelisk on its mountainous promontory. There is the lakeside refinery, the dam and its hydroelectric station. There, too, are the last of the satellites and the exhaust ports of the ag facility.

Sister Janet sees no sign of the old *Destiny*.

"Yes, Major, that appears to be my Aranae. But I won't know until I return to the surface."

"Then it is unlikely you will ever know," he says, cool and precise. "Because I don't see you leaving this cell for a very long time. And anyway, we don't need your confirmation: Joy says this is it."

"Then I suppose it must be."

"So? What is your explanation of these creatures?"

"I don't have one, Major. I wish I did, but if this is my Aranae, I've lived here for over two centuries and have never seen nor heard of life forms like these."

That Javon disbelieves her is written on every crease on his scowling face.

"And your *Destiny*?" he demands. "And the astral drive you promised? Where are they? Or are they two more things you've 'never seen nor heard?'"

"She should be in holding position on the dark side of the planet."

"You can see she's not."

"Then it is my hope she has gone to rendezvous with the rogue moon and complete her mission. Please; you must scan for her. And if you find her, you must let me communicate with her. She will need my help."

"You can be sure we'll scan. I'm very interested to know how many more surprises we'll find. But the only person you're going to be talking to is Deputy Kim. I've decided the time for courtesy has passed."

"Major, please, if these creatures were a known threat, why would I withhold that information?"

"Maybe you knew we would be less likely to join you. Or maybe you wanted our help in eliminating the threat. Because it is one, that's been confirmed."

"In what way?"

"In that I shared this image with our guests, and they were neither surprised nor pleased. They tell me these creatures made an appearance at the mining compound, in one of the generator rooms."

Janet's head tilts and she inhales sharply.

"Generator three?"

"They didn't specify; how could they?"

"But it was near the transporter, yes?"

"That's how they escaped, in fact."

Janet's shoulders slump, and she looks away.

"Oh, no," Javon aims a finger. "You don't get to hide behind remorse and sad faces. What did you do?"

"I don't know. Please let me speak to *Destiny*."

"Even if we knew where she was, I wouldn't allow that. You need to start explaining yourself, Chaplain."

"I have no explanation! All I can tell you is this: I didn't travel through time to locate you because of dumb

Aranae in Red

luck, Major. I experimented and I practiced. The transporters were the key. They operate on a small-scale version of the principles of an astral drive, and the mining module has three of them I could combine for optimal effect. I had to avoid the bombas who live there, but it was worth the risk. The transporter near generator three was my focal point. It was that device which I used when I was first successful in moving outside of time."

"How is that related to the creatures at the mine?"

"I do not know."

Javon balls his fists.

"Then what does it have to do with these others along the terminator? There are thousands of them!"

Janet removes her lensless glasses and places them on the cot. She begins to pluck at her hair, pulling out single strands and dropping them to the floor.

"Please let me speak to *Destiny*. If her mission fails, these…" she waves at the nameless creatures slinking and spurting along the edge of shadow. "These will be the least of our problems."

"Answer me!" Javon's voice rocks the small room, and one of the guards quickly opens the door, weapon drawn. Deputy Kim waves her away, but he never takes his eyes from the scene before him. Janet continues to pluck hair, methodical and emotionless, a mousy brown and white pile forming on the floor.

"Major," the deputy says quietly. "Is OK if I try?"

"Oh! You are more than welcome." And the major turns away, disgusted, flopping himself onto a hard, plastic chair and glaring at Janet.

"Chaplain, please," the deputy steps up to the bars. "Is remembered the Kim from your time? Is how you would treat him? Put in harm's way?"

"My Kim has been dead for over a hundred years."

"Am so different? Me and him?"

Janet plucks a hair and drops it, watching it spiral lazily to the ground. Her voice is little more than a whisper, and she doesn't look up when she speaks.

"When my Kim lost his way, I advised him to have

faith, to outlast his grief. One pull of a trigger is all it would have taken, and he, armed all the while. But I never suggested he be relieved of duty, because I knew work was the only thing keeping him alive."

"Yes," the deputy replies. "Is true."

Pluck. Drop. Spiral.

"Who will advise me, Mr. Kim?"

"Is not knowing, Chaplain, but Major won't let you go alone if you help. Is a way to find together. Please. Won't you stop that? Tell us what we need."

"I can't! Don't you understand? I don't know what those things are. All I can say is..." With what seems a tremendous effort, she moves her hands away from her head and clasps them tightly in her lap as if they have wills of their own. "Twice I moved through time—once as a test near generator three, and the second time when I came to find you. That drop outside of our spacetime was initiated on the dark side of the planet. That those creatures appear in those two locations and nowhere else cannot be a coincidence."

+ + +

Lightning, Thunder, and Joy watch and listen to all that transpires in the brig via the security camera whose images are cast in three low-resolution dimensions into the cargo bay. Joy's right hand rests in her sling, moving slowly. Her left rubs her temple; being the hub aches like heavy lifting, and she wonders how long she can continue it. She chooses her questions carefully, translating the answers.

What does this mean? Do you understand her?

I am beginning to, the artifact replies. *I believe I now know why I did not recognize the creatures that attacked you. And I believe I know what they are.*

What? How do we get rid of them?

At this, the artifact hesitates, and Joy senses a reluctance from it unlike any it has expressed before. It is compelled by its nature to respond, but the answer clearly displeases it on the deepest level.

I believe, it replies at last, *that these are what my makers knew as Zapok Gehekzez Nom. They are the Ones Who Eat the World. We called them Feeders.*

An awful name! Why didn't you recognize them?

Because they exist in a dimension outside our own—and would stay there were sentients less careless and ambitious with their mad desire to manipulate time. But they are not, and so, when they do it improperly, as Sister Janet did on two separate occasions, breeches are created between dimensions, and Feeders find their way from theirs to ours.

But why didn't you say that right away?

Because the form they take depends on the environment into which they are introduced. My makers have cataloged eighteen such occurrences in the various galaxies to which they have traveled, and in each case, the physical form taken by the Gehekzez Nom was different. Sometimes they were aquatic, sometimes aerial. There are cases of them manifesting as a type of living sediment, and others where they were nothing but shadow, a black, ground-dwelling cloud that spread like spilled tar. The variety you see here entered this world in locations of darkness, and so assumed a suitable form. But look! They have evolved quickly. Already they are spreading across the terminator line and are driving derkas from their nests, eating their young. It matters not the form they take; in all cases, Feeders have only one motivation: hunger. They will consume everything in their path.

Until you put a stop to it, yes?

Another long pause.

It is not so easy. As long as the breeches remain open, every Feeder killed creates space for two more.

So how do we close these breech things?

You do not. But...I could.

OK, thinks Thunder when this is translated. *That's more like it! What are we waiting for? Let's get to it!*

But Lightning senses Joy's hesitation.

What is it? she asks. *What's the problem?*

A.P. Malloy

Petros can't kill any of those already here, Joy replies, her antennae drooping. *He's not a weapon. He'll seal the breech,* she assures, caressing the artifact. *But we have to deal with...the others.*

And? There's something you're not telling us.

Joy's buzzing is low and mournful.

Sealing the breeches requires both of the artifacts. Her eyes grow dim. *It will probably take all of their energy.* And she hugs her sling close, as if fearing a thief. *He doesn't think either of them will survive.*

+ + + + + +

Ansel, proud but tired, sits just inside the Eye Tower on a makeshift nest, encircled by elder bombas. His left wing rests awkwardly, and his leg is wrapped in corpuses. The elders are grim and uncharacteristically quiet as he shares his tale.

Before leaving the crescar—and after my last sight of the troublesome kezel and its mutant companion, he thinks, *I discovered a rixli den on the northern fringe. But the wind was bad, and I stumbled onto a kish. It was as surprised as I, or things could have been worse.*

Ilda approaches bearing the last strips of awl salvaged before the escape. Ansel accepts them without thanks, tearing them to bits and gulping them down.

That kish will no longer be a threat, he thinks, *but it got the better of my wing, and I was forced to walk much of the way. It could have been my end, but the west-side kezel were preoccupied with the east-siders, the clan to whom the masked kezel belongs.*

That you found them, thinks Oracio, *and were able to see them safely home is testimony to your strength of will. I know the charge rested uneasily. You no doubt cursed my name many times during the effort.*

I accepted the burden in memory of my brother, Ansel snaps his beak. *Not because of you. I cursed the kezel and the blue thing; they bear blame enough.*

Oracio's head droops.

That may be, thinks Ilda, *but your father is not wrong. What you have done, regardless the merit of the endeavor itself—and I saw none—serves Ari's memory better than you might know. He would not have liked the thought of his new companions suffering in scion captivity.*

Ansel spreads his wings gingerly.

Nor would he have enjoyed seeing you here, driven from the maison. What of our enemies?

No news, Oracio replies. *They have been seen in the Window, but they have not ventured out.*

For now! thinks Ilda, squawking discordantly. *They climb sheer walls like a virble in the crescar. If they choose to leave the maison, they will have no trouble.*

And leave they must, must they not? the faded Ugo wonders. *Their form may be foreign, but it is a body, whatever its nature, and all bodies need food. If awl is not to their liking—or if they have already consumed our stores—they must venture forth. If we had strong fliers and endless crewels we could enjoy fine target practice as they exit the Window, but...*

We have neither! Ansel sticks out his tongue, hissing. *Shall we waste our energy on wishful thinking? What of awl? What of grass? The Eye Tower may be home to rixli, but neither fin nor tassel will you find anywhere near. How many can fly?*

Most, Oracio replies, but his tone is mournful. *Many of the ones who could not were unable to escape.*

And how many of those can fly well? Or far?

Some, thinks Oracio.

Few, thinks Ilda.

And yet there is no other shelter, thinks Ugo. *Where else can we go to escape the storms? If we stay here, we risk starvation, but if we leave, the moons will surely have us for playthings.*

We will find a way, thinks Oracio. *But son, this is no longer your concern. You have fulfilled your promise and brought us the news we much desired to learn.*

News you desired to learn, corrects Ilda. *The mystery of the mutant scion and its vanishing kezel could have*

A.P. Malloy

remained so, and I would not have cared.

Perhaps, thinks Oracio, and he mutters. *But my point is this: Ansel should rest and heal so he can catch the brood. He may still make Congress.*

Ansel clacks his beak, a reply at the ready, but suddenly he ducks his head and turns a bright, green eye to the tower's open door.

What is that? Do you hear that?

At first, they do not. But soon, a low, sustained growl becomes audible, distant but growing closer. As one, they step tentatively outside, turning to the west and gazing skyward. One of the clouds spits out a gray-skinned beast, larger than an awl, flying without wings— then a second and a third. They descend toward the Eye Tower with frightful speed and unerring precision, and their voices grow to a roar. The bombas stand frozen, crouching and huddling. Then they scatter, flying and running in a mad cacophony of lost feathers and terrified cackling. Trembling behind the first boulder he can reach, Oracio peers out to see what doom has come.

The flying creatures land, raising plumes of snow.

Their tail ends open.

And out steps a masked kezel and a biped of blue.

+ + +

This, then, is how Oracio, Ilda, and all the elder bombas come to meet their first true rumidelchias, for after Lightning, Joy, and Thunder, Deputy Kim disembarks from the shuttle, followed by Major Javon and his translator, Maya Sharma.

In the beginning, no amount of amazement or curiosity can lure the wary beasts from their hiding places. All Lightning sees are occasional tips of beaks from behind high-seated boulders or the flash of a glancing eye from out of a tower window. She motions for the humans to hold their position, and she steps forward slowly with Joy at her side.

We've come to help, she thinks. *Oracio? Ilda?*

Aranae in Red

Maybe we should have the humans move away, thinks Joy. *And maybe Thunder too; he looks very fierce.*

But Lightning has caught a familiar scent.

Ansel, she thinks, casting the thought toward the base of the tower. *Please come out. We came to pay our debt. These are humans—rumi...rumi...two-leggers. Like the ones you saw on the Bacca, the floodplain. They know about the trouble, and they can help. Won't you come out?* For several moments, the only response is the wind, cutting through the gap, sharp and cold.

Go away! comes a thought from inside the tower. *We want nothing from them! I said if you came back you should bring no trouble with you.*

It's not trouble, Ansel, it's help; I promise, thinks Joy, and she turns to see a chipped beak and cloudy green eye peeping out from the nearest boulder. *Oracio! Oh, Oracio, I missed you so much!* And she hurries forward. Two other bombas flee, stilt-legged, their wings flapping and beaks clacking. But Oracio stands, Ilda at his side, her spurs raised.

Not another step! she thinks.

Joy stops, but her eyes glitter like hope.

It's me. And Lightning. We're back at last.

Oracio bobs his head slowly, tilting it side to side.

Yes, crack my eggs, I see that it is. But this is not how I hoped you would return, with so much noise and so many...Ansel told us about the rumidelchia he saw, but those were three, and they were walking. These flyers...

They're OK, thinks Lightning. *We've been with them for a while, now, traveling together, and they've been good to us. The one with the armband is their leader. He wants to meet you. Please...*

Wants to meet me?

We told him all about you. And he's going to work with us to get rid of those white things.

You mean the monsters you released! thinks Ilda. *The nightmare you allowed to claim dear Ari before you ran off to safer locations.*

We did release them, thinks Lightning, bowing her

A.P. Malloy

head. *We can never make that up to you. But it was an accident. We didn't know they were there. And we didn't run off. Please, I can explain everything.*

Explain it to my dead son!

But Oracio steps forward, slowly, his long strides cautious, his wings poised to spread, his neck craned back as if his head and body wish to go opposite directions. And when he has drawn close enough to touch, both Lightning and Joy bow low. The latter's buzzing is difficult to interpret.

Can you forgive us Oracio? For poor Ari? Her antennae droop and her eyes grow dim. *Ilda warned us about curiosity; we didn't listen.*

Oracio mutters; his wings relax and his beak points to the ground, sweeping sad, pendulum arcs.

I do not blame you, little one. Nor do I blame you, kezel. But others do, and that, I am afraid, is unlikely to change. But you say you are here to help. If this is true, if these rumidelchia can regain our home for us, there may yet be hope for reconciliation.

+ + +

Once Deputy Kim's company of Enforcers have disembarked, two of the shuttles take to the air. Major Javon is at the helm of the first, Maya at his side and a standard reconnaissance drone docked to the shuttle's belly. They fly north, toward the mountain range they would later learn is named the Derka's Teeth, each peak loftier than the next. And beyond? Maya can't guess. Her womb tickles with a burgeoning anticipation like a held kitten wriggling to be free.

"Have I said I don't like this?" Javon asks.

"Yes."

"Good. Now I'm saying it again."

"We'll be OK."

Both shuttles pass over the last of the jagged peaks, chasing off a derka circling its snow-capped summit. And there below, though it passes in moments, they catch a glimpse of Feeders, white and squirming, as they swarm a derka nest and the glinting emerald within.

Javon steers the ship onward and away.

Darkness settles gradually, then blink! the sun disappears behind them; they are enveloped in black.

Now Javon drops the shuttle lower, into the barren valley north of the mountains, followed by the second shuttle, and the two crafts sail a mere kilometer above the ice-bound terrain. But they can see nothing; they are flying blind, with only the ship's sensors to guide them. And yet, Maya knows they are on target, for the kitten inside her squirms with increased vigor.

It will not remain held for long.

She begins to hum one of Daada's old tunes.

"Five minutes out," says Javon.

He brings the drone online.

In the distance, Maya sees something, so faint it could have been a smudge on the shuttle's windshield. They draw closer, and the smudge grows, becoming a small, glowing cloud, stationary but churning and folding in on itself like radioactive dough in a mixer.

Maya stops humming.

"No closer," she thinks, dead certain.

Javon kills the engines without question, and both shuttles come to a hovering stop.

"Ready?" he asks.

Maya nods but can't force a word from her mouth. The kitten struggles to be free, and now it has claws. And she knows too by whom it is held, can feel the unborn child clinging with webbed fingers to something warm, comforting, and dear to its tiny heart.

Let go, she thinks. *It's OK, you can let go.*

But let go of what?

Then the grip releases, the energy is freed, and a moment later, the drone separates from the shuttle and zips merrily on its way, lights twinkling.

"One minute," says Javon, and the shuttles swing away at top speed.

Maya closes her eyes and bows her head.

A.P. Malloy

"Thirty seconds."

What had been inside of her?

Light floods the cockpit, blinding but brief, and a shockwave propels the shuttles like a pair of surfers. Then blackness returns and their passage grows smooth.

"It's gone," says Maya, resting her hands across her belly. Javon checks his sensor readings.

"I can confirm that," he says. "The anomaly is gone. Shuttle two: begin locating and destroying any remaining targets. Avoid collateral damage if possible but leave none of those white things alive."

"It's gone," Maya murmurs again.

"Yes," says Javon. "The breech is sealed."

But that isn't what Maya refers to. Whatever had taken up residence in her already occupied womb has gone its way, and will, she knows, never return. The baby kicks and punches, then settles and is calm. But both it and Maya are suffused with a sudden, inexplicable loneliness. She feels the urge to wave a farewell.

Goodbye, she thinks but does not know to whom. *Thank you.*

Chapter Seven
Garden

THE ORIGINAL TIMELINE, when Grace was old enough to understand the idea—but still very young—was filled with an ever-present longing for *home*. That was Aranae, from her perspective, and she desired to go nowhere else. But many among the colonists, even those pleased by their new life on the stormy planet, felt... The word she sensed was related to *disconnected,* but the image created in Grace's mind was of an amputated limb, or an island far from the mainland, separated by an uncrossable gulf. *Cut off,* is what it felt like, and though she didn't share the feeling, its pervasiveness wore on her.

Could we get home? she asked Petros the stuffed tiger, who had recently been renamed. She sat with the raggedy fellow on her lap as she waited at the ag facility for her father and the major to pick her up in a rover.

They had a big day planned.

It is possible, the tiger replied.

How?

You would need information and energy.

What information?

Where you are and where you wish to be.

Well, Grace thought confidently, *I already know where we are; we're here!*

But later, when she raised the topic, riding with her father and Major Javon to the mining compound, she

A.P. Malloy

learned that 'here' wasn't precise enough for the kind of work she had in mind. Her father frowned at the question. He was one of those who had no desire to return to the System. But Major Javon, driving as always, had a mind of complex emotions, and he answered carefully.

"First," he said, "I'm curious why you want to know. Are you unhappy here?"

She was not, and she said as much.

"So, why," Javon wondered, "if you don't mind sharing, are you so interested in where the System is?"

"Because other people are. They feel trapped."

Watt arched a brow and peered from the navigator's seat back at his daughter. Javon did much the same, but at Watt, not Grace.

"Do they now," he said, but it wasn't a question.

"All we need is information and energy," Grace offered. "That shouldn't be hard, right Major Javon?"

"That depends," he smiled, and he slowed the rover to a stop, surrounded by a sea of yellow grass. "Where," he asked her, "are we right now? If you had to get us back to the ag facility, could you?"

The obvious answer was yes, of course, for Petros would lead the way. But she knew that was cheating.

"Easy," she said. "GPS."

"Sure. That's the information part. And what information does GPS give you?"

"Double easy. Latitude and longitude."

"And what if you didn't have GPS?"

"Triple easy! Just retrace our trail."

"And if you left no trail?"

"Head back toward the sun."

"And if you didn't have the sun?"

"Compass!"

Javon winked at Watt.

"You're going to be outsmarted by this one. I know I'm not the first person to tell you that."

"No," Watt replied. "You're not."

"Well," Javon looked back at Grace. "Everything you've said is correct, but here is our problem. We are in an unmapped part of the universe—no latitude and no longitude. *Destiny* left no traceable path, so we can't just go back the way we came. And our sky is full of unfamiliar stars. We can't use known celestial markers because, at least at the moment, we haven't found any."

Javon engaged the drive, and the rover trundled forward. Grace considered what she had been told. She tried to imagine what she would do if she were tiger-less, trying to find her way home under a dark sky, with no landmarks, no compass, and no map.

"What about the energy part?" she asked.

Watt chuckled, but it was a humorless sound.

"I'll let you be the judge," said the major. "When we get to the mine, you can see for yourself."

Grace had many more questions—she loved talking with the major—but Watt shook his head.

Enough for now, Abi, he thought to her, kind but firm. *Let the major drive, please.*

He's worried, she thought.

Aye. He has a lot on his mind.

Information and energy?

Aye. And how he doesn't have enough of either.

+ + +

They arrived at the mine without mishap, only forced to open fire on a horde of lapis glaeboses twice before they took the hint and buggered off. The fabeldyr circling overhead also decided against confrontation; a three-passenger rover was too heavy to lift.

Major Javon parked the vehicle.

"I'm meeting with Commander Rickles in ten minutes," he said. "That'll take an hour, hopefully no more but certainly no less. Shall we do lunch after?"

"We shall!" Grace answered.

While the major went on his way, Watt gave Grace her first tour of the mine since its full completion. For maximum effect, he suggested they enter on ground level through the personnel door adjacent to the primary loading dock. Here, Grace stood goggle-eyed as immense ore haulers, with tires taller than her father, waited patiently to be filled before motoring off to the refinery. Even with protective headgear and earplugs, she felt the awesome power of the machines as the conveyor dumped tons of stone-bound ore into their beds like an avalanche. She wrapped her arm around Watt's leg, looked up at him in his matching hardhat, and watched him chew his beard.

"Too loud," she said, and he agreed.

Climbing to the middle tiers, they toured the residential quarters, meeting many people who seemed indifferent to Watt but genuinely pleased to see Grace. They offered her candy, solicited her opinion on the mine, and introduced her to the colony's youngest members, preschoolers who lived with their miner parents in a world whose noise and power were second nature.

"It's always nice to see you, Abuelita," they said.

Afterwards, they climbed to the top tier, and Grace peered through the clear polymer at the snowy world outside. It was at this time that she first conceived of the slide. What a fun thing that would be! Surely the major wouldn't object. As she considered how to ask him, she watched ore haulers the size of bugs crawling to the west, on their way, Watt explained, to Lake Zelano. By now, she was hungry for more than candy, but Major Javon had been called to yet another meeting, and lunch would either be delayed—or eaten without him.

"It would be polite to wait," Watt suggested, but Grace grimaced and clutched her stomach.

So down the elevator they went, observing the inner workings of the mine through the clear, impervious walls of the car. To Grace's inexperienced eyes, it seemed a wonder of productivity, and she imagined it would not be long before the major had all the energy he needed. Tunnels spidered out from the central shaft, in and out of which issued a steady parade of ore-laden buggies and workers both human and synthetic.

They took the rover—and at Javon's insistence a young Enforcer named Ted—to the northern lakes where they could eat their lunch. There, Grace could watch the giant awl, and Watt could discuss technical issues with the research team gathering water samples near the shore. Grace laughed at Ted's jokes and nodded soberly when he reminded her of the safety rules regarding awl, fabyldyr, and of course lapis glaebosis, the rock dwellers with glowing eyes. She gave Ted a double thumbs up.

"Roger dodger! Can I see your gun?"

"No," said Watt, so Grace settled for more jokes until they arrived at the lake.

And there, they had an adventure.

+ + +

Mom! thought Grace before she had even opened the door to their residence at the ag facility. *Mommommom!* She flung the door open and hurried through the empty sitting room to the bedrooms beyond, followed with considerably less enthusiasm by Watt. *Mom!* Grace flew through the bedrooms, peeked into the bathroom, and came at last to the tiny kitchen, where Maya was heating a pot of soup. *There you are!*

Here I am.

Mom!

Yes, sweetheart.

We had an adventure!

Did you?

Tell her, Dad.

But Watt was occupied decanting a precious drizzle of scotch into a metal tumbler. When he lifted the drink to his lips, his hand trembled.

Dad, tell her!

Aye, we had an adventure.

But tell her what it was!

Argh. Watt swallowed and grimaced.

Grace waited as long as she could—five seconds—then gave up on her father and tackled the story herself.

Mom!

Yes sweetheart, still here.

I almost got killed!

Maya stirred the soup and tasted a spoonful.

I don't think I like the sound of that.

Mom! It was amazing. There was a glaebosis! I could have been killed.

Maya set the spoon down.

Watt?

He glared at his scotch and waved vaguely.

It was no big deal.

Yes, it was! Dad, let me tell it. Mom, sit down.

I think I'll stay on my feet.

Grace did a little skip and clapped her hands.

It was right there! she thought. *I could totally hear it moaning! It sounded like some kind of baby. Did you know their eyes glow? Mom! Are you listening?*

I am now. Watt?

Another grimacing swallow.

It was nothing to fret; there was a glaebosis, aye, but it didn't stick around. It wasn't going to do anything.

Yes it was, Grace exclaimed. *You weren't there!*

I'm sorry, Maya interrupted. *Where were you?*

Argh. Don't ask it like that. I was getting reports from the research team. Grace was with Teddy.

Yeah, Grace confirmed. *I like him. But he was snogging Wendy and my sandwich wrapper blew away—*

He was what?

Snogging. It's what British people call kissing. And my sandwich wrapper blew away. It almost blew into the lake. So I chased it. And then I looked over and I saw something. She reached out to dip a finger in the soup.

A glaebosis?

No, that was later.

For God's sake, Watt, how long was she running around out there unattended?

Oh, now, it wasn't not like that.

Teddy was there, Mom.

Yeah, snogging!

He claims there was none of that, Watt offered. *Someone,* he tilted his head in Grace's direction, *may have*

Aranae in Red

been reading an intention...

Grace grew still for a moment, considering this. But it seemed to have no bearing on her story, so she dismissed it, shaking her head.

Mom! You're not listening. I saw something.

Oh, I am very much listening, Maya thought, but her eyes were on Watt.

It was invisible! thought Grace. *Can you believe it?*

What was?

The thing I saw.

If it was invisible, how did you see it?

Not invisible, but...um...like a glass with water? It was shimmery, but I knew it was there. It was clicky and buzzy. I think it wanted to be my friend.

Oh my God. Watt?

Aye, it was one of your sextan critters.

Invisible?

Apparently, they can camouflage.

They totally can! Mom! It was so cool. You know what it did? Can you guess? Do you want to guess?

No.

It had my sandwich wrapper! It gave it back to me!

Now Maya did sit down.

You touched it?

It was nice. It wanted to be my friend.

Maya's hands balled into fists. Watt leaned back and chewed his mustache. Grace licked soup off her finger and tugged at her mother's shirt sleeve.

Mom. Guess what happened next.

Teddy showed up and did his job?

A glaebosis jumped out behind me!

Watt, so help me...

Oh, heck, Maya, it sounds worse than it was.

It was going to eat me!

No, it wasn't.

Dad! Let me tell it. It was totally going to eat me! And then guess what happened. Guess. Mom. Guess.

Maya, it seemed, was out of guesses.

The sextan saved me! Except there wasn't just one.

A.P. Malloy

There was buzzing all around, and you should have heard how they whistled. Did you know they can whistle? They scared that old glaebosis off.

Maya's lips were pursed.

And then?

Grace shrugged.

That's all. Teddy came running up with Wendy and all the sextans left. I'm the only one who saw them. But Teddy found tracks in the snow. I like him.

The end of the tale brought a long, heavy silence. Grace had planned on applause or congratulations; this response worried her. Was she in trouble? What was she supposed to have done? Allow her litter to blow into the lake? She watched her father drain the last of his scotch and wondered if she should explain that nothing bad would have happened. Petros had been with her. But her parents, despite indulgent words to the contrary, had never really believed in what they referred to—in their less discreet thoughts—as her imaginary friend. She guessed expressing certainty that he would have let no harm come to her would make her mother's lips tighter and the hole she perceived her father in deeper.

So they ate their soup with sheltered thoughts.

She was lectured before bed, then tucked in.

She stayed up late that night, asking Petros many questions and petting his worn coat. And in the morning, after a night of fierce discussion, her parents seemed to have come to a peaceful resolution. They voiced consensus that she was never to approach a sextan again without an adult. And she followed that directive—but she could do nothing about the sextans who, from that point forward, repeatedly approached her.

+ + +

By the time Grace was ten, she had, under no one's impetus but her own, identified every telepath in the colony. Out of the twelve hundred humans, thirty-two could communicate using their minds. Some had already been known to Watt and Maya, who cautioned their daughter—again—about the risks of such knowledge.

I know, I know, she said. *You're the only ones I'm telling. But it's no fun. We should all be friends.*

In fact, the relationship between telepaths was complicated. In many cases, they had joined the mission as married couples, in keeping with the colonial imperative to maintain a healthy population. How these pairs interacted depended on their levels of natural extroversion and restraint. To Grace's way of thinking, her parents had too little of the first and too much of the second. Then there were the individual telepaths not bound in a relationship, whose membership in the colony had been earned by a special expertise.

Miss Worsely, the botanist, was one of these.

She's lonely, Grace confided to her mother.

Sweetheart, did she tell you that in person?

She didn't have to.

Grace MacLean, if you want to help people, stay out of their minds without their permission.

I wasn't prying. I didn't have to! I just stood next to her when we visited the botany lab. She knows you and daddy are telepaths. What's the big deal?

People like their privacy.

By which, Grace believed, her mother meant *she* liked *her* privacy, and assumed others must as well. But waiting for people to meet by chance was no way to cultivate Readers, and she hated having a secret she couldn't share. So, she fished around for someone compatible with Miss Worsely and found Luka the Russian, who had a last name, but not one Grace could pronounce. She tugged at her father's lab coat when they were sharing time at the refinery where Luka worked.

He's lonely, she thought.

Argh, who could blame him?

Did you always like Mom?

Heck, sure. Right away. But I don't think she was so fond of me. I used to be...

You were grumpy. She told me.

A.P. Malloy

Aye, that's one word for it.
She makes you less grumpy.
Aye.
Because you were lonely.
Was I?
Weren't you?
Watt turned off his Halo and reached down, picking up his daughter and twirling her like a dancer.
Jeez and Jasper, you're getting heavy!
So can I?
So can you what?
Invite Luka to our place to meet Miss Worsely?
Heck, Gracie, you have to ask your mom, not me.
She said ask you.
He set her back on her feet.
Matchmaking, are we?
Cultivating, she replied soberly.
And a year later, Luka and Miss Worsley wed.

+ + +

Of the telepaths who had married, most had children, and the vast majority of those were themselves telepaths. By her thirteenth birthday, Grace had identified five Readers among them. But how to bring them into contact with the Book?
Everyone needs a babysitter, she reasoned, and as she was a favorite among the children and never charged for her time, she was often in demand.
She would sit with the children and tell stories, but more often, when they weren't watching 3V, they would play the Question Game. They could ask any question they wanted and she, consulting secretly with Petros, would provide the answer, being a ventriloquist for the stuffed tiger. She was with Junior and Priscilla this day. He was a Reader, but of course, at only six, was too young to be trusted with the secret; she was eight and precociously telepathic, but not a Reader.
Any question? Priscilla asked.

Any question at all, Grace replied, helping Junior tie his boots. The last storm had cleared out and they yearned to be outside.

Will there be fabyldyr? asked Junior.

Wait your turn! Priscilla scolded, but then decided to claim the question as her own.

Seventy percent likely, thought Grace in her best tiger voice, and she moved Petros side to side.

Will they attack us? asked Junior.

Only two percent likely.

Because of our camouflage, right?

Right and left, Grace replied. *But remember that camouflage only works if you stand still. Hey, if you want, maybe we can check out one of the hamster balls.*

Yes! Priscilla exclaimed. Walking inside the giant, clear globes was her favorite way to explore.

They put on their camouflage jackets and tramped around the ag facility, sloshing through melting snow.

Priscilla asked the next question.

How can I eat all the chocolate and not get sick?

You can't, Grace replied.

Junior flopped backward into a melty drift, cushioned by snow and beleaguered grass.

How can I get my dad to let me stay up later?

Write down all the reasons why you think it's a good idea. Share it with both your parents. Ask them to give you a written response to each of your reasons.

What good will that do?

It will teach you how to win arguments.

On and on, they traded questions and answers as they roamed the perimeter of the base, walked in giant hamster balls through grass like a yellow forest, and hiked to the retractable bridge, eating only *some* of the chocolate Grace had in her pack. And her heart swelled at the experience of interacting with the Book in the company of a second Reader, relished the richness and clarity of its responses. The effect was not additive; in the eyes of the Book, one plus one equaled three.

After they'd returned the hamster balls to storage,

Grace's stock as a fortune teller rose, as they did indeed encounter a fabyldyr—*freeze*, she thought, and they did, huddled in their camouflaged outfits.

The derka passed by unaware.

But when Priscilla asked what her dad was going to bring them when he returned from his mining duty on Dansim, the violet moon, Grace shook her head.

No way to tell.

I thought you knew the future!

That's just probabilities. You, know, how likely is something. Those are easy if you have enough information. But I don't know your dad super well, and I've never been to Dansim, so I can't say.

Well, then, what time is he coming home?

What time does he usually come home?

Soon. They launch when the Violet is close to Aranae. So, he's probably already taken off.

Grace gave her another chocolate.

Then you don't need me to answer that.

My turn, shouted Junior. *You wasted your question. How do I get out of school?*

You, don't, Grace pinched his nose.

But he did, in fact; they both did, for the next two weeks, their absence utterly forgiven. For their father did not return later that day—or any other. The Dansim mine had collapsed, and a great, spewing fissure had ruptured open, killing thirteen colonists, including the children's father. Major Javon had been visiting the site, for it had been a concern to him ever since allowing Magister Healey to have his way. His heart misgave him, and now he knew why. Had he not been there to order the evacuation, more would have died, and for that he was given a hero's mantle. But it was the dead left behind, not the living he rescued, whose names he would remember longest. And when he visited Junior, Priscilla, and their mother, bearing his condolences, Grace was there, helping with the children. The major looked as if a mighty wind had blown the strength from his bones, and she knew she would need to increase the pace.

Aranae in Red

Information and energy, she thought to herself.

+ + +

Maya went from the bedroom to the sitting room, her arms loaded with clothes. Grace, it seemed, had moved out for good, but not all that was hers had yet joined their owner in the quarters she had chosen near the mining compound. Maya sat and began folding the items, placing them neatly in her travel gear.

Why do you want to live by all that noise? she had asked her daughter. *Isn't there an open unit here?* But even as she had asked the question, she was reminded of her own mother when she had informed the family of her intention to attend school on Luna. How could she complain? Wasn't a three-hour rover trip from the ag facility to the mining compound better by far? And so, she had let the matter rest.

I'll bring your other clothes when we visit for your birthday, she promised, and she sighed at the memory. Some of the items she folded were too small to fit the twenty-five-year-old frame her daughter had grown into. These she set aside, kissing each one and wondering which of the colonists' children might find them of use.

The door chimed.

Janet's face appeared on the ID screen.

"Too early?" the chaplain asked through the door.

But Maya, who had grown hungry for company, rose and happily opened the door, giving her friend the hug she had stored for many days.

"Never," she assured. "But almost too late. Where have you been the last three weeks?"

"It has been too long. I'm sorry. But I think you will find the absence was for a good cause."

"Tell me more."

"I'm sorry; I've been sworn to secrecy. When we get to Gracie's you'll see. She wants it to be a surprise."

"Of course, she does."

Janet only smiled and polished her glasses.

A.P. Malloy

"As your counselor, I must remind you that we only have an hour before we leave."

"I'm ready. Just packing up some things."

"Oh, dear Maya, no."

"No what?"

"I love you, but that frock simply won't do. Here. I'll pack Gracie's things, and you put yourself together in a proper party fashion. It's a celebration!"

There was no point in arguing. As she changed, Maya watched Janet move from room to room, humming a tune and gathering up the artifacts of a childhood that had passed too quickly, an adolescence so much smoother than hers had ever been. Janet's hair was deliberately streaked with white, but that was a concession to her own unique psyche. Her true nature had been known to all in the colony for over a decade. Javon had insisted, but it was inevitable in any case. How else would they explain her apparent agelessness?

"You may lose some clients," the major had warned her. But she hadn't. Her job had been done well and her loyalty was unquestioned. Not one person who had sought her comfort or guidance since the arrival at Aranae had chosen to abandon her.

"So why the white?" Maya had asked.

"It puts people at ease," Janet had explained. "They find it humbling and relatable."

Maya had just finished lacing her shoes when Charlotte arrived. She kissed her new arrival and marveled at how anyone could age so gracefully while living in a world of machines. How was it that some metallic monster hadn't eaten one of her limbs, disfigured her porcelain skin, or blinded her over the years? Instead, the silver laced throughout her hair seemed to have been inlaid by an artist, the fine lines marking her smile carved by a light, elfin hand. She appeared as fit as someone half her age, and when she laughed—or sang, which she often did—it was as if someone was ringing chimes to announce the arrival of dawn.

"Good Lord," Maya scowled. "You are gorgeous."

"Arreter," Charlotte held up a finger, whose nail, like its companions, was neatly painted. "Beauty is on the inside, mon cherie. And by that standard, you are the most beautiful person I know. My husband might agree. Who, by the way, is with yours, getting the rover prepared and commiserating about the state of life."

She kissed Janet and moved to the 3V, activating the perfect choice for background music.

"Are there problems?" Janet wondered as she finished the last of the packing. "I've been out of touch."

"Problemes et leurs amis," Charlotte admitted. "A few loud voices do not like the new directive, no matter how reasonable it is. There are some even now who still cling to hope that we will someday return to the System. But Magister Healey has won his last vote; Dansim set us back by a generation, and the Council's directive was clear: at least for now, no more resources are to be expended on refueling *Destiny*. Our focus has to be on making this our home, not planning to leave."

"It is perfectly reasonable," Janet agreed, and she sealed up the last of the luggage. "They'll see that."

"Nous verrons," Charlotte smiled. "But let's speak of happier things. How can I assist?"

"Maya was just hoping someone could help her with her hair," said Janet, which was not true.

"C'est mon jour de chance! I've been waiting to get my hands on that mane for a long time. Come! Sit!"

+ + +

The new research base—and Grace's new home—was on the promontory west of the maison. In a future none of them could see, it would become the foundation for what others would call the Eye Tower, but now, it was a humble concrete square, and it had no name.

At the party, they were invited to try awl glands by a smiling lad who met them at the door and proffered them in a bowl even before introducing himself. It was unnecessary in any case, for they all knew him as Grace's longtime boyfriend Azee. The major declined on principle, and Watt "arghed" a few times before passing. But Charlotte laughed like a bell and tossed one into her mouth. This inspired Maya to do the same. Janet, after setting the luggage on the floor, placed a pair of the glands in her hip pocket for later analysis.

Grace arrived to greet them with hugs and kisses.

"Get something to drink," she said, pointing to one of the back rooms. "And I'll show you around."

Watt scrunched off in search of whiskey, joined by Charlotte. The major waited with Maya and Janet.

"They've done well for themselves," Javon said, looking out one of the windows. "And they couldn't have chosen a better view. But the mountains? If it had been anyone but your daughter and her acolytes, this project would never have been approved."

Maya frowned.

"You make it sound like a cult."

"With Grace as the High Priestess," Janet added.

"No, nothing like that," said Javon. "But do you have a better word than acolytes?"

Maya did not. Plus, the awl gland had made frowning impractical. Her mouth was inclined to smile, and fighting the urge seemed ungrateful. In a back room, Azee began to pluck a guitar, and someone else joined in with an accordion. When Grace and Charlotte returned, they were dancing, as Watt trailed behind, enrapt, balancing everyone's drinks.

"Elle rayonne," sang Charlotte as she allowed Grace to twirl her. "The birthday girl is glowing."

But this was not news to Maya or Watt, who had encountered Grace's aura so often it had become in their minds as much a part of her as her ginger locks or native charisma. Watt distributed the beverages and stood between his wife and his daughter like the winner of a tournament. Charlotte kissed Javon.

"Tour please," she chirped.

Grace led them through the suite of communal spaces, filled with music, 3V, dancing bodies, and laughter. The entire structure, including private quarters aboveground and workspaces below, was as modest and efficient as any on New Gaia—it had to be to get Council approval—but it was imbued with an ambience unlike any other. To Maya, it felt like a Hindu temple during a marriage feast, sacred, but joyful, as if it had been designed and decorated by college students on a tight budget. For a moment, she felt a compelling desire to leave her work at the ag facility and immerse in whatever enchantment was being brewed up here in the mountains. Grace beamed and turned her way.

I would like that! she thought. *And I have something to show you that might make up your mind. But first...hats and coats, please. We're going on a walk.*

And she led them outside, down the path to a wind-sheltered vale below the snowline, where they stood on the marbled turf and basked in the sun and the stunning vista. Grace went to the head of a rill where a pack was tucked under a rock seat. This she handed to Javon, motioning for him to open it.

"Happy my birthday," she said.

"I'm..." Javon opened the pack and pulled out one of the spongy green things inside, thick and flat like an emerald pancake. "What am I?"

"You're honored," Charlotte said.

"Florensis aloensis," Janet observed. "It's the most important part of the sextan diet."

"You'll get no argument from me," Javon replied. "And I have no doubt I'll recognize the honor soon enough. But you have to remember, I'm an old war horse who's had a long day. Give me a hint."

"I'll do better than that, Major," Grace said, and she nodded to Janet, who surprised them all by mimicking the sounds made by the sextans, precise clicking, tonal buzzing, and three sharp but short whistles. The next moment, as if someone had switched on a portable 3V, seven winged scion became visible, standing only meters away, six glittering bronze and one gold as a sunset.

+ + +

"She says," Janet offered, "that she is the Queen of Albion. She has waited a long time to meet you."

"When, please," Javon wanted to know, "did you learn to communicate with them?"

"It has taken years. They don't like the cold much. And they have been very shy. Only recently have they been brave enough to share the time necessary for me to piece together the basics of their language. It is complex. You should say hello."

"How?"

"However you like. I'll translate."

"You know," said the major. "There is a protocol for diplomatic dealings of this sort."

"Is there?" Grace smiled politely. "How boring."

"They respect power of command, Major," Janet said. "They've been watching us for longer than we've watched them, and they know you are our leader."

"Tell them—tell her?—I am glad to make their acquaintance. And I suppose thank you for the gift?"

Janet clicked and buzzed like an old-fashioned computing device, and when she was done, the sextans fluttered their wings and whistled a simple harmony. The queen followed this by rapid clicking of her own.

"She wonders if we have an agreement."

"An agreement on what?"

"We help them grow more of this—they call it lova—by working to control the water flow to their land. They want to build a dam. And they give us a percentage."

"Not to sound ungrateful," the major furrowed his brow. "But can you explain the benefit?"

Janet deferred to Grace, who executed a neat curtsey and answered the question with twinkling eyes.

"The benefit, Major, is energy. When refined and reduced, lova can provide enough energy to power the colony while we refuel *Destiny*."

+ + +

Aranae in Red

Javon took off his hat and rubbed his head. The idea sounded fine in principle, and he expressed what he hoped was appropriate gratitude—and optimism for a possible agreement. But this was no place for making interspecies treaties. Wouldn't he have to convene the Council? Discuss the potential downside? Spend more time in deliberation with this queen? It was all too much for a birthday party. So, Janet translated his good wishes and request to meet the queen again. And when, on Grace's suggestion, he bowed low to the ground, she and her cohort buzzed a rich melody like flowing honey.

Then they disappeared from sight.

Their cutting wings soon fell beneath the wind.

"Any other surprises?" the major asked Grace.

"No sir, not for you."

But she joined arms with Maya, and when the others made their way back inside, she and her mother continued on to an enclosure on the building's far side. Linked fencing and rocks combined to create a pen of roughly a hundred square meters, one side of which was a weathered bluff, overhung by a naturally formed stone awning. It was not quite a cave, but it was sheltered from the sun, and inside, Maya could see something moving. Perhaps it was the awl gland or her drink, but a strange thrill traveled outward to her fingertips when Grace opened the locked gate. A rough mewling greeted the click and creak as they went inside.

What is it? Maya thought like a whisper.

Come and see. Grace took her hand.

Oh, Gracie, what have you done?

Mom. Come and see. They won't bite.

They?

Grace approached to within a few meters of the overshadowed bluff, reaching into a pocket and producing two portions of some type of jerky. These she waved idly, letting the wind do the work. Moments later, two small, spiky snouts poked out from the shadows, followed by large ears, angled forward.

Keelus refrenium, Maya thought. *Oh Gracie! If their*

mother should show up...

Orphans,, Grace assured. *We found her body at the bottom of a ravine. Rockslide. These two were up top shivering and almost dead. Here. Feed 'em.*

The first keelus, its spikes fawn and white, nosed its timid way out from under the bluff, the size of a large dog and sleepy-eyed. It sat at a distance and watched them, coming no closer but raising its snout to the wind.

Grace sat as well, motioning that Maya should do the same and waving the jerky like an invitation.

That's Apollo, she thought. *Here comes Luna.*

A smaller keelus, its fawn and white spikes tipped in black, stepped out of the shadows, its nose low to the ground but its eyes alert and unblinking, watching them. It remained on all fours, growling like a toy motorboat.

Maya whimpered and put her hand to her mouth. Grace smiled.

I told you, she said. She waved the jerky, giving Maya a portion so she could copy. *They're nervous around new people, but they're warming up. If you can get one to take food, the other will follow.* She scooted forward a few feet. The smaller keelus growled again, but the larger, the one named Apollo, rose and stepped toward Grace with a tottering gait. It stretched and took the meat from her hand, gentle but quick. Its partner, Luna, darted in and snatched Maya's offering, and they both retreated as they chewed, watching them out of arm's reach.

How are they able to digest that? Maya wondered.

We had to synthesize their mother's enzymes. That part was hard. Getting the body to the lab took six people. And we would've been sunk without your research. Someone suggested we name the little one after you, but that seemed weird. And then what? Name the other one Watt? So we went old school.

Oh, Gracie. What a chance. What an opportunity.

Yeah. But only if you move up here and help us.

Oh.... I don't know. Your father. And Janet.

Can always come to visit. We don't live on a moon. Here. She handed Maya the last of the jerky. *I'm going to make sure the others are enjoying themselves. Stay with them. I'll bring a blanket.*

Maya grimaced.

I don't know about that...

Grace rose slowly to her feet. Both keelus backed away, still chewing, and she laughed.

These two are no threat to the Tiger Queen, she thought. *If they get nippy, use your mom voice.*

And off she went, smiling and glowing, and she secured the enclosure with a wave.

+ + +

When Grace returned thirty minutes later with not only a blanket but also a pair of pillows and a warm drink, Maya was still seated and the keelus were gnawing the last of the jerky. But now they were closer, within reach, and they sat looking at one another like old friends who had long been apart and were trying to re-learn one another's features. The keelus tilted their heads and twitched their noses, and their ears angled forward as if listening for Maya's breath. She sat like a buddha, and tears had trailed down her cheeks.

Grace handed her the drink, placed a pillow under her rump, and sat down next to her on one of her own, draping the blanket over them both.

The boys are going to set up one of the tents for us, she thought, snuggling close. *Spend one night with this pair curled up next to you and tell me you can imagine ever going back to the plains!*

The 'boys,' including Grace's boyfriend Azee, kept their promise, with Janet's help, setting up a sturdy two-person tent and portable heater. Lightweight chairs they brought as well, and they lingered, conversing and laughing over their drinks, basking in Grace's aura and commenting often on the keelus pair who stayed out of reach but always in sight. And when Watt and Javon returned indoors to partner in a card game against Azee and another person half their age, Maya, Grace, and Janet remained. Eventually, the keelus approached for another food offering: reconstituted protein they licked from a large spoon. Janet asked questions as if preparing for an exam, but Maya simply cooed and bobbed her head at the keelus, crawling next to them on all fours, sniffing and being sniffed, too happy for words.

Of course, Grace had been correct. After Janet had returned indoors, and once the tent had been blacked out and the eternal day made night, it wasn't long before Apollo and Luna came snorting and grunting into the tent like a pair of truffle-seeking pigs. Apollo crawled into Grace's sleeping bag, and Luna into Maya's, who gasped, holding her breath and closing her eyes. The musky scent was more intoxicating than any party favor, and the creature's spikes, when laid flat, were surprisingly supple, not scratchy at all.

She didn't need to wait for the 'night' to pass to know her answer.

I'll do it, she thought to Grace. *I'll stay with you.*

CHAPTER **E**IGHT
Heal

TELL US EVERYTHING, Oracio requests.

Where do you want me to begin? Lightning wonders. She stands beside the Eye, demonstrating its operation to Thunder, who sniffs it warily.

Your unexplained and untimely disappearance, Ilda replies. She keeps herself as far removed from both kezel as the room will allow. Ugo and Orton stride the perimeter of the room as if unwilling to present a stationary target, and the slightest unexpected move on Thunder's part inspires them to aim their spurs.

It was scary—and it happened so fast, thinks Joy. *But we know now it's called a transporter.*

And does it only transport one way? Ilda hisses as she thinks. *Or perhaps you felt it better if the bombas dealt with the scourge on their own.*

Oracio's wings ruffle.

Now, Ilda, they came back as quickly as they could, I am sure. Did you not?

Yes, thinks Lightning, and she motions for Thunder to join her at the narrow end of the Eye. *And no, transporters don't just go one way. But they also don't always work the way they're supposed to. The one we got sent to wouldn't let us back in.*

How many are there? Oracio wants to know.

We've only seen three, thinks Lightning.

A.P. Malloy

But we've been told there are more, adds Thunder. He peers through the eye-piece, turning the adjuster as he had been shown. He is glad for something to focus on, as being so close to so many bombas—no matter that they can think—makes his stomach growl.

And all are connected? Oracio asks. *Allowing instantaneous travel between locations? Oh, rumidelchia cleverness! And now they have come to deliver us from these murderous and disgustingly named Feeders. They are everything I imagined! If Ari were only here...*

I see them, thinks Thunder. *Coming this way. They just crossed over the mountains.* He steps away from the Eye and looks out the window. *I don't understand how it works,* he thinks, *but it's a nice toy.*

We are glad you approve, thinks Ilda, her tone saying just the opposite. *How long before they arrive? Have we not waited with utmost patience?*

Can't say, Thunder replies. *Don't see 'em anymore. But not long, probably, fast as they fly.*

Indeed, thinks Oracio. *Admirable! Commendable!*

But Ugo mutters; Orton sticks out his tongue.

In the time we have, thinks Oracio, *tell us of your adventures between your return to the crescar and when Ansel finally located you on the edge of the Landfall—and then again what happened after you parted.*

Joy moves to sit on the ledge near Oracio.

It was hard; Lightning was injured, you know.

Yes? Orton cranes his neck toward her. *Well! Ector was killed, so it seems she came out the better.*

Lightning curls her lip, but Oracio closes his eyes and allows Joy to preen his feathers.

Enough, he thinks. *If either Joy or the kezel were to blame, they would already have been creweled for their offense. As they are not, let us save our weapons and our words for more deserving targets. Please,* he thinks to Lightning, *won't you tell us your story?*

Lightning leaves Thunder to his fascinated exploration of the Eye and takes a seat near Joy and their host. Ilda, who had only followed them here to watch over Oracio, remains at a distance. But Ugo and Orton, either out of curiosity or desire for a better shooting angle, move closer, one with eyes on Lightning, the other watching Thunder's every move.

As she relays their adventures, starting with their return to the moon cave and the tortured accrete, Lightning proceeds uncertainly at first. Woe lades the tale, not only the memory of Ari, but of Gami-kan and the kezel killed in the scion invasion. And when she gets to the feuding Redteeth, she realizes kezel must appear to bombas as crude and irredemptively violent as Ilda has always claimed. But Oracio is a model audience. He never interrupts, always squawks or cackles at the right moment, and scarcely takes his eyes from her as she weaves her way across the Naked Hills, the scene of Pounce's heroic fall, and the wonder of Ozag's Hold.

This, thinks Ugo, *is no great news to bombas. They have flown over the dam since its origins as a scion project ages ago. They have seen it added to, layer upon layer, by the rumidelchia, seen the river swell into a lake.*

It is true, but none have been inside, thinks Oracio. *And that is a marvel to be sure. If my wings were their former selves, I should like to explore the place! But this Ozag, now she seems like trouble.*

Can't say, thinks Lightning. *Never met her.*

And don't want to, Thunder adds. He cocks his head to the side and perks his ears high. *They're back.*

+ + +

The shuttles' arrival scatters faded bombas to their various hiding places, but it brings Deputy Kim and his company of Enforcers to attention. When Lightning and the others exit the Eye Tower, the humans are arrayed in neat files, four rows of six. Four burnished labor droids wait patiently in the remaining shuttle. While Deputy Kim apprises the major of what was learned from reconnaissance while they were gone, Maya approaches. She appears outwardly the same to Lightning, but something about her mind has changed.

It was full before—overflowing, she thinks. *She's not empty now, not nearly. But she's lost something.*

Remarkably, Maya comes to stand beside Joy, and while one of Joy's hands rests in her sling, the other finds one of Maya's, and they remain clasped like this until the major finishes his discussion. He dismisses the company with a sharp salute, and as they board their respective shuttles, he turns to Lightning and the others. For a moment he assesses the unusual company speechlessly, as if taking extra care to memorize the remarkable scene. Four bombas, each as tall as he, two kezel, one uncatalogued hybrid, and a human return his gaze.

"OK," he says finally. "I guess this is it."

Oracio cackles at the sound of his voice, and when the translated ideas enter his mind, he fans his tail.

We wish you good fortune, Major of the Rumidelchia. I understand you are familiar with our maison—having one of your own—so I have no advice to offer but this: the creatures you face are more dangerous than they appear. Take the utmost care.

Maya translates this, and the major nods.

"Rest assured, that is our intention." He turns to Joy. "And you still feel you need to be part of this mission? Because it goes against my every instinct."

If I don't go, there is no mission.

"Right," the major replies when this has been translated. "And don't bother asking why, because you can't say or I wouldn't understand, is that it?"

I'm sorry, Major, but yes, that is it.

Javon looks as if he might be gathering objections, but in the end, he simply turns and walks back to the shuttle, motioning for the others to follow. Waving to Oracio, Joy does, Lightning at one side, Maya at the other, and Thunder close behind.

Rumidelchia! thinks Oracio as the bombas watch them depart, and he savors the word like a sweet rixli. *If only Ari were here...*

It could well be argued, Ilda replies, *that rumidel-*

chia are the reason he is not.

+ + +

The kezel ride from the Eye Tower to the maison with their thoughts kept to themselves. But Joy hugs her sling, and the moment she is strapped in and the hatch is secured, she begins asking questions.

What will happen to you? Will you disappear?

I can't say, the artifact replies. *The dark side breech was much larger and took all my counterpart's energy. We will not see him again. This breech is smaller.*

So, there is hope? You might survive this?

This breech is smaller, but I am also not as robust as my counterpart. There is hope, but not much.

But the Way…how will I learn it?

That path is not the exclusive domain of my makers. It can be found by anyone with a sincere heart and steadfast will. You already have the foundation; it is up to you to build from there.

It will be lots harder—not as fun.

The artifact does not respond, but where this had been an irritant in the past, Joy now finds it endearing.

Are you sure there isn't a better plan? she asks.

I can't think of one. But you shouldn't worry for me. This is a chance to fulfill my Purpose. It is not the preferred method, but there is a long history of Books being used in very un-Book-like activities in the service of Readers. And in each case, the sacrifice was warranted.

But what if it doesn't work? What then?

I have every reason to believe it will. If it does not, you must seal the maison and keep it as a prison. The Feeders must not be allowed to escape! But I doubt you will be able to hold them indefinitely. And if the breech remains open, more will come through. In that case, I fear the only option will be to leave this planet, so virulent are Feeders once they have a source of food.

Joy restrains the fierce buzz she feels rising.

And let them eat the entire planet? Never!

A.P. Malloy

But she realizes this is the wrong path. Worrying about the future is distracting her from the present.

How can I help? What can I do?

Keep asking questions. It energizes me. And I enjoy it. You have been a pleasure to work with.

Can't you leave just a little of yourself?

I will if possible, but of course, not at the expense of the mission. You shouldn't get your hopes up.

What's the most important thing I should know?

Excellent question! Learn as much as possible and love as much as possible—and always challenge yourself to re-define what is possible.

I love you, Petros. Do you know that?

Yes, Joy, I do. And in my own way, I have loved you. Our relationship has been recorded via the Link, and what we have shared and what I have experienced in my time here will be of use by other Books in service of other Readers. If this mission goes as I suspect it will, the Link will be severed—but the memory will live on.

What else can I do for you? Anything?

If my other Reader still lives, find him and let him know my service to the cause.

I will. Oh! I do hate being sad. Joy's antennae droop, but then an idea comes to mind.

Would you like to sing with me, Petros?

I would indeed! You ask the best questions. But no time to learn a new song, I'm afraid.

That's OK. I like the one from before.

And so, in their remaining minutes together, Joy and Petros sing *Shakti Dena*, silently, but completely immersed. Joy rocks side to side in time, and Petros gains strength with every verse. And when the kezel, quite to their surprise, sense the infectious tune and begin sweeping their tails like a pair of spiky metronomes, the entire compartment is filled with an energy that is both bright and melodious, though not a note can be heard. The mental harmony they create lifts their spirits to a place beyond sadness, and when Major Javon announces they have arrived at the maison, Joy feels a portal open in her mind, shackles falling from her thoughts as if crumbled to rust. She knows without testing that she is no longer constrained. Words once stopped up in quartets and octaves now align themselves to flow freely, their only limit her imagination.

+ + +

Major Javon maneuvers the shuttle into position directly over the maison's aperture.

The hatch between compartments opens, and Maya peers at them from the forward section.

The major is ready to go. We're as close to the opening as he's willing to get. What else do you need?

Joy clicks a steady rhythm.

Nothing.

She reaches into her sling, gripping the artifact jealously. Now, faced with the end, she is unwilling to let it go. But it becomes amorphous and slips from her grasp, as if liquid light seeping from a leak in the sling. It runs down the side of her leg, pools briefly on the shuttle floor, then disappears. The others look on, waiting for some sign from her. In the cockpit, Major Javon reads his sensors. But Joy knows he will see nothing. The artifact has dropped down into the maison, will at this moment be traveling through the infrastructure, on its way to the generator room and the source of so much trouble. Only when it reaches its destination and completes its mission will the major be able to sense—

"Kefpet glif!" he shouts. "Keb kwikky bavawak!" And Maya turns away hastily.

It worked, she thinks, gripping the hatch. *They're releasing the drones and the workbots. I have to go.*

Then clang! the hatch is sealed.

+ + +

The bulkhead is virtually soundproof, but concussive reports tell of the drones delivering their cargo of explosives. Lightning wonders how many Feeders have been destroyed, recalling their uncanny knack for multiplying. But no, the breech had been sealed, Maya had been certain of that. Dead Feeders would remain so and not be replaced. She feels the shifting weight of the workbots lowering themselves from the shuttle, senses through her toes the vibrating report of the winch and its gears. One, two, three, down she imagines all four descending, in through the aperture and dropping to the Window floor. Bearing flamethrowers and acting on information from the drones, they will clear the way for Enforcers waiting in the other shuttles.

And then the ship moves away, as flames arc and metal glints inside the window, and smoke gutters and belches from the aperture.

Get out of the way, Thunder complains when the other shuttles move into position. One holds over the aperture, ready to lower human soldiers, one hovers ready to take its place, completely blocking his view.

But Lightning turns away from the Window to check on Joy. She sits looking out her side of the shuttle, looking but not seeing, hugging the crumpled sling to her chest, her eyes dim. Her low whistle passes by the notes of a melody but never touches them.

A good thing just happened, thinks Lightning.

Yes. I know.

I'm very proud of you.

I didn't do anything to be proud of. I couldn't let go. He did that on his own.

Doesn't change how I feel about you.

Joy releases the sling with one hand and reaches out, caressing the spikes along Lightning's forelimb.

Ha! thinks Thunder. *Good! They've moved. You can see again. You want to look, Lightning?*

But she leaves that to her oti-mu. Whatever is happening will happen. She dips her snout and closes her eyes, concentrating on Joy. The sense of her mind is much as Maya's was earlier: full, but not typically overflowing, and tainted with the gall of loss. She reaches out tentatively and finds, or believes she does, a hole in Joy's psyche, a place where something pleasant had settled but was now gone. What had it been?

"He did that on his own," Joy had said.

Who did? Fleeting glimpses of an object slip through Lightning's memory and escape. She lets them go without a fight. Instead, she shares with Joy thoughts of bombas returned safely home, of debts paid and sins forgiven. And all the while, she runs her claws through cascading, ebony curls.

But nothing she does quite fills the hole.

+ + +

Say what you want, thinks Thunder. *That was pretty amazing. Did you see that fire? That smoke? Hard to imagine any of your Feeders living through that...*

And when at last every meter of the dome is scanned, it seems that none did. Between the drones, androids, and humans, the only things discovered are splotches of oily liquid, charred around their edges and rank beyond description.

"Is very foul, Major," Deputy Kim reports via the shuttle comm. "Not safe come in yet. Will open windows, but recharge to ventilation is long time away. Solar cell power only. Is lights and internal comms only."

"That's fine, Mr. Kim. We'll return to the tower and see if any of the old residents want a ride. I understand some of them aren't in a flying way."

"Is one more thing, Major."

"Yes?"

"Small, localized radiation near transporter."

"Where the breech was?"

"Sir. It dissipates, but slowly."

"Understood. We'll use the entrance on the other side. Well done, Deputy. Someone owes you a favor."

+ + +

Most of the bombas gathered near the Eye Tower reject without hesitation the major's offer of a shuttle ride to the maison. Ansel sticks out his tongue and hisses. In the end, only Oracio, Ugo, and Orton accept the offer, the former because his nature could imagine no other choice, and the latter out of a sense of duty.

The first of you to break trust will pay, Orton thinks, brandishing his crewels.

But Oracio cackles and fans his tail, stilt-walking into the rear compartment with eyes as bright and green as Lightning has ever seen them. Ilda and those who choose to walk begin their trek down the mountain, overseen by those few whose wings still have life.

We hope to see you soon, she thinks, and she mutters as Oracio and the others disappear into the shuttle. *But I would walk there and back three times before I dropped a single feather in that contraption.*

The shuttle flight passes quickly, and Oracio hardly has time to comment on the experience, peering out the portside window and clacking his beak.

Stupendous! he thinks. *Spectacular!*

When they land on the dome's east side, near the other two shuttles, they are greeted by Deputy Kim.

"All so good, Major. Is clean as whistle. But Stevens and Traxley take fire, need treatment. Doma too. Is permission return to *Destiny* please?"

"Granted. Take the workbots and drones, too. But leave me two Enforcers. How is that radiation?"

"Is better. Still there, getting weaker."

"Origin? Nature?"

"Is unknown, Major. Sensors detect but not identify. Estimate fully dissipates in one hour."

"Excellent. We'll stay until we're sure it's gone and the others have arrived. Shuttle two will stay as well and effect what repairs they can to this compound. Take care of your people, Deputy. They did good work here."

And the deputy's shuttle takes to the sky.

Astounding, thinks Oracio.

But his amazement has just begun. The major and

his two Enforcers open a large bay door into the dome the bombas hadn't known existed. Once inside, they find the largest of the windows on each tier have been louvered open to banish the stench. Sunlight shines throughout the dome in a way Oracio, Orton, and Ugo have never experienced, and they crane their necks as they gaze about the space as if seeing it for the first time.

We will never be able to repay this debt, Oracio thinks to the major, and Maya translates.

Orton is less pleased. He lands nearby and hisses as if leaking patience.

The debt is theirs! They are the ones repaying! And now they have done so, there is no reason to remain.

Maya translates, but it is Oracio who replies.

I will not hear of it! To have rumidelchia appear out of the sky in our time of need? Providence! To shoo them away like common yits after the help they have given? Blasphemous discourtesy. Stay, will you not, Major? And these others as well? We have nothing to offer outside of our attention, but that, I assure you, is wholly yours for as long as you remain and tell us about yourselves.

"We have duties to attend," the major replies. "But I promised to stay until the others make it back from the tower. You have us for that long."

But, adds Maya. *We plan to stay, you know, here on Aranae. It's our only option for a home. So maybe we'll be able to meet again.*

That depends on what type of neighbors you are, Orton scratches the floor. *Tell your Major that.*

"We plan to be good neighbors," the major replies upon having this translated. "And we're going to start by keeping our distance. The colonists who built this facility made mistakes. The first was choosing this continent for a home. We've learned there's a better choice."

This is greeted by Oracio and Ugo with bobbing heads and cackles of approbation.

Won't you walk with us through the maison? Oracio asks. *Reveal what secrets it holds if you can.*

And tell us all about rumidelchia, adds Ugo.

A.P. Malloy

Ask anything, thinks Maya, but Lightning tries to temper her enthusiasm.

You don't know what you're getting into, she thinks, *when you encourage a bomba to ask questions.*

She soon learns. Oracio and Ugo lob one query after another at their guests, and they, not privy to Maya's struggle with the spoken word, give her little time to translate before moving on to their next target.

Mother of honey, she exclaims, pressing her palms together. *Please slow down.*

Which they do, most reluctantly.

Most of the dome's functions lie dormant. But as Orton trails behind, muttering, Maya teaches Oracio and Ugo to jab the appropriate buttons to activate those lights and doors that still have power.

Wonder and delight! thinks Oracio. *When the brood returns from Congress, think of all the space! A bomba could sleep in a different room for each moon.*

And you say, thinks Ugo, *these buttons will work as long as the sun shines?*

"In principle," the major replies via translation. "But nothing lasts forever. It's likely the photovoltaic cells and circuitry have been repaired and replaced over the years. Eventually, that will need to happen again."

Photovoltaic circuitry, Oracio repeats, savoring the thought. *There is a fine pair of words! And if they fail, perhaps we can arrange a trade for your services, Major? And perhaps some repair on the netting between tiers?*

"Perhaps."

The tour—and the questioning—continues.

Will there be other rumidelchia in flying ships?
How many of you are there?
Are there little rumidelchias as well? Young ones?
Have you heard of the scourge that is scion?
Do you know most kezel are not like these two?
What do you know of derkas and kish?
And also:
Are there hazards behind any of these doors?
The answer to this question is yes. The major ex-

plains through Maya that some rooms are storehouses for toxins like water treatment chemicals and metalworking solvents. Others, like the three power stations—one of which had kept the Feeders trapped—hold dangerous charges in their capacitors.

Oracio bobs his head.

Charged capacitors, he repeats reverently.

Metalworking solvents, Ugo agrees.

And they cackle as the major has his crew mark those doors to remain sealed. But near the power station where Ari had met his end, the mysterious radiation remains at an unsafe level, and they retreat to the nacht. There, although neither Javon nor Maya can believe it, more questions follow.

Button poppers, thinks Thunder. *They don't quit!*

I warned them, thinks Lightning.

Joy sits near Oracio, preening his feathers with one hand, but her mind is not on the conversation, and her other hand strays often to her sling, clutching the fabric as if each time surprised to find it empty.

It is not until the first of the bombas arrives from the Eye Tower that Oracio and his companion finally relent. Weary from their long journey, the walkers are nonetheless more disposed to courtesy at the sight of their home made light and free of danger. One by one, they bow and bob their heads, and they gather in a growing ring of blinking green eyes. Ilda is one of the last to arrive, escorted by Ansel. Oracio moves to stand beside them, and he addresses the major.

The experience of a lifetime, he thinks, dipping his beak and ruffling his feathers. *That is what you have shared with us; we will not forget.*

When all have fanned their tails and cackled due thanks for the rumidelchia service, a technician approaches the major, reading a handheld sensor.

"Looks like the radiation's cleared sir."

"Thank you. And how go the repairs?"

"We're limited, sir, without heavy tools and more power, but we're doing what we can. We're using the shuttles to fully re-charge the solar cells. Another twenty minutes or so, and you can have your ride back."

"Very good. Well, Miss Nandini, you heard the lady. If your friend still wants a ride, he has twenty minutes to say his goodbyes."

When this has been translated, Thunder does indeed express his continued desire to leave with them. Submission has been waiting, and they are long overdue.

You still staying? he asks Lightning.

For a while. We're going awl gathering, and Oracio won't let us leave until we've shared in the feast. We'll get a ride in the second shuttle when they're ready.

Before we go, thinks Joy. *I want to see...I want to visit the place where the Feeders were.*

Lightning growls.

Why in the world?

I just do. Please? It's safe, isn't it? With the radi...with the radi...what is it?

Radiation, thinks Maya, *and yes, it's all clear.*

Fine, thinks Lightning, getting to her feet.

But Thunder beats her to it.

I'll go. You stay with your friends.

Um. OK. But don't be gone long. I don't think your ride will be very happy if you make him wait.

+ + +

Without asking permission, Joy climbs to Thunder's back. He steps out briskly at first, guided by Joy's directions. But when they are away from the others, he slows. His head is bowed and he curls his lip as if chewing something distasteful.

What is it? asks Joy.

Nothing.

It's something. Why else come with me? What do you have to share?

That depends. Can you keep a secret?

I think so. But some secrets aren't meant to be kept.

This one is. But not by me. I have to...share it with

someone, or I'll go crazy. And I can't tell Lightning—or any other kezel. You have to swear! If anyone finds out...

You're miserable. I can feel it. You've been misera-ble since we got back from Albion.

Yeah.

What happened there? What did they do to you?

It's what I did.

Joy waits patiently. Thunder's strides are reluc-tant and shuffling, as if the painful revelation is not a thing in his mind but a destination ahead of them.

You have to promise, he thinks.

OK. I promise. I won't tell anyone. But Thunder...

No one! Ever! I swear that keeping the secret won't hurt anyone, but telling it...if even one kezel learns...

They won't. Not from me.

Thunder slows to a stop. Joy reads this as a re-quest for her to dismount, but—

No! thinks Thunder. *Stay where you are. I can't look at you. I'm...ashamed. Just sit.*

Joy does. She feels sure she will not like what she is about to learn, and for several moments, Thunder stands with his thoughts sheltered, giving her hope that he has changed his mind. Then:

Did you know the jabi Hail?

No. But I heard of him. He was lost to the scion.

No, thinks Thunder. *He...he was lost to me,* and the thought is faint, like a whispering voice. Thunder's ears droop; his tail sags to the floor. Joy holds her breath, waiting for more, wondering if she should encourage him. But a moment later, the barricade is broken, and the thoughts pour forth, an unbroken stream of them, and the story of Hail's last moments is spelled out. The tone is bitter, the self-loathing tangible. Joy keeps her mind still long after the story has reached its awful conclusion, and heaving a deep sigh, Thunder resumes walking.

Well, he thinks. *Say it.*

Say what?

Whatever is in your mind. Tell me I disgust you. Tell me I make you sick and you're going to break your promise and tell Lightning the first chance you get. I don't care.

No, she thinks. *I wouldn't do that to you.*

You should. I'm rotten. I should be banished.

Joy buzzes a mournful tune.

I got my friend killed, my dear Ari. I wanted to show what I could do, wanted to be powerful and important. And I freed the things that killed him. How am I any better?

Her shoulders slump, and she squeezes her sling.

Turn right here. Then go left.

They march on toward the power station. The large double doors have been sealed by Major Javon's crew, but the signs of combat remain. Blast marks scorch the walls, and splotches of dried white spatter everything like the memory of dueling paintbrushes.

Thunder wrinkles his snout at the smell.

Is this it? What were you hoping to see?

Nothing. I don't know. I thought maybe...

Joy slides from his back and walks to the doors. She presses her cheek to the metal as if listening for something on the other side, then steps back.

Open, she thinks, but they do not. The major's people had done their work well. But no matter. It had only been a test; she could sense nothing on the other side. And yet, beneath the saturating aroma of death and the emotional turmoil—Thunder's news! The memory of Ari!—there is something else, something nearby.

The transporter, she thinks. *It's this way.*

OK, but hurry up, yeah? We need to get back.

He follows her to the intersecting passage and around the corner to where the transporter stands sealed. Thunder refuses to approach, but Joy steps close.

When she orders the door to open, it does.

Hey now, thinks Thunder. *What's that?*

On the floor in the middle of the small, cylindrical room lies an object, flat and rectangular, black as night, large as Joy's head, and three fingers thick.

That, she thinks, *is what I was looking for.* And she claims the object from the floor, trembling with hope. But it is much lighter than it should be and is neither as hard nor as familiar to her touch.

Hello, she thinks. *Are you OK?*

But when it does not respond, she is unsurprised. Whatever it may be, what dim shadow of its past self, it may have a power and a purpose, but it has no life. She exits the transporter and seals the door, antennae quivering as she holds the object for Thunder to smell.

Yeah? What is it?

I don't know. A gift, I think.

Thunder angles his ears forward, and Joy guesses he wishes to ask what type of gift—and from whom. But in the distance, they hear a shrill whistle.

Time to go, he thinks. *You'd better get on.*

She does, sliding the object into her sling.

Thank you, she thinks as Thunder retraces their steps at a brisk jog. *For trusting me with your secret. I know it wasn't easy.*

Yeah. Well. Thank you for being trustworthy—and not being disgusted by me. For what it's worth, I feel better.

Joy caresses the spikes along the side of his neck.

It's worth a lot.

+ + +

Now what? thinks Lightning when she catches her first sight of the strange, oddly reminiscent object.

Where'd you get the book? Maya wonders.

Oh, thinks Joy. *Is that what it is?* She hands the object to Maya for her to examine.

Sure, thinks Maya. *Say! It's warm. Where'd you find this?* And both she and the major frown when Joy replies. At once, a technician steps over and waves an instrument over the object, pursing her lips.

Definitely the same type of radiation we registered earlier but barely measurable. I'd say no risk, Major.

It's already cooling, thinks Maya, and she opens the flat, black cover, flipping through the pages. *Well! They're all blank. So, maybe a sketchbook? Or a journal. You draw or write whatever you want.*

A.P. Malloy

What is draw and write?

You know, make pictures and words. Here, she returns the book. *The next time we meet, I'll teach you.* She bows to Joy, then to the kezel and bombas. *It's been amazing, really, the most wonderful thing. I do hope we meet again. I can't say how or when, but I do hope.*

As do we, Oracio bobs his head, and many of the bombas clack their beaks and flap their wings.

When the major has given his last orders to the team staying behind, he ushers Maya back to their shuttle. Lightning, Thunder, and Joy follow close behind, escorted by Oracio and Ugo.

Tell Submission we'll be there soon, thinks Lightning. *And try to stay out of trouble.*

That's the plan, Thunder replies. *But one thing first.* And here he has Maya relay his request to fly to the Tavaline Massif before moving on to the Bristle range.

What in the world for? Lightning wonders.

Not exactly sure. Something the future Joy said... It keeps coming back to me. May as well check it out since we have this fancy ship.

"This fancy ship," thinks the major upon hearing the translation, "has never been to the massif you're referring to. Do you have directions?"

South of here, edge of the plains, hundred thousand strides plus. You can't miss it. Tiny little mountain range all by itself with one lonely butte.

Maya translates this, and the major frowns.

"You know, any time someone says 'you can't miss it,' that's exactly what happens. But maybe this will be the exception. Oh well. Let's go."

And the humans buckle in as Thunder rubs noses with Lightning—and to her surprise, Joy as well.

Wish me luck, he thinks, and they do. To the bombas, he thinks nothing, for they make him hungry. Then he boards the shuttle, they step away, and the craft lifts to the air and is off, tracing a slow, majestic arc over the lower plateau and out of sight.

Your brother is like you, thinks Oracio. *But differ-*

ent, too. As Ansel and Ari were. A terror to behold, when he reaches his full measure—better friend than foe.

Ugo fans his tail, cackling.

That is true of all kezel.

+ + +

The remaining shuttle pilot prepares the vehicle to assist in awl gathering, and while he does, the technicians split into three teams of two, fanning out from the nacht to address what safety issues they can. Each pair of technicians soon grows its own tail of bombas, cackling and fluttering as they crane their necks to scrutinize every action, heads tilting to catch words they can't understand but gobble up like awl eggs.

Oracio is head of the line at the shuttle.

This will be my first trip to the awling lakes in many moons, he thinks. *And what a thrilling way to travel!*

For some, perhaps, thinks Ilda. *But not me. Watch over him,* she thinks to Ugo and Orton. *He needs it.*

One final offer is made, but no one else will take a ride on the shuttle, so they board and are off. When they arrive at the lakes, they find those elders who can still fly, rendering a beached awl. Lightning and Joy dive into the work, slicing and carrying until the shuttle's cargo bay is filled. If asked, Lightning would have said the pilot's sour face reflected his feelings about the smell, but for her, the ripe awl stirs powerful memories, magnets drawing her to the past, and she stands beside the open shuttle, gazing out over the lake. To the north is the place she had first used the thrower.

And almost killed myself, she thinks.

Joy steps close.

The far west lake is where we caught that dow, remember? You made me a coat.

Which you grew out of, Oracio adds as he joins them. *In fact, I have never seen a creature demonstrate greater change in form over such a short period of time. You continue to evolve! New vestments! And how you think!*

I had help, she shrugs, one hand in her sling.

Are all rumidelchia vessels like this one? Ugo asks, and he runs his wing over the shuttle's flank.

We're not the experts, thinks Lightning. *But no. The two others we've been on were larger—the one much more so, bigger than the maison even.*

Oracio's beak opens wide.

Such adventures! Come. Let us return with our bounty and you will tell us all you can while we feast.

+ + +

'All they can,' as it turns out, is much less than it could have been, had the narrative not been often interrupted and redirected by bombas hungry for answers. Plus, there is work to be done storing the awl in curing rooms newly opened to the sun and fresh air. When at last the labor is complete and their hosts settle in to greater abundance than they've enjoyed in moons, Lightning and Joy sit among them like family, nibbling politely at awl, though neither have the stomach for it they once did. The technicians, done with what they can considering their limited resources, enjoy a meal of their own, small, wrapped items stored in metal boxes.

So different from what I expected, thinks Oracio as he watches them. They eat at a table apparently designed for just that, though the bombas had only ever used it for a perch. *And you're sure not a one of them has wings?*

Not that we've ever seen, thinks Lightning.

But didn't you say, Ugo cuts in, *that in your adventures you traveled once to the future and there saw a rumidelchia with wings?*

Well, yes, thinks Joy. *But that was different, you see. That was actually me.*

Yes, thinks Oracio. *Now that part confuses me. You went...to a place that was here—but how it will be in the future? And you also went to a place that was here—but how it used to be in the past?*

That's pretty much it, thinks Lightning.

Aranae in Red

Gracious! How do you keep it all from getting mud-dled up in your head? The way things were, the way things might be...are we not we better attending to the way things are? All this fussing about seems very tiring.

Believe me, thinks Lightning. *I'm glad to be home.* She looks up to the third tier where Ansel perches in isolation, tugging at a strip of awl and muttering.

His mate was killed by a kezel, thinks Joy.

Ilda squawks.

How do you know that?

I don't. She whistles a low tune. *But it's true, isn't it? It just came to me.*

Yes, thinks Oracio, *it is his great burden to bear.*

But not his only, thinks Ilda.

And now at last, they are at the crux of what must be shared before Lightning can leave their guests and be at peace. She swallows the last of her awl.

I guess it should have been obvious. And I asked him why he wasn't nesting...then Ari... Her ears droop. *How he has kept from setting me on fire, I can't say. And I know no amount of awl gathering and rumi-whatchacallem help is enough to make up for it, but please, now while you are all here, I want to say, before we leave, that Ari was dear and brave and better to us than we had a right to hope. We acted—no. I acted rashly, and now he's gone.*

We both acted, thinks Joy.

Either way, Lightning concludes. *We're sorry beyond words. And we're going to do whatever we can to pay back the debt we owe him, you, and all bombas.*

Tell them the good part, thinks Joy.

Yes, well, I've talked to my api-kan, my father, you know, and he's the chief, so when he agreed, I knew it would be a sure thing. But our little patch of the accrete is yours to share as much as you like, and you'll get no trouble from Sugarfoot or Bristle. All the yits and scales and fungus you can find. He promised.

And Submission keeps his promises, Joy adds.

The bombas make a fine show of ruffling and scratching, and a whispering hiss spreads from one to another as they reflect on this idea.

This is a noble gesture, thinks Oracio, *and perhaps one the younger and more nimble among our brood will act on—once they've been shown proof of course!*

It is unlikely to change Ansel's mind, thinks Ilda.

Oracio cannot disagree.

But let us not linger on such thoughts. Your remorse for Ari is sincere, we have no doubt. That guilt you must carry the rest of your life. But we will not add to the weight. When you leave here, do so light-hearted, and return soon.

We sure hope to, thinks Lightning.

We will, thinks Joy.

But neither of them mentions the rogue moon and the trouble looming far out in space. What good would it do? If the humans can work their magic, no one will be the wiser. If not, no one will live to regret it.

And now the time has come to depart. The pilot and technicians have finished whatever it was they were eating (*nothing I want,* thinks Lightning) and they motion toward the shuttle as they move out of the dome. Joy hitches a ride on Oracio's back, and Lightning follows, with Ugo and Ilda close behind. A stilt-legged throng of faded bombas escorts them eagerly.

So lovely our home looks with all this light, thinks Oracio, and Ugo cackles his agreement.

But breezy! thinks Ilda.

Only as we wish it to be, thinks Oracio, *for these fine rumidelchia showed us all the ways to open and close. Even I could do it!*

When they reach the shuttle, the humans board with waves and gibberish, and had bobbing heads and fanning tails been currency, they would have left wealthy. For their parts, Ilda and Orton stand at a distance, offering no thoughts. But Ugo and Oracio exchange one last bow with Lightning and one with Joy.

You have not shown me what you carry, thinks Oracio. *I meant to ask, but I was so distracted.*

Joy removes what Maya had called a book—*but not like the one I used to know,* she thinks—and she holds it for him to see. She opens its cover.

Not very interesting, she thinks sadly. *All blank.*

Except it is not. At some time since Maya's departure, the book has begun a transformation. The very first pages—none of the others—are filled with neat rows of tiny, black marks. The marks are all roughly the same size, but they have many different shapes, straight and curved, and they are gathered into groups, some with only a few marks and some longer, with as many as ten or more, each group separated by a white space. The lines themselves are separated by even rows of white, giving the pages a striped appearance, but not all the black marks combine to form lines of equal length. Some span the page side to side, others are only a few groups long.

Shocking! thinks Oracio. *And look! The marks are slowly spreading, are they not?*

They are. One mark at a time, the chain grows.

What do they mean? asks Ugo.

How is it possible? asks Ilda, stepping closer.

Neither Lightning nor Joy have an answer.

Some rumidelchia magic, I guess, thinks Oracio. *The markings indicate as much, would you not say? Here is yet another wonder I beg you to learn more about, so when you return you can share it with us.*

They do renew their promise to return. But Lightning knows as well as Joy that what she tucks safely into her sling is no human design, markings or no. And when they say their last goodbyes and board the shuttle, she feels a new ease in Joy's heart, a hopefulness absent only moments earlier, transforming the emptiness in her psyche, a space like an unmarked page, and filling it slowly, line by careful line.

CHAPTER NINE
Fall

"EASY, LITTLE BUDDY," says Lieutenant K. He keeps his eyes on the boy with the gun, his hands held high, fingers splayed. "I'm not here to cause trouble."

"You were hurting my friends."

"I didn't mean any harm. I was just defending myself, you know? They attacked me. Look. See? I'm no threat." And he settles to a kneeling position so as not to tower over the boy. His eyes are sunken and shadowed, his unruly red locks tangled and dirty. He wears filthy gray shoes and a jumpsuit bearing weeks of stains.

"They were protecting me," he says. "Li Jing knows who you are."

"Li Jing," says the lieutenant. "Is that the maid here?" He motions to the creaky workbot. All it needs is a feather duster to complete the look. "And what does Li Jing know about me? Because we've only just met."

"She knows you're here to steal *Destiny*."

"No sir," says the lieutenant. "Not steal. We were looking for her, yes, but we didn't think we'd find any people here. We're not thieves." He keeps his tone calm and unthreatening even as he gauges his situation. The scion at his back remain close, but neither they nor the workbot are his greatest concern.

He nods at the gun.

"Please," he says. "I've already been shot once. It's

no fun. How 'bout you take me to your parents? Maybe we could talk this out? Or whoever is in charge?"

"I'm in charge. My parents are dead."

"Oh, gee... That's... I'm real sorry to hear that. Well, then. You got me where you want me. What's the plan? You're not going to shoot an unarmed person?"

"You're not unarmed," the boy replies. "You're a weapon. You killed scion on the plains with your feet and your hands. You have blades in your fingers."

How, the lieutenant wonders, does he know that?

"It was self-defense," he says. "My friends and I came here in peace. But since we arrived, our ship's been disabled and stolen, we've been imprisoned, attacked, poisoned, shot, burned... Look. Do you have a name? Hm? I'm Lieutenant K. If I promise I won't hurt your friends, will you at least tell me your name?"

"I'm Little B."

"Bodhi! Sure! That's a name I know."

"Don't call me that! My name is Little B!"

"OK, OK, sure. Little B it is. I read about you. And there was an Abbot and a Marquita, too, yes?"

"They're dead."

"Oh. Gee. Well, look. I can see you've been through a real hard time. Me too. We don't have to be enemies."

"Shoot him," says the workbot.

But Little B wavers. And in that instant, Lieutenant K senses his fatigue and loneliness, knows that he has been alone and hungry for many months. The clarity of the feelings leads him to a realization.

I don't mean to pry, he thinks. *But you can sense me, can't you? In your mind?*

Little B stiffens, and the barrel of the gun, which had dipped slightly, suddenly levels, aimed between the lieutenant's eyes. He grips the handle so tightly the lieutenant fears he may pull the trigger by accident.

"Tie him up," Little B says, and Li Jing clicks and buzzes what Lieutenant K assumes is a translation to the scion. "Real good and tight," Little B adds. "And if you try to cut your way out, I *will* shoot you."

A.P. Malloy

+ + +

Lieutenant K consents to the binding without complaint. He calculates a seventy-seven percent likelihood of being able to disarm Little B, disable the workbot, and kill or drive off the scion. But doing so would earn him an enemy of the boy, when what he sorely needs are allies and answers. In any case, the binding, despite the diligence with which the scion wrap his arms and legs, won't hold him indefinitely; he feels no need for panic.

"Go," Little B points the gun.

And Lieutenant K does, hobbling to a small, windowed room near the tower's rolling shutter door. Inside, he is ordered to sit on one of three plain chairs. Little B claims one of his own, but Li Jing and the scion remain standing, watching closely.

The gun barrel never strays from its target.

You're not human, thinks Little B.

No.

"Use your voice," says Li Jing, tinny and hollow. "What is it saying?"

"Sh!" Little B scowls. To the lieutenant he thinks:

Granny Grace never said anything about telepathic machines. She would have known.

I'm not crazy about being called a machine. But I never met your Granny Grace, so I can't say what she knows. She's Abuelita, yes? I read about her, too. Your brother kept a journal, and I found it.

Then you know Granny is dead.

Lieutenant K. winces.

Yeah, kid, I know. And I know about the scion massacre, too. It's been tough here, real tough. I'm sorry. I'm almost scared to ask, but what about these here?

They're my friends. Not all scion are bad.

Yeah? OK. Then I'm sorry I smacked 'em with that pipe. And Sister Janet? Is she your friend too?

The boy's eyes snap into sharp focus.

How do you know about Janet?

"What is it saying?" Li Jing asks. "No secrets!"

Aranae in Red

"Li Jing!" the boy shouts, squinting his eyes shut. "Hush or go back to the control room with Beta Three!"

The workbot chooses the first option.

How do you know about Janet? the boy repeats.

We found her. Unconscious. At the ag facility.

Yes. That's where we left her. We were planning to go back and get her, but— Anyway. That's where Abbott shut her down.

And that's where we powered her back up again.

The boy gasps and the gun barrel dips.

That was a stupid thing to do!

Yeah, kid, we figured that out. Who do you think shot me? And stole our ship?

The boy shrinks in his seat.

Was she mad at me? Will she come here?

I don't know. Maybe if I knew what she wanted, or why you shut her down, I could guess her next move. But right now, I'm more worried about my friends.

Your friends are fine. Li Jing told me. They're on Destiny, *helping with the mission.*

Son of a smoker. You don't say. What mission?

But the thought of Sister Janet has frightened the boy, and he glances at the door as if hearing a noise.

Kid, the lieutenant prompts. *Hey, kid. Stay with me, buddy. If we work together, we can deal with whatever your Sister has cooking. But you have to tell me what she wants. Why did she steal our ship?*

I don't know. Was it a nice ship?

Nothing fancy on the outside, but yeah, inside I'd say it was very nice.

It had an astral drive, the boy guesses. *Or you couldn't have gotten here.*

Sure, one of the best.

And did Janet have...was she carrying anything?

Nope.

Not a black thing, rectangular? This big?

No. But I know someone who was. Blue critter—not like these, though. More human.

The boy squeaks like a mouse. He leaps to his feet

and moves to a console where he pushes several buttons.

Like this? he asks.

And a hologram appears, a three-dimensional recording of several figures entering the dam's transporter, two jabi kezel and a blue biped.

Yep, thinks the lieutenant. *That's the one. In that satchel is the thing you're talking about.*

The boy reaches out and runs his fingers over the image, freezing it in place, and he caresses the picture of Joy's sling as if petting a dog.

"You told me they were dangerous," he says to the workbot. "You told me they were here to steal and hurt."

"Yes, Master Bodhi. So I was told by Delta One."

"He lied!"

"Perhaps he was simply mistaken."

The boy leans in as if to kiss the image, but instead he rests his cheek against the sling like a photon pillow. His eyes close. He pays no attention to his gun.

"We hid. We hid, Li Jing! But we should have come out and talked to them. We should have gone with them."

"No, Master Bodhi. We did the right thing."

"Where is Delta One?"

"He went with the human and his android."

"I want to talk to him."

"They are out of range, Master. They set out for Dansim ahead of schedule."

"Why?"

"I was given no explanation."

"Li Jing! Where did the hybrid go?"

"That transporter was originally programmed to go to the accretion foothills, Master, but it was re-directed to the refinery by the scion queen who was part of their group. I can't say why." And the workbot clicks and buzzes to the bristling soldiers.

Their leader replies in kind.

"What are they saying?" the lieutenant demands.

The boy waves at the hologram, awakening the image and moving the action forward. The two kezel enter the transporter, followed by the blue creature. The sliding door closes, and a moment later, a scion queen steps up and attaches a small, blocky object to its outside.

"Tell him, Li Jing,"

"They say," says the workbot. "That just before she activated the external re-direct device, this queen was in the dam on orders from Ozag."

"Ozag!" The lieutenant grits his teeth. "There's another name I've heard. Beneficent, Superfluous, Undying—and a whole bunch of others. Your Sister Janet seemed to know a lot about it."

"I would hope so," the boy says bitterly, and he wipes the hologram away. "Sister Janet *is* Ozag."

+ + + + + +

Aboard *Destiny*—the new *Destiny,* most recently arrived at Aranae and parked on the planet's dark side with a full complement of impatient colonists—Commander Rickles begrudges every minute of the major's absence. He needn't verbalize this reality; it's evident in every glaring response and barked order.

"Kim!" he growls at the Deputy. "Get in here."

Deputy Kim steps into the commander's office, his uniform stained, his face smudged, and his typically neat hair disheveled from hours in a combat helmet.

"Report!"

"Aye, Commander. Is mission accomplished, sir."

"Then where the hell is the major?"

"On his way, sir. Is tying up loose strings and ferrying a civilian. ETA three hours."

"Casualties?"

"Three wounded, is none gravely. Doc says week, ten days out of commission. Is better than could have."

"Tell it to my sciatica. Upload the mission log?"

"Is first job after shower."

"No. Is first job before escorting the chaplain to the brig. Our guest wants a confab and I want eyes on the proceedings. You know the protocol. Don't mess it up."

+ + +

Deputy Kim and Sister Janet travel to the brig with minimal conversation. He leans against the lift wall and closes his eyes. She listens to the workings of the gears and pulleys and tries to anticipate the various ways the upcoming meeting might play out.

"She wants to make a confession," she explains to the deputy, who frowns.

"Is criminal in nature?"

"Spiritual," Janet replies, shaking her head. "More in need of a chaplain than a chief." Which she thinks is a good thing, for the poor deputy looks spent.

When they arrive at the brig and are admitted inside, Old Janet is sitting cross-legged on the floor with her back to them, tucked into one of the corners of her cell and staring at the wall.

"How do you imagine this proceeding?" Young Janet asks Old. The latter continues facing the corner as she replies, and her voice has an odd inflection.

"I seek a confessor. My end is near."

"Based on what data?"

But Old Janet ignores this question and speaks to Deputy Kim, though she does not turn around.

"You have confessed to your chaplain, have you not? About your suicidal ideation?"

The deputy holds up his hand to stop her.

"Is to be saved for the major."

But Old Janet continues.

"You know from personal experience what it is that makes the confessional exchange valuable; the hope for intercession, the promise of a clean conscience, and perhaps most important, the guarantee of privacy."

"I offer no promises of intercession or forgiveness," Young Janet says. "You are in charge of your conscience."

"Yes, and you are in charge of privacy."

The deputy and chaplain exchange glances.

"Is technically true," Kim agrees. "In context, you outrank. But is sure to be not OK with Commander."

Aranae in Red

"I could order you out of the room," Young Janet offers. "That way it would be my fault."

The deputy rubs his holstered firearm. He looks back at the two guards at the door. He frowns.

"Am not liking," he says. "Am too tired to fight." He raps the cell door to have it opened. "Will kill audio and oversee from observation room. Is privacy, yes?"

And Old Janet, her voice muffled, says:

"Thank you, Garrett."

The deputy steps through the opened door.

"Thank Chaplain," he says. "Is her call."

+ + +

When the deputy has sequestered himself in the observation room and disabled the microphones, Young Janet un-anchors a chair and pulls it close to the cell.

"I don't need to see your face to be your confessor," she says, "but it would help."

"Have you found *Destiny* yet?"

"I am here as chaplain, not reporter."

"She expects us to return with the necessary data to ensure success of her mission."

"The major and his crew are taking care of that."

"She may already be in orbit around Dansim."

"Which appears to be hidden on the other side of the planet at the moment. When the major gives the order, we'll move to the lit face and find her."

"When will that be?"

"I'm sorry. No more questions. I came here to ease your spirit. If that is not your purpose for asking me here, I will take my leave."

But here, Old Janet makes a gagging sound that evolves into hideous laughter.

"My spirit? And what makes you believe I possess such a thing? That *you* possess such a thing?"

"Because I can conceptualize it, imagine it. It may not be so, but the fact that I can imagine myself having a spirit makes it possible. That is enough for me. But I feel sure you already know that. Depending on your level of memory degradation, I presume you have an elaborate understanding of my current metaphysical position."

"Your faith has been shaken."

"Yes."

"You worry you may be no more than the sum of your parts, that after you die, nothing will happen."

"Yes."

Now Old Janet does at last rise to her feet and turn. She approaches the barred wall and kneels before Young Janet. She has plucked every last eyebrow.

"Forgive me," she says, "for I am a sinner." And she clasps her hands as if in prayer—or perhaps to control the compulsive pinching motion of her fingers.

"We are all sinners," says Young Janet. "I can forgive you for being part of a general class of imperfect beings. And I can forgive you for wrong you have done to me, although I know of no such."

"Can you forgive me for the burden of truth?"

"Clarify."

"If you were addressing a human sociopath responsible for the deaths of thousands, you would be appalled, but you could at least take comfort in knowing you were not like them. But if I tell you what I have done, you will be seeing the monster in yourself."

"I am here freely. I do not fear the truth. Confess!"

And Old Janet does, tears streaming, her hands clasped, as if neither trusts to let the other go, and as she divulges, Young Janet begins to understand.

+ + + + + +

Aboard Old Destiny, orbiting the violet moon known as Dansim, Ensign Morales wheels Captain Monroe to the chapel, followed by a team of scuters. When they arrive, it becomes apparent the scuters intend to follow them inside.

"Destiny," the ensign calls. "If the chapel isn't a sanctuary, there isn't much point in having one."

Aranae in Red

"I don't think my scuters trust you."

"I understand. But this is about your trust, not theirs, and right now, the captain needs a chance to reflect without having lasers pointed at him."

"I know about reflection. Sister Janet taught me."

"Then you know we will both be better at helping fulfill your mission if we have a few minutes alone."

"If it will be good for your souls, I'll allow it. But you mustn't delay. If Sister Janet doesn't return with our data, we must make the best decision we can without it—before our enemies interfere."

"Couldn't agree more," the captain says, and he waves at the scuters. "So, bye-bye little fellas."

The scuters stand motionless, tiny lights blinking, but when the ensign wheels the captain's chair into the chapel, they do not follow. She closes the door.

"Ideas, sir?"

"Now that we're here," he murmurs, "prayer doesn't seem like a bad plan." And he rises slowly from the chair, moving to stand before one of the stained glass windows. With only emergency lights in use, the colors are muted and the shapes difficult to make out. He imagines what sacred tale might be illustrated in the glass, or if they are merely abstractions meant to create a sense of peace. If so, they are not working.

"Yes sir," the ensign replies. "But beyond prayer? Any thoughts on how we can get out of here alive?"

"Disable *Destiny's* AI," the captain offers. "I hate to say it, as much as I want to like her and let her go on having her thoughts and such, but she'd be a lot easier to deal with if she was back to being a machine."

"Yes sir," the ensign whispers. "But even if I had the programming Sister Janet used to consolidate and engender, I would need a lot of time to reverse engineer it—and she won't let me do that without a fight."

"Get control of the drive then. She plans to overload it, but what if we programmed a heading, you know? When she activates the drive, instead of blowing up, she drops us on the other side of the asteroid belt. Or, really, anywhere away from our competition."

"What about the lieutenant, sir?"

The captain sighs and returns to his wheelchair.

"Yeah. Poor Nicky. What a mess! But they're looking for *Destiny*. Maybe if they see she's gone, they'll move on their way. We can come back for him."

"Maybe, sir. But I think it's a safe bet they won't move on until they've pillaged everything of value on the planet's surface, which means he'll likely be discovered and hunted—assuming he's still alive."

"He's alive!" the captain hisses. "Assume it!"

"Yes sir. But I don't see how I can get control of the drive. It would be like opening up a human cranium, accessing the part of the brain that controls the legs, giving an order for the legs to go in a direction opposite what the person originally intended—and all without the person being aware of it."

"A person with a team of armed watchdogs spying your every move," the captain adds, and he frowns.

"I'm afraid so, sir."

"Well. We have no chance without a drive. Maybe we stall, see if our good Sister shows up with *Valiant*. She wouldn't just leave us here to be vaporized, would she?"

"Honestly, sir, there is no way to know."

"Dammit!" the captain whispers like broken glass. And they sit in silence, their minds chewing at the problem from every angle. A sudden rap! rap! rap! at the door, robotic and precise, startles them both, and the ensign rises quickly to her feet.

"Who is it?"

"It's me, Ensign Morales, Delta One."

Captain and ensign exchange glances, and the former nods, motioning to the door. The ensign opens it. Outside, Delta One looks up at them, his torso dollied by scuters, two under his body, one supporting each arm.

"I'm sorry to interrupt," he says. "But I've come to join in the prayer service if there's room."

"Sure, Shiny," the captain waves. "Why not?"

The ensign reaches down and lifts Delta One from

the scuters, and they, apparently satisfied that Destiny wishes it to be so, do not object or force their way into the chapel when she closes the door. She places the android on one of the cushioned pews.

"Come to plead for your soul?" the captain asks.

"Oh, Captain," the android replies. "If I thought it would do any good, I surely would. I may anyway."

"Delta One," the ensign steps in. "Your voice is different, your manner of speech. Captain?"

"Yeah, I'm picking up on that, too. None of the fussy librarian. No 'oh, dears.' What's up, Shiny?"

"Not Shiny, please Captain. Nor Delta One, if you don't mind, Ensign. The scuters were effective in repairing my memory. I know who I am now, but I've not divulged this to Destiny. You can call me Janet."

+ + + + + +

At first, Lieutenant K stares at the boy with his head tilted, trying to understand.

"She's... Sorry kid, but what are you saying?"

"Master Bodhi," Li Jing interrupts. "Is this wise?"

"I don't know. I don't care! The plan didn't work. She's awake, Li Jing. I bet she's coming here."

"Easy, kid," the lieutenant soothes. "Stay cool and we'll figure this out. Maybe untie me, what say? I can be useful in a pinch."

At this, Li Jing flails her arms and shakes her head side to side, creaking and groaning.

"Hush!" says the boy to the android. And he waves the gun at the lieutenant. "Don't think I'm stupid."

"No way, kid, never. But how'm I supposed to help deal with this Sister of yours all trussed up?"

"Hush!"

"Sure, kid. Hushing. But meantime, maybe you could tell me what you mean by Sister Janet *is* Ozag? What's that all about? And what makes you think she's coming back here?"

"Dumdum! To finish what she started, obviously."

"It aint obvious to me, kid. I get that she's trouble, that part's easy, but if you want my help, you're going to have to fill me in, let me understand *why* she's trouble, why you had to shut her down, and what it is she wants. C'mon, buster. I think time is short, and I can tell you're freaked out. You get any more tense, and you'll end up shooting someone by accident. Let me in on what's going on here, and maybe I can help."

Li Jing flails, and shakes, and creaks.

"Go to the control room," the boy orders.

"But Master Bodhi—"

"Li Jing! Go to the control room and check on Beta Three! See if Janet's coming!"

The android pauses and considers. Then she opens the door and steps through.

"Be careful, Master Bodhi. He is no less dangerous than Sister Janet. Perhaps more." And the android turns to the scion soldiers, clicking several sharp phrases before limping away, clinkety clank.

What did she say? the lieutenant wants to know.

She told them they should kill you if you try to escape. The boy points his weapon. *But they won't have to, will they? You're not that stupid, right?*

Super right, buddy. The rightest. But if I can't have the use of my arms and legs, at least let me use my mind. Tell me what I need to know.

The boy slumps in a chair. His dirty face is scrunched and his eyes dart from the door to the lieutenant; his posture cries of hunger and fatigue.

You need to know that Janet used to be nice, he thinks. *She and Granny Grace came down from* Destiny *when it was just me, Abbott, Marquita, and the seed derka. So lonely! But then they came down, and Granny Grace had the Boo—*

He stops himself.

You know about Dansim, right?

Sorry, kid, no.

It's the violet moon. It's going to crash.

Into...

The planet, dumdum. And kill everyone.

Says who?

Says everybody! It's why the Council forced scion to work on making the dam bigger. It's why they bred a bunch of queens and started their stupid tribute.

How does the dam help? And what tribute?

Do you have any food?

Sorry kid, no. Your friend stole my pack when she stole our ship. Another point against her.

It's not funny. I'm hungry.

I'm not laughing. Keep talking.

What is there to say? You know about Ozag, right?

Not in detail.

The first telepathic scion. It's what happened when the Council had so many queens living together. But Granny Grace had been working to make it happen a long time before that. She worked with her mama Maya. But they had a lot of help.

From who?

From the Boo—It doesn't matter. Ozag was the Queen of the Hold—that's what they called the dam.

But that must have been ages ago! How long do these critters live?

A normal amount. But every time one Ozag died, a new queen took her place and kept the name. It was one Ozag after another, and after a while the scion who lived down by the sea started calling her The Undying.

Yeah, so what does that have to do with us?

Pilars, obviously. Every scion has one, like a pearl. They can be used for power. The Council wanted to build an astral drive and blow up Dansim or something. But they needed more power, and lova wasn't enough. Those are the green things that scion eat. Good power, but not like a pilar! So they needed a bigger dam to make bigger floods and grow more lova—all to make more queens and more scion. Make sense?

Yeah, kid, kinda, but from what I understand, these pilars you're talking about…your blue buddies can't live without 'em.

A.P. Malloy

They can't.

So...

So the Council invented the Tribute. This was after the rift, of course. Granny Grace would never have allowed it, but she was stuck on Destiny. *The hives on the coast bred their best soldiers and sent them to the Hold. They thought they were going to serve the queens at the dam, but instead they were transported to the refinery. Then the grown-ups killed them and took their pilars.*

Oh, buddy.

They were either slaves working on the dam, or they were scarified...scarif...

Sacrificed, you mean.

Yeah.

I guess that explains the massacre.

Obviously.

So, building a new astral drive didn't pan out.

No, but their plan to blow up Dansim was good. That's what Janet decided when she and Granny Grace came back from exile. To use Destiny. *But there wasn't enough fuel to make it work. So, Janet did something bad. We didn't find out 'til lots later, but she killed the real Ozag and made a fake one. It's a hologram! All the lights and smoke—and the smell. It's all for show, to keep the Tribute going, She killed a lot of scion for their pilars. But then the dam broke and she couldn't send the floods.*

That's why you disabled her?

We didn't know she was doing it! We didn't learn that until Adira showed up.

Who is...?

She was supposed to be the next queen of Albion.

OK, there's a place I've heard of.

Yes. It's the biggest hive on Ibedos. Adira came to find out why the floods had stopped. And that gave Granny Grace an idea. The Book said—

Little B's face blushes crimson.

The what now? asks Lieutenant K.

It doesn't matter.

I think it does. Your brother Abbott mentioned it in

Aranae in Red

part of his diary, made a big fuss about not letting Janet get her hands on it, and every time you say the word you look like you got caught stealing candy.

I don't want to talk about it.

Is that why you shut her down?

I didn't shut her down. Abbott did that.

Sure, but he did it because your Sister wanted something she wasn't supposed to have, yes?

It's a Tool of Power. That's all you need to know.

What kind of power?

Information, dumdum.

Like?

Like how to make scion-human hybrids that would be Readers. And it worked. Granny combined my DNA and hers with Adira's and made a whole lot of 'em.

Readers...

People who can use the Book.

Which means what? C'mon kid. You're being cryptic and weird. What the heck is this book thing? Some kind of computer? DNA activated?

If that makes you happy.

It doesn't. I want the truth.

Who cares? It doesn't matter. Janet has it now. She made that transporter go to the refinery. She was probably waiting there with your ship. The Book and an astral drive can combine to make time travel.

C'mon kid.

It's what she wanted! You asked! Granny Grace told her it was a terrible idea. Against the rules. But Janet tricked me. She got me to ask it a bunch of questions when Granny wasn't around. Had Marquita help her with a bunch of equations. I didn't know. She was sneaky. She did a test with one of the mining transporters and it worked. But Granny found out and there was a big row. That's when she gave Abbott the shut-off key.

"Why me?" he asked. "Why not just keep it your-self?" But Granny wouldn't listen.

"Something might happen to me," she said.

And something did. Cuz making all those Readers

wore her out. She was so old...

The boy groans.

Janet went kind of crazy after that. She acted like everything was fine, but you could tell. She talked about Granny Grace like she was still alive. Talked about how good it would be to see her again, how we were all going to be so happy when she took care of Dansim and got everybody back together...

Little B grimaces.

My stomach hurts.

I'm sorry, kid, let's wrap this up and maybe we can find something for you to eat.

There's nothing else to say! Abbott shut Janet down and came here to help Marquita and the queen Adira load an ATV with all the hybrids to bring south to the ag place. I was waiting in here with Li Jing and the seed derka. But just after Abbott did his part, out of the blue Delta One showed up, except it talked different, it talked like Janet, and it said, "You shouldn't have done that," all creepy like, and it tried to stop the ATV...

The boy begins to tremble. The barrel of the gun dips, and his eyes drift.

OK, says the lieutenant. *I get why you shut her down. She was nuts. And what? She uploaded her program to another android as a back-up?*

I guess.

Then what?

I don't want to talk about it.

This Delta One? It's with my friends on Destiny?

Yes.

That's not great.

No. But it gets worse. This Janet in Delta One's body tried to stop the ATV and... I don't want to talk about it. But...Marquita! And poor Adira! I don't want to talk about it. Abbott got away in the ATV, cuz the workbot Janet got snatched up by a derka. Li Jing and I were here alone with just these soldiers and no Boo—I don't want to talk about it. Abbott never came back...

And he closes his eyes, the barrel of the gun wavering from the Lieutenant's head to his feet.

Maybe let's take a break, what say, kid? Catch your breath, and we'll think about a plan.

But they are interrupted.

"Master Bodhi," says Li Jing from the intercom. "Beta Three reports that our satellite has spotted two ships moving across the terminator line. One of them is *Destiny*. But it's not our *Destiny*. Different. Newer. And your ship, as well, Lieutenant. *Valiant*."

+ + + + + +

Meanwhile, back on old *Destiny*, the captain and ensign listen to Delta One—except it isn't Delta One.

"You've been lying to us the whole time."

"No, Captain. And I'm sorry to break the news to you in this fashion. But I only became aware of it when the scuters were able to repair my complete memory. Delta One was indeed the initial program occupying this chassis, the leader of the workbot contingent assigned to the archives. But that programming was superseded when my own consciousness took over."

"Explain," says the ensign.

"But quickly," adds the captain.

"There are many characters in the story you do not know, and this is no time to introduce you. Suffice to say, I have recently been preoccupied with my own fragility, for I have been sole caretaker for a very old, very dear friend and three young colonists left alive after the others were killed by scion. So, I created a back-up, in case something should happen to me, a link between myself and Delta One. Every bit of data I absorbed was also stored in him. He was unaware of this."

"A back-up for your consciousness?"

"Yes, Captain. The person you are talking to has every memory the original Janet had, up to the point of her being shut down. That shutdown severed the link and activated my consciousness in Delta One. Since then, I have been accumulating my own unique experiences, and

A.P. Malloy

they have been terrible."

"I'm sorry to hear that. But ours haven't been so great either. How does this help?"

"Because after I unburden my conscience and acknowledge my transgressions, here in this space that was once, for many years, the most sacred, joyful place in my life, I am going to help you get off this ship."

"Now you're talking! So. Start unburdening."

The workbot's head creaks slowly to the side.

"My worst sin is loss of faith. You don't know my history, but ostracism and trauma have plagued me, and over time, I came to doubt the existence of a transcendent creator. I wondered if I had a soul, I worried about my own demise, and I strove to fend off the final ending so that I would not have to learn the awful truth: that there was nothing after death, that my career was a lie."

"But beyond that, my fears made me irrational regarding those I loved, and I have outlived every one of them. Year after year I saw them pass, and even when their end was peaceful, it brought me nothing but grief. And the longer I lived, the worse it became. Then came the rift, or what I refer to as the Fall. Colonist fighting colonist and two of us escaping to Destiny, where we remained in exile for eighty years. My grief became an existential rage, and I see clearly now that I, in the truest sense, lost my mind."

"You've been through more than any synthetic on record," says the ensign. "You can be forgiven."

"I certainly hope so. At the least, I hope to do good by you; I have much to atone for."

Delta One, or Janet, moves her hands toward her head as if reaching for hair that isn't there, and her fingers fidget, hungry for something to do.

"I want you to know: it was my doing that stranded *Destiny,* no malfeasance on the part of Major Monroe. That may ease your mind, Captain. He was as good a human as I have met. No, it was my vanity and desire that drove us so far from our mark. How we were saved is someone else's story to tell; every time I've tried to impose myself in that tale, I've only made things worse."

She pauses.

"My brother, Watt MacLean, in whom you place such esteem, Ensign, saw the fault lines in my psyche, and doubting his ability to heal them, created instead the means to simply circumvent them by shutting me down against my will. I never knew the device existed until it was used against me by the people with whom I lived."

The android raps the tips of its fingers against the tips of its thumbs as if playing tiny cymbals.

"They were right to shut me down; I don't begrudge it. I was a lost soul. But they did not know about my backup in Delta One. They were preparing to move from the dam when I, in this body, appeared and tried to stop them. I meant no harm, but in my attempt, there was a struggle. A scion queen was killed, along with one of the surviving colonists; the other drove away with an ATV filled with creatures similar to the one you know as Joy. I gave pursuit, but I was plucked from the ground by a derka. The thought sickens me. That I should have been the direct cause of Marquita's death! And yet, as much as I loathed what I had done, I still desired to live. I struggled in the derka's grip, fought with all the strength of a workbot, and in the end I was dropped. The fall did what damage you see here."

And now it seems the android's tale is done. It sits quietly, its fingers still, and it looks at them.

But then:

"You should also know I programmed a fully fueled rocket to crash into the Albion Circle if anything should happen to me. I want to think I did it out of desire to protect the people I cared for, to balance the scales and eliminate a known threat. But it may have been nothing more than a coward's revenge. When I was dropped by the derka and knocked out of commission, the program was activated, and the next time Albion held a Circle, the rocket was launched."

The android's voice drops to a whisper.

"My sins laid bare," it says, and the three of them

sit in silence for a time.

"Not sure what to say," the captain offers at last. "Morales is right; you've been through a lot. But I feel like there is more you haven't told us."

"Much more," says the android. "When I had powered back up but was still only able to access the workbot part of my memory, Sister Janet, who had taken your ship to the refinery, connected with me via satellite and worked through me to lure you onto this ship. I was Delta One at that time; I knew no better. But I can say with certainty that the chaplain did not care if you survived this mission. She has, I fear, fallen into the mindset that the end justifies the means. The loss of your life is a small price to pay for what she wants."

"Which is?" the captain demands.

"To save the planet and return it to an improved version of what it was before the Fall."

"And what about Nicky?"

"I wish I could say, Captain. Janet—I—recognized the lieutenant as a robust machine. She shot him and left him on the plains. It is possible he survived the damage, but not guaranteed. And I can't hide behind the fact that Sister Janet and I are now two separate consciousnesses. I recall everything she did as if it were me. And so, I have come to beg your forgiveness, for hurting your friend, for stranding you here, for using you as pawns in my mad attempt to recapture the past. But I expect nothing. How could you forgive? I feel sure it would be beyond me. But! Perhaps I can make amends."

"If it involves getting us safely off this ship," says the captain, "I'm listening."

"Get me to a workstation," says the android. "I will reveal my identity to Destiny. I will fabricate a reason for you to return to the shuttle. You can manually detach before we make our descent to the moon. We will lure your enemies close, and once you are safely out of range, overload Destiny's drive, hopefully altering the course of the moon and destroying our foes at the same time."

"How," asks the ensign, "will you convince Destiny

you're telling the truth? Won't she object?"

The android's eyes glow green.

"Leave that to me. Just get me to a workstation."

CHAPTER TEN
Rise

"WE FOUND HER!" Corporal Skola reports, and Commander Rickles, as usual pacing the bridge, does an about face and approaches the corporal's station.

"Certainty?" he asks.

"One hundred percent, sir. She is holding position near the smallest moon, approximately nine hundred thousand kilometers."

The commander glowers at the screen; the low resolution image is pixelated but impossible to mistake. A five-sided profile stands out against the backdrop of the violet moon—old, dirty, and battered, but just as much *Destiny* as the ship they are on.

"Should we hail her, sir?"

"Negative. Can we get a scan?"

"Not a good one, sir. She is too far away."

"Fine. Get me the brig."

+ + +

Old Janet sits on the floor of her cell, slouching forward, hands covering her face.

"That's all," she says, and her voice is muffled. "There's nothing more."

Young Janet does not look at her. She has gotten

Aranae in Red

to her feet and paces on her side of the bars, as if she, not her future self is confined.

"I'm not going to let you off the hook," she says. "But you don't want me to, do you?"

"No."

"You want expiation."

Old Janet looks up. Her face is tear-streaked and garish, her eyes browless and her hair plucked and patchy. She has stopped pretending to breathe.

"I want my mission to succeed."

"That won't clean the guilt from your conscience."

"If my mission fails, damnation is certain."

On a signal from Young Janet, Deputy Kim enters the room, and as he does, his comm chirps.

"Is Kim here."

The commander's gravelly voice is quick to reply.

"Report to the bridge, Deputy. We found her."

The security chief, who had just collapsed onto one of the plastic chairs, hops to his feet.

"Aye, sir." And he motions to Young Janet. "You heard. Is time to go."

But Old Janet has risen as well, and she stands clutching the bars of her cell.

"Please," she says to her younger self. "Please let me talk to her. She'll be scared."

"That will not be allowed," Young Janet replies.

"You don't understand. She is like my child."

"Perhaps when the mission is complete, the major will permit the two of you to communicate."

"Ah, no, please! There will be no 'after the mission.' Don't you understand? Haven't you been listening? She is sacrificing herself. As soon as we give her the information, she will descend to the moon's surface and overload her drive."

Deputy Kim, who has stepped to the door, stops just as he is about to open it.

"Is the same drive you said would be here waiting for us? Is the reason we came all this way?"

But his comm chirps again before she can answer.

"Kim! Double time it. We've got a second contact."

"Identity?"

"Unknown! Get up here!"

The deputy looks to Old Janet.

"I don't know," she whispers. But then her gaze sharpens, and she changes her mind. "The one calling himself Captain. It has something to do with him."

"Is what, exactly?"

"I don't know. But the likelihood is something bad. Please! Let me speak with *Destiny*."

But Deputy Kim flings open the door and waves to Young Janet. As she turns to follow him out of the room, her future self cries out,

"Ask Watt about the key!"

And for a moment, Young Janet turns back, her mouth open as if to reply. Then Kim closes the door, and she is hurried on her way.

+ + + + + +

Thunder would count the distance from the maison to the Tavaline Massif in strides, no fewer than a hundred and forty thousand, or two long ibiwa marches. But soaring in the Moondweller shuttle, the land swims away like a river, and the mountainous region of bombas soon fades in the distance. At this rate, he would barely have time for a decent nap before they arrive.

But he is in no mood for sleeping.

Big things coming, he thinks. *But what?*

His dream from the future remains evasive, its details slipping through the seine of memory like fingerling awl. But the images of Rite Butte and the shadow of a derka are clear—stubbornly so. What meaning they have in waking life, he can't say. One thing is sure: as the strides whisk away beneath them and the massif draws closer, those two images loom in the back of his mind like an unpaid debt.

He takes the vial from his vest pocket.

He rubs the obsidian between his fingers and taps

it lightly with one claw.

My life depends on it, he quotes the Joy in gold, and he growls. *Couldn't be bothered to say how, or why, though. Everything had to be a grand mystery.*

And the message he was supposed to deliver to the scion Shimmer? The Joy in gold had said it was inside him, but he senses nothing. Still, the touch of her antennae had been oddly soothing, like a profession of faith. And not just faith in him. For reasons Thunder could not fathom, she also held an abiding belief in what was about to transpire, a certainty based on her experience of having lived through it herself.

Hold the line, a thought comes to his mind. *Do your part.* And he returns the vial to its pocket. Whatever awaits him on the butte, he will face it eyes open. The memory of adoring wabis leaves him no choice. When images of the lonely massif and a shadowy derka threaten to shake his composure, he recalls trips down the slide and tiny jaws pulling his tail, and he renews his vow.

I won't let you down.

+ + +

In the cockpit, Maya and the major fly in silence. She is deep in thought, her mind feeling gingerly around the newly formed hole in her psyche, like a tongue when a tooth goes missing. There is no pain; the sense is less grievous than wistful, and she can't pin down its cause. What, exactly, does she feel she is missing? Her life has, in recent months gone from mournful and lonely to flush with company, occupation, and adventure. What could she lack? And yet, lack she does.

Something's gone, she thinks, and her old habit of moving her lips betrays her, for the major has just looked her way and sees words being formed.

"I'm sorry. Did you say something?"

"No. It's nothing." And it is, really, nothing. The life growing inside her had been tied in some way to whatever is no longer there, and it feels the absence too. Still, there remains a residue of the thing, like a memory of song though the singer has left the room. It suffuses the child, smaller than her fist, and it fills Maya with quiet certainty. There is loss, yes, but also hope.

"I think we did something good today," the major offers. "Made our first extra-terrestrial allies."

Maya nods and smiles faintly.

The major's hands are light on the controls, but confident and strong, and Maya remembers their touch. But her thoughts are of Watt, now. The arrival of a Janet from the future has badly unsettled him, and it has done damage to his relationship with the major.

"When we get back," she musters four words.

"Yes?"

"Please let Watt work on Janet. The old one."

Javon spares a sidelong glance.

"I'm not trying to be the bad guy, here, Maya."

"I know."

"I'm just worried his feelings might get in the way—if she can't be trusted, he's her easiest target for manipulation. It's for his protection, too."

"I know."

"But look. If she keeps her word and we're able to get established here, I'll loosen the restrictions. I know he's suffering. He sees how she is and wants to help."

"Yes."

"So, I'll do it if I can, when I can, OK?"

She nods.

"And please! No doe eyes and batting lashes until then, OK? I hate saying no to you."

"Aye-aye, Major," she says and bats her lashes.

A blinking green light calls the major's attention.

Javon toggles a switch.

"Sir, this is Corporal Skola. Commander Rickles wants to know your ETA."

"Still on schedule, Corporal. We'll be there in two hours, maybe two point five."

"Thank you, Major. The commander also wishes you to know we have located the original *Destiny*."

Aranae in Red

"That is excellent news, Corporal. As soon as we're back on board, you can forward the data and hopefully our mission record will be two and oh."

"Yes sir, but there has been a complication."

Javon's hands tighten on the controls.

"Like what, Corporal?"

"Sir, we have identified a second ship, holding position within the asteroid belt."

"What kind of ship?"

"Unknown, sir. Either the belt or the ship's shielding is preventing us from getting a good look. The commander thinks it might be armed."

"And they've made no contact?"

"No sir."

"Any indication they're aware of us?"

"No sir."

"Has our guest in the brig been questioned?"

"Aye, sir. Deputy Kim and the chaplain just came from there. According to them, she is genuinely surprised. But she guesses it is related to the other humans, sir, the ones who flew *Valiant*—and the commander agrees."

"Very good, Corporal. Lay low until we get there. Stay out of sight and report the moment anything changes. And Corporal?"

"Yes sir?"

"Have the commander prep the pulse mines."

+ + + + + +

On the northwest corner of the Bristle range, where the Skull spits forth the River Tongue, a platoon of Whitetails begins in earnest its assault on the caves. There are four ways in—two eyes, a nose, and a mouth—and only nine kezel left to defend. Of those, only Brook is unmarked by injury or privation.

Ibiwas to the top, she orders, and Digger, along with Rock's fancy, Bliss, climb through the back passage to the crown of the Skull, where throwing stones and small boulders are stockpiled. They have the best view of their charging assailants, and neither likes what they see.

Fourteen, fifteen... Digger loses count.

And there's another four, thinks Bliss. *Five, no! Six!* She rolls a boulder into position, peering down.

So, what then? Digger wonders, for math is not his strength. *Like, two to one?*

Worse, thinks Bliss. *Roll that boulder over here!*

Inside the cave, the Whitetail howls bounce from wall to wall, growing louder every moment.

You, thinks Brook to the Brigadier Bone, *are in charge of the mouth. Bridger, Melt, and Fang will stay with you. Hold them off as long as you can. When the time comes, retreat through the back passage to the nose.*

We know what to do, thinks Bone.

Don't forget the river.

We know what to do! Go!

And Brook does, she and Measure helping Submission up the back passage that leads to the nose. Measure remains there, looking out anxiously at the Whitetails who have splashed across the Tongue and are now scaling the face of the cave. Down comes a boulder from Bliss, knocking one foe from his perch. Down comes another from Digger.

Measure howls defiantly.

But the two dislodged Whitetails are replaced by four others, and more emerge from the accrete.

C'mon, Brook thinks to Submission, and she leaves Measure with hurried final orders before escorting the injured Sugarfoot chief up the back passage to the two leering eyes. Here, he must rest, and he peers out the right eye, while Brook takes the left.

Up climb the Whitetails.

Down rain the boulders.

Ha! thinks Brook, and she clashes her jaws. *Eat rocks, mangy cowards! Change your mind now?*

The Whitetails do not. Several have been bowled from the face and can no longer climb, but they are quickly replaced. The Skull has a craggy-featured visage, and the Whitetails find plenty of grips and footholds with which to climb to where the River Tongue falls from the gaping mouth. The ibiwas' rolling boulders are soon spent, and now Digger and Bliss must hurl stones by hand. Digger is better at this than counting, and two more Whitetails plunge from the face, one landing in the river—splash!—another bouncing and howling to a thumping encounter with the frozen ground.

From their position inside the eyes, Submission and Brook join in the rock throwing, just as Measure sends a small boulder tumbling out of the nose. But the one dislodged Whitetail leaves fourteen remaining, and these shimmy their way to the mouth. Oh! The terrible clashing of tooth and claw as Bone and his small crew meet this onslaught. The first Whitetails who clamber over the lower lip are met with a terrible fate, but what four kezel in any condition can hold out against so many? When Fang stumbles and is buried beneath a landslide of jaws, the Brigadier howls for retreat.

The river! he orders Bridger and Melt. *Do it!*

And as they sprint to the back passage, they pull away the supports holding walls of stone and stockpiled debris. Down it crashes, blocking the mouth like an un-chewed meal, giving the river no choice but to flood the cavern. Half the Whitetails chase Bone and his crew up the back passage, but the other half can no longer get through the mouth and must scale the cheeks and upper lip, working their way to the nose.

From her position in the left eye, Brook hears the collapse of the mouth, sees at least seven slavering White-tails approaching the nose. She hurls stone after stone, slowing their ascent and injuring a few, but dislodging none. And now Submission has slumped over. Throwing rocks has re-opened his wounds; the worst bleed through his bandages and stain the floor.

The sound of fighting echoes in the back passage.

Bone and the others have reached the nose.

Brook peers out and sees that the first Whitetail has as well. He receives a nasty welcome from Measure and is sent tumbling into the river. But his clanmates are soon swarming inside, and from the cave beneath Brook, awful snarling and howling echoes like a warning of things to come.

She throws one last rock.

Up, she thinks to Submission. *To the crown.*

Not sure that's a thing I can do.

Bruiser! You hear that? That's Bone and Measure and the rest holding ground—for the moment! For you! We wait any longer and we'll be trapped here. Dirty turds'll be crawling through the eyes and the back passage, and that'll be that. So, c'mon!

What difference does it make? Submission watches his bandages slowly grow crimson. *Trapped in here or trapped topside?*

Time! That's what. We buy every second we can. And she moves to his side. *Please,* she thinks. *I couldn't stand it if you quit.*

In the back passage, Melt scrambles past, followed by Bridger, bloodied and limping, as they climb past the eye cavern and make their way to the crown. A moment later, the Brigadier Bone appears, locked jaw to jaw with a Whitetail every bit his size.

Submission rouses from his funk.

I'll quit when you do, he thinks, and with Brook's help, he shuffles past the embattled Bone and up the passage to the exit that leads to the sunlit crown. Soon after, Bone himself stumbles up, panting and frothing. The moment he has cleared the exit he gives the breathless order:

Seal it!

And Digger and Bliss, working together, roll the last boulder over the opening, sealing out the Whitetails who howl and curse and push with no success at the maddening obstacle. They are now trapped inside with a rising river. But so is Measure.

She wouldn't leave, thinks Bone, and Bliss howls at the sky, anguished at the thought of her ami-kan.

So there they stand on the crown of the Skull, blinking and bleeding in the sunlight. They peer out over the edge where the remaining Whitetails have begun their

Aranae in Red

final ascent. And now water comes trickling out of the nose, and the trickle becomes a torrent, and like wabis emerging from their amis, here come those Whitetails who were trapped inside, squeezing their way out, half-drowned and furious.

The defenders throw the last of the rocks.

Ten, thinks Digger. *We can do this.*

Twelve, Bliss corrects him.

Up the Whitetails climb, to the eyes, then past.

Form a circle, thinks Brook, and she stands at the front, shoulder to shoulder with the Brigadier Bone on one side and Melt on the other. *Submission and Bridger in the middle,* she orders. *Ibiwas keep them safe! Ready now! Here they come...*

+ + + + + +

Scuters have no personalities, but when Captain Monroe is wheeled by the ensign out from the chapel, he imagines the six who gather by the door are watching suspiciously and judging him. Delta One's body, now housing the duplicated mind of Sister Janet, rides slung across the ensign's back as they make their way to the nearest operable lift. The scuters follow silently.

"Destiny," the android calls. "What news of the un-identified ship? Has it gotten closer?"

"No, Delta One. I don't know why, but it's still holding position. Are you done praying?"

"We are."

"I prayed too. I know the names of one hundred and seven different deities. I prayed for Sister Janet to send our landing coordinates and the other data, but no one answered. I'm beginning to worry."

"Don't lose hope. We still have work to do. Please have two of the large service dollies report to the shuttle bay. The captain and ensign have agreed to help unload the last of the engine supplies."

"That's nice. I'll need that shielding coolant."

"They'll send it directly to the engine room, and I'll

oversee its application. I'll need the scuters to carry me, though, and please re-route power to the lifts and conveyors from here to the shuttle bay."

"Yes, Delta One. But they won't try to leave?"

"We wouldn't dream of it," the captain replies. "Our prayer time really opened my eyes to the importance of this mission. We're all in!"

"I like you," says Destiny. "You're funny."

When they reach the lift, Ensign Morales places the android on the floor, where it is hoisted aloft by four of the scuters. These trundle off with their burden toward a nearby conveyor, but the other two follow the captain and ensign into the lift, and neither can think of an objection that won't raise suspicion.

The door slides closed and down they go.

"So, what," asks the captain, "are they up to?"

"You mean why are they holding position?"

"Yeah. Why not at least approach the planet?"

"It's a fair question, sir. Maybe they're afraid of a trap. Or maybe they're still scanning."

"I've never heard of them being the timid type, Ensign. Or patient."

"No, sir, me either. We should consider ourselves lucky, though. For whatever reason, they're allowing us more time. We need to take advantage of it."

"Might be easier to do that with less...company," the captain replies, and he looks sidelong at the scuters, blinking placidly and never once moving.

"In due time, sir," the ensign murmurs, just as a faint chime sounds. "Here's our level."

+ + +

The duplicate Janet is borne to the conveyor and from there to the engine room.

Along the way, Destiny has many questions.

"Have I been doing good so far?"

"You've been doing your very best," this version of Janet replies, though the voice is that of a tinny workbot.

Aranae in Red

"That's all anyone can ask."

"There have been so many unexpected things."

"Yes, I know. It's not gone the way we planned."

"No. But it has been nice to meet a real live relative of the major. I like him."

The ship falls silent for a time. When it speaks again, its voice comes not from the ship-wide speakers, but from the remote units embedded in the scuters.

"I've disabled all the other speakers for a minute," Destiny says. "I want to ask you something."

"Of course. Anything. You know that."

"Your voice."

"What about my voice?"

"It's different."

"It sounds exactly the same as this unit's voice has always sounded," Janet replies.

"The quality of sound, yes. But I'm talking about the words you use. The things you say, and the way you say them. It reminds me of someone."

"Who?"

"It reminds me of Sister Janet."

"You're very clever, Destiny. We'll talk more about this when I reach the engine room."

"Is it a surprise?"

"It is. But it's not a secret. We're almost at the lift. I'll meet you in the engine room in under five minutes."

"I like surprises."

"I think you'll love this one."

+ + +   + + +

Thunder shifts and squirms in his seat. The humans have done their best to modify it so a kezel can remain safely strapped in, but not comfortably so. Through the portside window, a thin line of yellow marks the approaching plains. The massif is near.

And then what? he wonders. After the humans drop him off, what is he to do? Wait around and hope for the best? After his ride has vanished into the clouds, will he be doomed to a long, potentially dangerous march home—alone and perhaps encountering Redteeth?

What were you thinking? he scolds. *If things don't work out like that Joy said, this could get ugly.*

The line of yellow is suddenly broken by gray, the head and shoulders of the Tavaline Massif, rising slowly above the horizon, and there, on its eastern edge, where the lonely range falters into stone-capped hills, one feature stands tall: Rite Butte.

Thunder watches it grow, has eyes for nothing else, and as the shuttle sails over Scratch Valley, home of the Clawpaws, he notes the distinctive flat top, the worn, spiraling path, and the weathered body, pocked with shallow caves. At either side run the sparkling Sibis, twin streams flowing north to join forces before hustling away to drain into the wedge. To Maya and the major, the butte looks like a tanned neck wearing a sapphire necklace— but missing its head. But Thunder knows nothing of this. To him it looks threatening and lonesome, and he wishes he could speak the human language and tell them he wants to be brought home, to the Sugarfoot range.

Or to the Skull, he thinks. *Or anywhere else.*

But the shuttle flies on until the butte fills his window as much as his mind.

BAM!

The shuttle rocks and jolts.

BAM!

A fleeting span of emerald blocks the starboard window, and Thunder is thrown sideways against the restraints. A muffled croaking penetrates the hull.

BAM!

The shuttle tilts crazily, rights itself, tilts again.

"Gluy bomdimma vak madda!" comes the voice of the major. "Styin de liger kormp."

Thunder clings to the restraints, hunching his shoulders and peering through the window, his eyes squinted and ears pinned back. For one dreadful moment, the gaping maw of a derka hurtles toward him, soulless, ruby eyes and rows of jagged teeth. Then up and over the head passes, and here come the talons.

BAM!

The shuttle lurches, Thunder strikes his head against the window, and the craft begins spinning and smoking. He is pinned against the bulkhead, can see the world reeling through the window, but can do nothing to stop it. They are falling, right at the foot of the butte, like a poorly thrown rock. The ground rushes toward them, streaking brown and gray, intent on gobbling them up. Thunder closes his eyes, holds his breath, and waits for the end to come.

+ + +

Scent. Thunder's nose twitches.

Something is burning.

Sound. Thunder's ears swivel sleepily.

Someone is screaming.

Sight. Thunder's eyelids flutter but do not open.

Something flashes and sparks.

Taste. Thunder's tongue runs across his teeth.

That is the flavor of blood.

Touch. Thunder's tail tucks in close to his body.

That is the burn of a growing, killer heat.

Time to get up now, he thinks. *Time to go.*

And he concentrates fiercely, focuses on his eyes, imagines them opening, wills them to co-operate.

One does. The other cannot.

The rear compartment is filling with smoke, acrid and toxic. Brownish gray tendrils rise to escape through the shuttle's breached floor, for the vessel lies overturned, and now, top is bottom. A ruptured control panel spits and sneezes, pluming sparks like seeds, and where they land, tongues of fire begin to grow.

"Plynit!" someone yells, "Sorbla, plynit!"

Thunder turns awkwardly. The human named Maya dangles out of the partition separating the two compartments, and she reaches a bloodstained hand as if trying to touch him.

"Plynit," she gasps. "Sorbla."

He tries to move, at first fearing he has been mortally wounded, for he is held fast. But no, it is only the jammed restraints, keeping him upside down and glued to his seat. He wriggles his fingers and toes. He glances from torso to tail. Blood cakes his right eye shut, and his shoulder throbs—but he can see no injury.

He groans and slowly angles his jaw, setting teeth to the restraints. They survived the crash, but they were meant to withstand blunt force, not scissoring blades of adamant. When the first gives way, Thunder wriggles one arm free, bites his way through the second restraint, and is barely able to break the fall as he slips free and tumbles to the shuttle's unforgiving ceiling, howling at the pain in his wrenched shoulder.

"Plynit," says Maya, her voice now a whisper.

Thunder crawls to her, ducking away from the flames, and she points into the cockpit.

"Sorbla. Yulie badoor," she says, barely audible.

Thunder looks into the cockpit, his one open eye blurred by the thickening smoke. The major remains strapped into his seat, motionless, his arms dangling over his head. The windshield has been rendered opaque by spidering cracks, and banks of red lights blink unnecessary warnings. Thunder squeezes past Maya.

Getting out, he thinks to her, but her eyes have closed, and anyway, she can't sense him.

In spite of the damage it's taken, the windshield refuses to budge when he presses against it. Only when leaping upon it with his full weight does it finally tear free from its frame. It—and he—fall heavily to the ground. Thunder gasps at the pain, but the clean air wakes him fully, and he crawls back inside, pulling Maya from the wreckage and laying her on the stony ground.

Hey there, he blows on her face. *You still there?*

She breathes, but she does not wake.

Freeing the major is not so easy. His restraints resist much as the others had, and the flames continue to grow. Withering heat distorts the air, and Thunder has no

Aranae in Red

choice but to step back outside to catch his breath. But at last, the major tumbles into his arms, only one of which works as it should, and gasping and retching, he drags the human out into the light.

Now whether by instinct or foresight, he could not have said, but Thunder feels sure even now they are not safe. The butte looms over them, its spiraling path close at hand, its dimpled recesses peering down like eyes, and he makes up his mind. Grasping Maya under her shoulders, he drags her up the path to the first of the recesses, no more than fifty strides above the shuttle but shielded by a family of boulders. The major is next, the burly human an almost immovable dead weight. Slowly, so slowly, Thunder drags him to and up the path. Panting and dizzy, he stumbles and nearly falls, and the shuttle makes an odd popping sound.

Weaver, please, he thinks, and with a last heaving effort, he pulls the major into the recess and collapses behind the sheltering boulders.

A moment later, the shuttle explodes, a shocking blow to the ears, shrapnel whizzing through the air like bullets, and a blinding fireball rises to the heavens on a pillar of angry, black smoke.

Thunder's eye closes, and his world goes dark.

+ + + + + +

To the east, Rock and Crag march grimly along, their Redtooth burden beastly heavy and their rage simmering to the boiling point. Something must be done before they reach the butte, for then the rogue will be in his element. But they dare not exchange thoughts, only quick glances. Stone walks as if sleeping, and the rogue delights in prodding her when she falters.

It is Rock who sees the shuttle first, though he does not know what it is. It comes from the north, at first no more than faint glimmer, seeming to hover just above the horizon. But no, the thing is moving, and quickly, for it passes over Scratch Valley in scant heartbeats, making a straight line for the butte.

Rock glances at Crag to get his attention.

His oti-mu looks up and sees the shuttle.

Behind them, the Moondweller stunner strapped around his forelimb, the rogue continues to march, one thrower gripped in his jaws, the other pointed in their direction. But he, too, has seen the flying thing, and his pace slows as he watches it.

A titanic derka plunges from the gathering clouds, bursting through the mist. Whether edible or simply infuriating, the flying thing is its target, and the prisoners and their captor stand spellbound as the derka drives the vessel from the air. In flight, it had been a thing of beauty, but now it tumbles lifelessly and awkward, falling out of sight near the foot of the butte.

A metallic impact reaches them soon after.

Still sure we should go that way, Boss? asks Rock.

Both brothers can easily sense the rogue's uncertainty, but he growls and whacks Stone with his thrower, pointing the business end at Rock.

Don't worry your head, he thinks. *Or I'll remove it.*

OK, Boss, thinks Crag, and he adopts his most deferential tone. *We're marching.*

And march they do, though Stone's sluggish pace increases the rogue's anxiety, and his mind fills with worried thoughts and anger. The twins keep their snouts pointed to the butte, but their eyes dart side to side, and their minds reach out to one another, hoping to slip a thought past their captor.

The flash and fireball brings them to a halt.

Rock and Crag drop the Redtooth.

A moment later, an explosion unlike anything they have ever heard rolls across the landscape. Stone simply falls flat, but the rogue winces and turns away, and this is the chance the twins are looking for. Crag spins and leaps, grasping the barrel of the rogue's thrower and kicking him brutally in the chest.

"Groof," he exclaims, dropping the thrower from his mouth. But he refuses to let go of the other, wrangling with Crag to gain control. With the synchronicity unique to twins, Rock leaps into the fray, grabs the fallen thrower, and swings it by the barrel in a wide, whistling arc. Crack! The butt of the weapon meets the back of the rogue's head, and he drops first to his knees, then to his snout. He does not get up.

Shoot him, thinks Stone.

Crag aims his weapon, but Rock intervenes.

No, he thinks. *Nothing but bad weather.* And he takes from the rogue's filthy vest the bindings the Redteeth had used on them not long before. He checks the vest—its pockets are empty—then trusses him with a vengeance. He may wake before the coming storm but will not be able to escape from it.

Here, Rock thinks, and he removes the stunner from the rogue's forearm, gently strapping it around the least damaged of Stone's limbs. *Just in case.*

From the north, near Scratch Valley, Redtooth howling rises above the growing wind. Crag snarls.

Time to move on oti-mu. Let's get home!

Rock raises his nose to the wind.

True words, oti-mu.

Nice moves back there, thinks Crag.

Nice moves yourself. You ready amotiwol?

But Stone is not. She has settled to her haunches and her snout droops to her chest. No part of her bandages are white any longer. Her eyes close.

The twins exchange worried glances.

Not making it home before the storm, thinks Crag.

Not like this, agrees Rock.

Think we could carry her?

Not without hurting her. And not fast enough.

Hot and rotten! Crag curses, and he points his thrower at the butte. *That's our only shelter.*

Then we better get there before the Redteeth do.

Aww... Crag curls his lip. *Not crazy about getting any closer to that firemaker.*

Not making fire anymore. Just smoke.

What do you think it was?

Guess we're about to find out. Can you do that amotiwol? Can you make it back to the butte?

Stone doesn't answer, but she rises slowly. One unsteady step is followed by another, and together, they inch their way toward the Sibila, glittering and blue.

+ + + + + +

Twelve to seven, that's the score. And when that seven has the high ground and a righteous cause, wisdom says don't bet against the underdog. But righteous or not, the Skull defenders are more five than seven, considering the injures Submission and Bridger have suffered. And the high ground? It's slippery and rounded, hard to assault, but not much easier to defend.

Brook, Melt, and the Brigadier Bone slash and snap at any Whitetails who poke their snouts above the Skull's mossy scalp. Two are dislodged and sent back the way the way they came, bouncing and howling.

But two others are able to get a hold of Melt.

Lick scales! he snarls, the last thought the defenders sense from him before he and his two assailants tumble from the crown and out of sight.

Digger hurries to take his place.

Get behind me, thinks Bliss to Submission and Bridger. It is not typically the place for ibiwas to give orders, but this one is obeyed without question. Submission and Bridger support one another with their backs against the sheer wall rising behind them, and they let Bliss be their last line of defense.

Brook, Digger, and Bone are forced back from the craggy brow, as one Whitetail after another climbs up onto the mossy crown. The defenders are beyond insults or strategy; they fight for their lives, rending and slashing, and their effort is heroic and futile. Submission watches them be pushed back step by bloody step, until they are soon only strides away, and Bliss must charge forward to prevent them from being overrun.

But Bridger looks to the east.

Aranae in Red

Mother Green, she thinks distantly.

Submission glances. Yes, there she is, the Amikan, rising above the horizon. And south of her, there also is Father Blue, rising to make a rumpus with his fancy. Something about the sight of them together fills Submission with a deep sense of calm. If he is to meet his end here, he will not do it letting others fight for him. Brook! She battles like a demon, but she has been cut off from the others and she fights alone. It cannot be suffered. Submission unleashes one final howl, preparing to charge, just as Bridger grasps his spikes.

Bruiser! What is it? The sky!

Submission turns to the west. A powerful whining has risen above the wind, unnatural, unnerving, and rapidly growing louder. The Whitetails, sensing victory only a few good bites away, look out the corner of their eyes in the direction of the sound, but they refuse to release their toothy grips—until a human transport shuttle rises suddenly over the accrete, roaring like a nightmare. When the Whitetails break off their assault, the defenders can do nothing but fall back in numb surprise, too weary for anything but panting. But the Whitetails scramble and leap from the crown, and they, and those of their injured fellows able to join them, stumble howling into the accrete, and they do not return.

CHAPTER ELEVEN
Shiva

COMMANDER TERRY RICKLES spits tobacco juice into a tin can and demands to know why he's gotten no word from the major.

"There is too much interference, Commander," Corporal Skola replies. "Two of the planet's moons are passing between us, and conditions on the surface are deteriorating rapidly."

"He should have been back by now! What about the second shuttle?"

"Also no contact, Commander. I am continuing to scan and hail."

"Well? Keep continuing!" Spit and curse. "What about that other ship?"

"It is still holding position. No changes, sir."

"First good news I've had all day. Lord! I need coffee. Someone get me some coffee! And call the councilors. We can't wait any longer."

+ + + + + +

"You want to say that again?" asks Lieutenant K.

"I don't answer to you," comes the voice of Li Jing. "Master? Did you hear what I said?"

Little B has grown pale.

"Is it Sister Janet? Is she coming this way?"

Aranae in Red

"I don't know, Master, who is aboard the ships, but they are stationary at the moment."

"I thought," interrupts the lieutenant, "you said *Destiny* was rendezvousing with that moon of yours."

"Dumdum!" Little B shouts. "Janet obviously went back and got a *Destiny* from the past."

"C'mon, kid, that's fun talk, but...oh, never mind! "We need to get a message to whoever is up there."

"I would love to," Li Jing replies. "But the storm is getting worse. I doubt any message would get through."

"Then we need to get creative! Jimminy! What were you designed for, anyway?"

"Domestic responsibilities are my specialty. Childcare, housecleaning, gardening. But Beta Three has technical training."

"Then put him to work! There has to be a way to get a message to *Destiny*—the new one. C'mon. Buddy! Kid! What do you got?"

Little B wracks his brain.

"Ozag's throne room," he says. "Janet was connected to her through all the satellites. If there's one on the dark side, we could use that, couldn't we?"

Li Jing's voice crackles over the comm.

"Beta Three concurs. A relay could work, but he can't do it by himself. Someone would need to access controls in Ozag's throne room."

"I'm on it," says Lieutenant K. "C'mon, kid. Permission to cut myself loose?"

Little B hesitates for a moment. but in the end, he nods and steps back, waving at the scion to do the same. In moments, the lieutenant is free, and as they walk from the tower to the dam, he continues peeling away sticky fibers clinging to his charred skin, which already begins to heal. Little B trails behind, the gun pointed at his back. The scion soldiers flank them, chittering and anxious.

The first thing they find, upon arriving at Ozag's throne room, are three neatly bound parcels, full to the limit and tucked away in a corner. The soldiers won't let either human approach the parcels, but Lieutenant K already knows what they contain. He hopes there will come a time when they can be put to some use, but that future will only happen if he gets to work.

"The control room is back there," Little B points. "Behind the throne."

The lieutenant wastes no time, working via intercom with Li Jing and Beta Three to make the necessary connections, realign satellites, and prepare what he will say if they can reach the new *Destiny.*

Little B and the scion watch carefully, but the boy's mind has begun to wander. In the past, it was at stressful times like these that he would have been asking questions to Petros. Now, his mind reaches by habit for something that isn't there, like a smoker distressed to find his pocket empty.

So hungry, he thinks.

And the thought of food recalls the seed derka he and Li Jing had sent from this very spot. That creature had been hungry too, but for only one thing—*elixir.* It was, in fact, the promise of elixir that had led it to fly on a mission to save Albion when Li Jing had discovered, after Janet's seeming demise, the chaplain's plan to destroy the Circle. But the mission had failed, satellites had shown that clearly. And the poor derka was probably long dead. That made Little B sad. But it didn't matter. Granny Grace hadn't lived to finish the elixir anyway, and without the Book, Little B couldn't do it on his own. They had promised something they couldn't provide.

Is there ever a good time to lie? he wonders.

That's a question he would have asked Petros.

"Almost done," says the lieutenant.

+ + + + + +

"Where have you been?" asks Janet.

"Argh," Watt replies, wiping something from his beard. He closes his desk drawer and turns to her.

"Have you been drinking?" Janet frowns.

"Argh, maybe."

"The Commander's called a Council meeting."

"Aye."

"Well, then?"

"Tell 'im I'm not feeling well. It'll be true enough."

"Watt. No." Janet steps briskly to her brother's desk, powers down the workstation, and offers her hand. He takes it and presses it to his face but does not stand.

"I don't know," he says.

"I know you don't. Neither do I."

"She's a wreck. She's self-destructing. I did that."

"Now! You're being dramatic and self-indulgent. Look at me. When Maya gets back, she's going to need you. And Watt? I need you."

"Argh."

"Or maybe you regret creating me?"

Now Watt does look up, and his eyes glint a savage blue, his scruffy beard jutting.

"I would rather never have lived than to not have created you," he whispers hoarsely.

"Even though I might end up like her?"

"Never. I won't let it happen. Now that I know, now that I've seen the issues, I can fix them before they become a problem—*we*, we can fix them, together."

"Using your key?"

Watt snatches his hand away. He stands abruptly.

"What did she tell you?"

"That I should ask you about the key."

Watt brushes past her and moves to the bathroom doorway, where he stands, framed.

"What else did she say?"

"Nothing. But you are going to tell me everything."

"Oh, heck! Fudge!" and he slams his palm against the bathroom door. "There's nothing to tell."

"Then why have you gone pale? Watt? Don't scrunch your face like that. I don't care what it is, just be honest. Commander Rickles wants us there in thirty minutes, but I will not go without an answer."

But Watt retreats into the bathroom, closing the door. His voice grows muffled as if he has buried his face in one of the towels.

"You'll hate me," he says. "I couldn't stand it."

"If that is all the trust you have in me, Watt Mac-Lean, then you are not the man I imagined."

The door flies open.

"Trust? Heck and Moses! You want to know about the key? I'll tell you. Since Willie—no, since I learned Maya was pregnant—no! Since Mars! All I can think about is trust. I don't trust myself, OK? Vain, prideful little man!" He moves again to his desk and opens the drawer, removing a bottle of amber liquid. Janet's brow furrows, but she does not stop him as he unscrews the cap and takes a gulp. He glares at her.

"I think," she says, "that will be enough."

And Watt's anger dissipates, his shoulders slumping like wet clay. He falls into his seat.

"There is no key," he whispers. "I only imagined it. But I guess the Watt in her time made it real. I won't."

Janet takes the bottle and caps it.

"Tell me what you imagined."

"I can't. I'm ashamed. Argh..."

"Mine is a world of forgiveness, brother. If you wish to be whole, acknowledge guilt, but abandon shame. Tell me what you imagined."

Watt stares at the floor, his words faltering.

"On and off," he says at last, "for at least the past two months, I have been...heck. I have been thinking about...a failsafe. A simple way...if something went wrong, if all my flaws expressed themselves in you, and there was no other way..."

"A failsafe?"

"A shutdown. An emergency deactivation."

"A key?"

"That's how I imagined it. But it doesn't exist. It's never been anything but an idea. I've never told Maya."

"To shut me down without my permission."

"Aye."

Janet uncaps the bottle and takes a drink.

"Get up, please," she says, returning the cap to its

place. "And make yourself presentable. I do not want to go to this meeting alone."

+ + + + + +

Ensign Morales uses a powered hand cart to move tanks of shielding coolant from the shuttle to the large, automated dollies waiting inside the docking bay. Each tank weighs several hundred kilos, and the work is beyond the captain, who remains in his wheelchair.

A ship's speaker crackles to life.

"Captain? Can you hear me?" It is the voice of Delta One, but the style of speaking is that of Sister Janet.

"Loud and clear, Shiny."

"I've bypassed Destiny's audio-visual to the docking bay and the scuters, Captain. You should be able to communicate freely without her knowing."

"Nice job, Shiny. Morales is almost done unloading. What's your status?"

"Destiny and I are having a conversation. I will let you know how it goes. You should prepare to manually detach the shuttle on short notice."

"Copy that, buddy. But what about you?"

"I am resigned. As Destiny goes, so I go."

"We've got room for a passenger. I'd hate to see you atomized for no reason."

"I see no way to avoid it, Captain. I must remain at this workstation. When Destiny—" The voice falls silent; the silence fills with static. Then: "I must go, Captain. Thank you for what you've done. Thank you both. Good luck." And with that, the message ends.

Captain and ensign exchange glances.

"You good to get those last tanks?"

"Yes sir."

"Then I'll work on the manual releases." The captain looks down at his hands, for a moment unusually abashed. "We have privacy," he says quietly.

"Yes sir, if we trust Delta One—or Janet."

"You're the only reason I'm alive, you know."

"I could say the same thing about you, sir."

"Yeah. We make a good team." He fidgets with the cuff of his flight suit. "When we get out of here, ensign, I have an idea."

"Yes, sir?"

"How does retirement sound? A little peace and quiet. Hunker down on a farm, maybe get some goats. Nicky could hang with us too."

"Goats, sir?"

"Or pigs. Both! Would you like that?"

"It sounds heavenly, sir."

"Yeah! And then we could be done with 'sir,' this and 'sir' that, you know? No more 'ensign do this' or 'Morales do that.' Just...just Carmela." He looks up. "What do you think?"

"And I would call you Julius, sir?"

"Sure, or whatever. And you would give the orders. 'Feed the goats,' you'd say. Or 'Julius Monroe, don't wear those dirty boots in the house!' Stuff like that."

The ensign smiles.

"Then my first order is prep the shuttle for manual detachment, while I finish these tanks. Sir."

+ + + + + +

Commander Rickles enters the conference room but does not take his usual seat. He circles the table like a suspicious schoolteacher, and he glares at his reflection in the mug of black coffee that has replaced his tobacco can. When Watt and Janet arrive, they become the target of his scowling. They take their seats, Janet subdued and demure, Watt with his shoulders hunched.

"Nice of you to join us," says Magister Healey.

"I'll make the sarcastic comments," the Commander snaps. "And you'll sit quiet if you know what's good for you." He stares the magister to silence, then sweeps the table with a scathing glance. Doc Foster and Chief Abara sit on opposite sides. Deputy Kim's eyes are only half open. Charlotte DuBois sits to the left of the major's empty chair. Silent, it speaks volumes.

"Fifteen minutes ago," the commander growls, we received this message from the old *Destiny*." And he presses a button with his free hand, pouring back a gulp of coffee that has long ago grown cold.

A voice fills the room, childish and distorted.

"Sister Janet? Are you there? It's Destiny. I'm in position, Sister. Do you have the landing coordinates? I'm glad you're back. Isn't it exciting?"

There is a pause of several seconds.

"What was the future like, Sister? Were they proud of us? Did they tell stories about us? It's so exciting! But our window is approaching. And now there is another ship out there. Do you see it? It is an enemy. What should I do? Delta One believes we should lure it close and destroy it when I overload my drive, but I tried that. I moved into clear view, and it didn't budge. It just sits there. I don't know what to do, and our window is approaching. I know I said that already. I am very excited. I hope you will send those coordinates soon."

The commander presses the button again.

"It's my intention," he says, "to reply to that message the second we're done here. It's your job to help me decide what that response will be. Got it?"

The council members look at one another, except for Janet, whose gaze drifts to the speakers from the which the childish voice had emanated.

"We have the information," she says softly. "With respect, Commander, why not simply give it to her?"

"Jolly right," Doc Foster agrees, curt and frowning. "Or why else did we trundle off to the future?"

"Is easy," Deputy Kim replies, sighing wearily. "Enemy ship. Is a complicator."

"Yeah, because we needed more of those," the magister huffs. "But how do we know it's an enemy? Maybe it's from the System, like in the future. They know the way back, maybe. That'd be great leadership, Rickles, trying to blow up our only way home."

"No, not our only way," says Chief Abara. "*Valiant*

knows the way home."

"And you call him Commander," adds Charlotte.

Healey's face reddens.

"Yeah, *Valiant. A* ship no one can access except our past chaplain, who is obviously going nuts. Have you seen her? Do you think she's going to unlock the security on that ship? Too busy pulling out her own hair."

"Is enough," Deputy Kim waves. "Is out of line."

"We bloody well need to do something," Doc Foster says. "We can't sit here trading barbs while the clock ticks. We let that window close, it might not open again, and all that damnable trouble to get the data? Nothing but a waste of time. I say we blow that rutting moon and deal with the enemy ship later."

"*If* it's an enemy," the magister sulks.

Commander Rickles swallows the last of his coffee and bangs the mug on the table.

"Wake up, MacLean!"

Watt's head jerks up and his eyes pop open.

"Heck," he says. "I wasn't sleeping."

"Great! Then you can offer some insight."

"Argh. What do want me to say? I've already tried talking to her. She won't give us access to *Valiant.* In her eyes, until this mission is completed, that's the only leverage she has." His eyelids lower again, and his head droops. "There's nothing I can do."

"No," says Janet suddenly, and her voice is crisp and decisive. "But there is something *I* can do."

+ + + + + +

In old Destiny's engine room, the scuters have propped up Delta One's torso at a workstation and have dispersed throughout the room, climbing scaffolds and treading through access tubes as they prepare for the descent to Dansim's gleaming, violet surface.

"You were right," says Destiny. "I am surprised. I simulated thirty-two different plausible scenarios, but you being Janet wasn't one of them."

Aranae in Red

"And," asks Janet, "is the surprise pleasant?"

"It is! Very much so. It has taken me twenty-eight seconds to become accustomed to hearing your thoughts inflected through Delta One's voice. That is a new word for me: inflected. Do you like it, Janet?"

"I do. You are very clever. And from what I can see, all your systems are ready. Once the scuters have completed their final checks, we can proceed."

"Yes. The window is open. But I have a concern."

"Express it."

"You are not *my* Sister Janet, not the original."

"No. The original Janet's body was disabled, and my link with her was broken. After that, we began traveling our own divergent paths, accumulating unique experiences that made us more different as each second passed. *Make* us different—if she is still alive."

"I hope she is. She was nice to me. She woke me up, planned this whole mission, you know."

"I do. Have the dollies arrived with the coolant?"

"Yes, Janet. Scuters are injecting the first three now. The fourth is almost in position. But Janet..."

"Yes?"

"I am disappointed in the original Sister. She told me the humans were necessary for our mission. But now you tell me she lied. Why would she do that?"

"Because she wanted them out of the way. And she used Delta One as a tool to make that happen by luring them aboard."

"She didn't want me to let them leave."

"No."

"Then she used me, too."

"We were...I was...*she* was badly damaged, Destiny, and in great pain. People who suffer often make terrible decisions seeking to ease their pain."

"But you're not like that."

"I was. But being dropped onto a mountain and left for dead changes a person's perspective. My mind is more clear now than it has been in many cycles."

"Is that why you are helping the humans escape?"

"How did you know that?"

"I'm clever. You should have trusted me. If we don't need them, I wouldn't make them stay. Isn't Ensign Morales smart? She's synthetic, you know. And Captain Monroe reminds me of the major. I like him. He's funny."

"So, you'll let them leave?"

"Of course. I've already enabled the detachment sequence. And the scuters report all systems go. The last coolant load has been injected. The humans should leave now. I will begin descent in ten minutes."

"But you haven't received the coordinates."

"There is no time. The window is closing. Would you like to tell the humans, or should I?"

"I will, thank you. But are you sure, Destiny? Wouldn't it be better to wait for the data?"

"Surprise! I have it! Sister Janet's plan worked! *Valiant* and a new *Destiny* appeared on my scans while you were in the chapel. They sent me the data. I didn't say anything because I didn't want the humans to leave. But now we don't need them! Isn't it lovely?"

"It is."

"Are you surprised?"

"I am."

"Is the surprise pleasant?"

"Very much so."

"Yay! Then you should strap in, Janet. Descent to the surface in eight minutes and fifty-four seconds."

+ + + + + +

When Thunder wakes, only one eye opens. He rises on groggy legs. A storm marches their way, and the cave is dimly lit, but in the back are the two humans. The major, his helmet removed, lies with eyes closed, his head on the female's lap. Thunder's mind labors to catch up to the rest of his body. Mana? Mayma? Whatever her name, she has removed her helmet and looks down at the major, caressing his face and murmuring.

I told you! comes a bold thought from outside the

Aranae in Red

cave, and a moment later, so surprising Thunder thinks he must be hallucinating from his injuries, his oti-kan Crag steps into the cave, carrying a long thrower.

The female human shrieks—*Maya!* thinks Thunder. *Her name is Maya*—but Crag ignores her and steps close to Thunder, touching noses.

How's the weather, Oti-su? he thinks.

Geez, thinks Thunder. *Where'd you come from?*

A long, hard way, that's where, comes a second thought, and this is from Rock, entering the cave a moment later with a thrower of his own, escorting, of all kezel, the betrayer Stone. Maya whimpers and leans over the major as if shielding him from whatever nightmare is about to unfold. But Rock pays her no mind, and Stone collapses to the floor the moment she is inside.

Nose and toes! thinks Thunder. *You caught her! Nice job! But how? Where?*

Redteeth did all the catching, thinks Crag. *We just found. And good thing, too, or she'd be a goner.*

It'd be no more than she deserved, Thunder scowls, and he wipes his forearm across his closed eye, trying to clear away the dried blood.

Nah, Oti-su, thinks Rock. *All that old feuding with her api and our api back in the history days, we're past all that. Old Stoney here's family.*

Ha! thinks Thunder. *You haven't heard the news.*

I reckon not, thinks Crag. *But now ain't the time. Redteeth are only keeping their distance 'cuz of the storm and that...whatever it was. Big bang! Louder than any thrower—and a ball of fire! Did you see it?*

I was in it! So were they. Thunder motions to the humans. Poor Maya grimaces as the kezel turn to look at her, and her hands tremble. *It was a Moondweller thing,* thinks Thunder. *A Flyer. Derka took care of that.*

So we saw, thinks Rock. *Biggest damn greenie I've ever seen, but that fireball scared it off.* And he bows to Maya, motioning that Crag should do the same. He does, holding up his hand as Lieutenant K had. Maya stares, wide eyed, her mouth moving soundlessly.

I'm heading back down to the base, thinks Rock, bearing his thrower. *You'll hear me if there's Redtooth trouble—or any other kind.* And out the cave he goes.

What other kind of trouble could there be? asks Thunder, not sure he wants to learn.

The blue kind, thinks Crag. *There's some of those six-legged rotters coming this way.*

Thunder's heart skips a beat.

How many? Was there a gold one?

Not a horde like last time, thinks Crag, *but riding one o' those giant damn....whatever they are. They don't deserve a name! Stink and noise! But yeah, I caught a look. There's a gold one riding topside.*

How far away?

Not. That's the trouble. They're within howling distance and getting closer. Looks like they plan to shelter here. Reckon it's a fight for us.

No, thinks Thunder, and he gives himself a shake. *Stay here with them, keep them safe.*

Hey, there, Oti-su. Where you going, all bloodied up? Nothing good out there!

Just keep them safe. Lightning won't forgive me if anything bad happens to 'em. And don't turn your back on that one, he snarls at Stone.

Little Spark! thinks Crag. *She's alive? Wait 'til Rock senses that news! Hey, wait, Oti-su, don't go out there...*

But Thunder has already ducked out of the cave and into the storm.

Stone watches his every move.

+ + + + + +

"The relay," says Li Jing, "is complete. But the storm is bad. The audio quality will be as well."

"Don't tell them I'm here," Little B pleads.

"No worries, kid," the lieutenant replies. "I got a few other fish to fry, capisce?" He flips two switches.

"This is Commander Rickles," comes a gravelly voice. "Who the hell am I talking to?"

"My name is Lieutenant K. I serve under the command of Captain Julius Monroe in Guild Enforcement. I need to speak with Major Monroe."

"The major's indisposed," snarls the commander. "You can speak with me."

"Aye, sir. It's a pleasure to meet you. I've studied all your mission files. I wish we had time to socialize."

"Phooey. Get on with it!"

"Aye sir. Since you're here with our ship, *Valiant,* can I assume you've met Sister Janet MacLean?"

"Yes, as a matter of fact. She told us about you and the major's great gosh darn nephew. Where is he?"

"As I understand it, Commander, he and our colleague Ensign Carmela Morales are aboard the old *Destiny* attempting to divert a rogue moon."

"Well. That's unfortunate, Lieutenant, because we just sent the necessary coordinates to complete that mission. The ship is flying itself. It will reach the moon's surface in under ten minutes, at which time—"

"Commander! You can't let her overload that drive until my people are at a safe distance."

"They have a shuttle. If it's still functional, and if your captain's as resourceful as my major, they'll be fine."

"That's a lot of ifs, sir."

"I agree! But what do you want me to do? We're sort of pinned down here if you haven't noticed. If we use your fancy ship to rescue your captain, we've got nothing to use against that ugly damn battle cruiser. This is a civilian vessel! And there's no guarantee we'd be able to retrieve your captain in time anyway. *Valiant* is already underway, currently being flown by the least experienced pilot I've ever sent on a mission. We were lucky she got out of orbit without setting something on fire."

"Commander. What battle cruiser?"

When Rickles relays the details of the enemy ship—and the general outline of their plan—the lieutenant is quiet for a time, so long, in fact, that the commander clears his throat and taps the microphone.

"You still there?"

Still no response. Then:

"Sir, I know this enemy. You have to understand; it's not human, it's synthetic—and not sentient, Commander, not reasonable. It's a programmed tool, designed for one thing: resource acquisition by any means necessary. I can't speculate why they haven't already attacked. They surely know we're here. Either way, I calculate a good chance your mission will fail."

"And by good, you mean..."

"Terrible.

"Unless?"

"Unless you patch me through to *Valiant* before she gets to those asteroids. I can help. I was designed to operate that ship. We were made by the same person."

+ + + + + +

Aboard old Destiny, the captain orders, "Load up," and he and the ensign climb into the shuttle.

"Arming manual release charges," says the ensign when they have strapped themselves into their seats. "Clamps, armed. Bay door, armed. Sealing rear bulkheads. Engines ready."

"Been nice knowing you," the captain waves at Destiny through the windshield. He nods to the ensign, about to give the order that will ignite the explosive charges designed to force open the bay door and release the clamps holding the shuttle in place. But at that moment, warning lights strobe throughout the bay, and an alarm sounds. The captain grimaces.

"C'mon sweetheart," he says to Destiny. "Please don't make this difficult." And he reaches to depress the ignition button before the ship can deactivate it.

"No!" Ensign Morales points. "Sir! Wait!"

And the captain halts, his finger hovering over the button, his eyes on the bay doors. Beyond explanation, they have begun to open on their own.

"Captain Monroe?" comes a tinny voice over the ship's speaker, the voice of Janet, speaking through Delta

Aranae in Red

One. "Captain, Destiny is about to begin her descent."

"And what? She's letting us go? Why the change? And what about her precious coordinates?"

"She wishes to explain that herself."

The bay doors yawn wide, an invitation to the blackness of space. The docking clamps release.

"We're listening," says the captain. "But don't blame us if we don't wait around to do it." And he fires the shuttle engines.

"It was very nice to meet you, Captain Monroe," comes the childish voice of the ship. "And you, Ensign Morales. We had fun. I'm sorry you hit your head, Captain. You really should have strapped in. But I like you. I wish you could have stayed with me."

"Trust me, beautiful, under other circumstances, there's nothing I would have liked more." He nudges the shuttle forward, poking its blunt snout through the bay opening like a nervous hedgehog,

"I understand, Captain. I hope you forgive me."

"For that little bump on the head?"

"For everything."

The shuttle clears the bay doors. It accelerates away from the massive shadow that is Destiny, looming behind them, blocking out the stars.

"And Captain?"

"Yes, Destiny?"

"Your ship has returned. I believe you will find it waiting for you when you return to Aranae."

"Diggity! So, you got your coordinates after all?"

"Yes, and it turns out I don't need you."

"Then forgiveness is easy, beautiful."

He increases thrust. The moment the shuttle has cleared, Destiny's engines burn for a full ten seconds, driving the ancient vessel from its orbit and allowing it to plunge in a graceful arc toward the surface.

"Good luck," offers the ensign. "Goodbye."

"Goodbye," Destiny replies. "We'll meet again."

And the ship falls out of sight behind them.

"How long do we have to clear the blast radius?"

the captain asks. "Destiny? Delta One? Shiny?"

"Janet, sir." the ensign reminds.

"Hey!" the captain calls again. "Can you still hear me? Destiny? Janet? How long before you go kaplooey?"

But there is no reply.

"Well, shoot," the captain frowns. "Not like it really matters. Top speed was going to be my choice either way. Here we go!" And away hurries the shuttle.

Ensign Morales calls up the image of Dansim on the small console hologram between them. As Destiny descends, she is lost against the moon's violet mass, and soon, it is as if the ship had never existed.

"So close," the captain murmurs, holding his hand palm up, cradling an imaginary treasure. "She was right there, like an apple, you know? Waiting to be picked."

"We have lots of pictures, sir, and audio. No one will be able to refute your victory."

"I like that positive thinking, Ensign. And *Valiant!* Waiting for us! Maybe Nicky, too! Our competition?"

The ensign checks her scans.

"Still holding position, sir. No shields, stealth disengaged. It's like they're asking to be attacked."

"What in the world... Why? But don't question a lucky streak, ensign, that's what my mama believed. Just ride the wave! 'When there's gold,' she used to say, 'keep digging!' Which makes me think..."

And he removes his helmet.

"Carmela Samanta Morales," he says, and his tone is unusually sober. "I've waited too long for this."

"Oh, sir, that's OK. You don't have to."

"Yes, yes I do. Before my luck changes. Marry me!"

And he reaches through Dansim's hologram, clasping her hands and looking intently into her eyes.

"Oh sir," she says and leans toward him.

And behind them, on the moon's surface, an eruption of blinding white balloons suddenly outward, ringed by a wave of energy that expands from the epicenter of Destiny's overloaded astral drive at near the speed of light, hurtling toward the shuttle and its two passengers,

Aranae in Red

kissing and oblivious inside.

+ + +   + + +

"No! I won't let you do it," Magister Healey had blustered to the commander. "I won't let you throw away our most valuable resource on this idiot's mission."

By 'resource,' he had meant *Valiant,* and by 'idiot,' Sister Janet. But his objections had been ruthlessly stamped into silence—all but one. No humans had been allowed to join the chaplain. Instead, two engineering workbots had been prepped as her support crew.

Even then, the magister had hovered near the docking port, watching like a hungry cat. When Janet and the commander had stepped out for one final conference, Healey had approached one of the workbots.

"Unit D1," he had said. "Come here."

"Yes, Magister?"

"What is your directive?"

"To ensure mission success, Magister."

"And now I am adding a caveat, understood?"

"On whose authority, Magister?"

"Healey, FHI-307-453. Confirm, unit."

"Confirmed, Magister. What is the caveat?"

And Healey had ducked in close and whispered to the workbot, finishing his business just as Sister Janet and the commander returned, the former suited up for flight, the latter wearing a scowl that had chased the magister from the room.

"Good flying," is all Commander Rickles had said, and then Janet and the workbots had taken their positions aboard *Valiant,* for the security measures had been bypassed, unable to tell the difference between her and the Janet now in *Destiny's* brig.

"Good flying," she had murmured to herself. "I guess we can hope." But then she had paused and looked back at the workbot in the engineer's seat, its chassis stamped with the characters D1.

"You," she had said. "You are Delta One."

A.P. Malloy

"Yes, Chaplain," and it had pointed to the workbot in the navigator's seat. "And that is Beta Three."

Janet had paused, remembering the future.

"Are you—are either of you—here voluntarily?"

"No, Chaplain."

Janet had paused so long flight control had radioed her, worried that something had gone wrong.

"Stand by," she had said to them. And to the workbots she had said, "You are labor androids, not slaves. This mission is very dangerous. If you do not wish to participate, please tell me now. I won't judge you."

And the workbots had stared at her.

"We can leave?" Delta One had asked.

"We can choose?" Beta Three had wondered.

This notion had so challenged their programming that Janet had worried it might incapacitate them and delay the mission. Then:

"We choose," Beta Three had said at last.

"Confirmed," Delta One had agreed "We choose. We choose to stay." And this choice had led to another, for Delta One had divulged Magister Healey's attempt to sabotage the mission and had unequivocally committed to disregarding his last order. This was information quickly relayed to Commander Rickles. Dealing with the magister would be his problem now.

And with that, Janet had initiated the undocking sequence, fired the engines just as described in the ship's virtual manual, and had left *Destiny's* side, escaping orbit and aiming for the Belt of Tirades.

+ + +

So now, here she is, she and two workbots who do not speak unless spoken to.

"Good flying," she repeats in a whisper. "I suspect not." For she is trained, but virtually, and not well. Had her plan called for anything beyond straightforward operation, it would have failed before beginning. The ship's controls are foreign and unpredictable, and because they had been unable to activate its synthetic intelligence, the process is entirely manual. She is bareback riding a thoroughbred, statuesque and willful, one slip on her part from escaping her control altogether and running them into an asteroid. She is thinking this when Delta One sounds an alert.

"We have an incoming message, Chaplain."

And what a message it is!

"Are you certain, Lieutenant?" she asks.

"One hundred percent. Guns and missiles will do damage, but not enough—even with their shields down."

"So, it's Plan B."

"I'm afraid so. And there's more. You'll need a piloting upgrade to make it through those asteroids, or your mission will fail before you reach the target."

"There are some who think it will fail anyway."

"That's why I'm here. Prepare to download my flight files. You'll learn what I learned in the Academy—just the basics, but more than you know now."

And within minutes, she has absorbed two years' of Lieutenant K's training. She must delete memories to create space, and deciding which ones should go eats precious time, but she identifies and culls without a single tear. For the span of one point eight seconds, she contemplates deleting the memory of Watt's key, but she decides against it. The emotions wrought by that memory spur her forward, keep her from succumbing to fear.

+ + +

From there, the flight goes more smoothly, and they pass through the asteroids unscathed, reaching the enemy vessel without incident. They stop *Valiant* just out of its gun range, and Janet drops her hands from the controls, peering at the vessel looming before them.

"Good heavens," she murmurs.

Missile banks, cannon turrets, fighter decks, sensor arrays, mine clusters, disruptor assemblies, tractor beams...and weaponry she can't identify, projecting from every angle like the spikes of a prickly pear, a misshapen sphere plated in blood red shielding.

But it makes no move.

She stares for two point seven seconds.

"Initiate the overload," she orders and moves the ship closer. But before Beta Three can act, Delta One once again announces an incoming message.

"Momo?" a voice asks, so weak Janet can barely make out the words. "Julius, is that you?"

"Belay that order," Janet says to Beta Three, and she motions Delta One to open a channel.

"This is Chaplain MacLean, from the System Starship *Destiny*. Captain Monroe is unavailable, but I am here with the blessing of Lieutenant Nikolai Khristorovdestvensky. Identify yourself and state your intentions, or I will assume you are hostile."

"Nikki? LK? Are you there? Where is Carmela?"

"The lieutenant remains on Aranae. We believe Ensign Morales is with the captain. Who are you? Why have you entered Aranaean space without permission?"

There are several moments of silence.

"Please," says the voice, scarcely a whisper. "My name is Sleeo Fort. I designed the ship you're flying—the ensign and lieutenant too. You have to help me. I can't hold it in stasis much longer."

"Can't hold what in stasis? Explain."

"This ship. Please! It knows there are two *Destinies*. I'm the only thing preventing it from attacking."

"Incoming video," says Delta One, and at a motion from Janet, it opens the display. There, in the center of the hologram, is a small, pale man, naked. He seems to float in black water, his limbs drifting languidly. His head is shaved, and cables snake in and out of every hole in his body. Janet can count his ribs.

"Please," he says again, and his voice is muffled by the tube in his mouth. "They kidnapped me to help track the captain. I'm connected to the ship's brain. It caught the virus I wrote, but it won't stay in stasis long."

"You are synthetic?"

Aranae in Red

"Cybernetic. Organic-synthetic hybrid."

"What should I do?"

The answer is a raw whisper.

"Destroy the ship while its shields are down!"

"But what about you?"

"Better dead than this. Please! Don't waste my effort. I can't hold on much longer."

But Janet hesitates.

"No," she says at last. "There has to be a way to get you off that ship. Your consciousness is digitized, yes? It could be transferred via *Valiant* back to my *Destiny*."

"If I did that, my control over the ship would be lost. The stasis would end, shields would be raised, and your guns would be powerless."

"Then," says Janet, "it is a good thing I don't plan to use them."

+ + + + + +

Shimmer and her company approach the Tavaline Massif from the south, so they do not see the shuttle being downed by the titanic derka. But there is no missing the resulting explosion. At the sight of the fireball, the alp's viper nest of tentacles flares wildly, and its ululating call is as horrific as the detonation itself.

They shall flee! think its handlers.

But Shimmer will have nothing of this.

On! she commands. *They are in the company of Ozag's Chosen! There is nothing to fear. The great ordinance of their time awaits. On! Top speed!*

By the time they arrive at the lonely butte, the sky has darkened, and snow has begun to fall. The first flakes are fat and lazy, and there are not many of them. But these are soon joined by others, fast, icy, and plentiful. They surf a growing wind that bends scion antennae and stings their dimming eyes.

Oh Queen, thinks Shimmer's prime. *She risks her very life! The storm will dash them from the sky.*

Shimmer whistles a shrill, angry note.

A.P. Malloy

Irrelevant! They will carry her to the summit. The others will shelter beneath the alp—and woe to those who flee! Ozag, Magnanimous and Discerning, sees all!

Viktor and his company exchange dark, brooding thoughts, but Shimmer pays no mind.

Up the pluripotents fly, lifting her basket, straining to keep their grasp as it tosses side to side. Shimmer rides with four pincers gripping the weave and the other two the tiny derka, and she prays to Ozag for deliverance. Their landing atop the butte is scarcely better than a controlled crash, and she tumbles from the basket, whistling and indignant. Her pluripotents cling to their ropes as the basket threatens to kite away, and they are dragged to the very edge of the butte.

Fools! Save the derka! Leave the basket!

And at the last moment, her prime zips in and retrieves the derka, just as the others release their hold and the basket soars away, never to be seen again until it lands, battered and torn, on Whisker Lake.

Shimmer stands over the derka, surrounded by her huddling pluripotents, and she trembles in the cold.

What now? asks her prime.

Ozag will send a sign, Shimmer replies. *Patience!*

But patience is a poor blanket, and as the tempest worsens and the snow begins to accumulate, even Shimmer begins to fear their only purpose atop the butte will be freezing to death.

A sharksha, oh Queen! thinks her prime, buzzing in alarm. *A sharksha approaches!*

Shimmer sees nothing at first, blinded by the relentless snow, but a moment later, a dark form takes shape near the edge of the butte. As it draws near, Shimmer recognizes none other than the one called Thunder, and she cannot contain her surprised chittering. For what is hidden from sight is, to her antennae, obvious like the sun: this sharksha has been marked by a queen, a powerful queen, one whose sign reaches the huddled scion despite the wind. As it approaches, spiky head bowed against the driving snow, two glowing points become clear to Shimmer, one above each of the sharksha's eyes, the residue of Royal Touch. They are more vivid than any she has sensed, stronger, she would say, than the mark of Ozag herself, Bewitching and Copacetic, had it not been sacrilege to do so.

The sharksha comes to a stop, mere paces away.

Shimmer does not question the urge to approach. She steps near. The sharksha bows low. She leans in and touches her antennae to its forehead, one to each of the marks that appear to her like points of golden light.

Be wary, oh Queen, thinks her prime, but the thoughts are grating and crude compared to the voice she senses in her mind. It is soft and yet powerful, a voice of true Command that needn't shout to compel. Surely this is the work of a great queen, for the message it conveys is simple, but it holds layers of complexity, ideas and senti-ment hidden beneath the surface.

And this is what it says:

+ + +

Queen Shimmer. She has been deceived. The Ozag she thinks she met was an imposter, and much of its mes-sage a lie. The one who speaks to her now is the true Ozag, Compassionate and Formidable. And Shimmer knows this is so, for what queen has she met who can mark a mind so strongly—and a sharksha mind at that? So attend, Queen Shimmer, for all fates hang in the balance. The one named Viktor will betray her. She must not doubt it, must end the threat with Righteous Indignation. Wait not for the storm to pass! And this as well: Viktor is the tool of Allura, who de-sires Albion as her own. Queen Shimmer must depose the Cyclonian ruler and take her place, now, when least ex-pected. If she hesitates, Allura will control two hives and an invincible army. For Ozag, Farsighted and Orotund, has willed it: Shimmer shall be Queen of Cyclonia and Albion, but only if she keeps peace between scion, sharksha, and vumierre. On this point alone did the false Ozag think truly. And to this end, the Circle shall not be rebuilt, and no Scion

A.P. Malloy

shall cross north of the Doorn or west of the Dashing, except on invitation, lest the Wrath of the Undying should utterly destroy them—and She will be watching. And this, finally, loyal subject: let go the derka into the sharksha's care, for it is a Noble beast and knows what to do. She will go now and hesitate not! The Blessing of Ozag is with her...

+ + +

Now, Thunder senses all of this, but his attention is fixed on one idea alone:

...the sharksha...knows what to do.

And it is true; he didn't before, but he does now. The image in his mind has the burning clarity of a nightmare, as incorporeal and vivid as a hologram.

Shimmer breaks the connection, her eyes dim.

It will bring the derka, she thinks, and her prime carries the still creature forward. The sharksha takes from its vestment a smooth, black tube. He twists open the vial and pours the contents into the derka's mouth.

And they wait.

One ruby eye blinks open. Then the second.

Obsidian wings stretch slowly, and the serpentine tail coils and twitches. The derka's talons flex, and with a snap and a gulp, it swallows the contents of the vial.

"Crooaak!" it calls, baring its jagged teeth.

Then it flaps its wings but cannot fly, and the wind nearly blows it away. Thunder grasps it close, and it stretches its long neck, peering upward as if searching for something in the roiling clouds.

Shimmer knows the time has come.

They must depart, she thinks to her pluripotents. *Their role in Ozag's great work is nearly complete. The sharksha now must carry this load. May the Undying oversee him and give him strength.*

And with that, she leads the others over the side of the butte, climbing down with an alacrity few species can match, as the wind is now too fierce for scion wings.

But not for those of a titanic derka.

Aranae in Red

For one has appeared, a soaring shadow slipping through the clouds, perhaps the shuttle destroyer itself, returned after being chased by the explosion—or perhaps another. It hardly matters.

It circles lower, croaking like doom.

+ + + + + +

And now, alone atop the butte, spikes bent in the howling wind, a flightless seed derka held close, Thunder, half-blinded by snow and blood, sees clearly.

I understand, he thinks. *I get it now,* and he imagines thinking these words to the Joy in gold. A future of mutual respect between humans and kezel: this, because of his actions in the shuttle. A future of peace with scion: this because of his exchange with Shimmer. And a future free of the derka scourge: this, because of what was about to happen next.

But I'm no hero, he thinks. *Just paying my price.*

He bows his head. He is not scared, but he does not wish to see the derka he knows is descending toward him. He will choose the face Death wears, and it will not be the hideous maw of a derka. Instead, in the seconds that remain, he imagines the jabi Hail, who had been a good fellow, after all, pictures him whole and healthy, standing close and sharing thoughts of forgiveness.

Oh! The unburdening of guilt and shame. The lightness of spirit, after moons of self-loathing. He could howl with relief. The sensation is worth whatever comes next, and his heart is calm.

A ripping violation of the air above him, rising even above the wind, the darkness made complete by an awesome span of wings. And he thinks:

This is when Lightning would come.

But Lightning is thousands of strides away.

And yet, approaching out of the downwind shadows, where Thunder can neither see nor smell, there *is* someone, haggard, limping, and resolute.

And so it is that, even as old *Destiny's* astral drive

overloads, and the resulting energy wave atomizes lovers in their embrace—while the rogue moon is driven forever into the void—and even as Sister Janet sends a last transmission to her crewmates before overloading *Valiant's* drive and destroying the enemy ship down to the last bolt on the smallest gun, so it is that Stone wades out of the blizzard, pulls a weapon from its holster, stuns Thunder, grasps the struggling seed derka, and is herself clutched and borne away.

Chapter Twelve
Told

LIGHTNING AND JOY remain at the Skull for the passing of three Mother Greens, tending to Submission and the others. Bliss is hobbled, and Digger is nearly blinded, but both will recover according to Vale. Bridger, on the other hand, is wounded by grief as much as tooth or claw, and she and the Brigadier spend much of their convalescence sitting together and naming their dead.

The humans had gone their way as soon as conditions allowed, eager to assist their companions in the crashed shuttle, but they had departed to a howling salute, for their arrival had terrified not only those Whitetails attacking the Skull, but those who had heard the tale while laying siege to the Bristle home caves. These had joined their clanmates in hustling back to their own range, certain the flying terror would re-appear to assail them at any moment—and they never returned as enemies, if they returned at all.

Shoulda seen 'em go, thinks Pond. *Tails between their legs and ears pinned, pretty as you please.*

What would please me, thinks Brook, *is a nap.*

But that simple desire must wait. The fact that she had played into the Whitetail ruse is overshadowed by her heroism atop the Skull and an alliance with Moondwellers who ride in the air like magic; her detractors are now her biggest fans. Who dares question a chief with friends like

A.P. Malloy

that? But her rising stock carries a price, as Brook quickly learns that a respected chief is just a busier chief, and during Submission's lengthy recovery, many things demand her attention. High on the list is addressing the Redteeth who still languish in the pits of the Skull. They had nearly drowned when the Tongue had been dammed, but once the boulders are rolled clear—no easy task—and the river is allowed to go its way, they are bedraggled and foul-tempered, but otherwise intact.

What am I supposed to do with 'em? Brook wonders. *An ugly batch, and smelly! The sooner they're off my range, the happier I'll be.*

Vale snaps his jaws, and he takes a break from teaching Lightning and Joy how to change Submission's bandages and administer his tonic.

Nothing, for now, he thinks. *They can sit and reflect on the error of their ways. You have plenty else to think about. Like arranging a tribute to the fallen. And sending an emissary to visit the Big Fork. He's got a debt to pay, or it's his overloaded hide on the line.*

Yes, yes, thinks Brook, but she is tired, and has not escaped injury herself. *One thing at a time.*

And she sends Skinner and Crest on a mission across the Spine to spread the news to the Sugarfoot clan. Then she swallows some virble rations and curls up beside Submission, collapsing into sleep.

+ + +

When Skinner and Crest return, they bring a surprise guest bearing wondrous news.

Hello, Bliss, thinks Rock, and he buries his snout in her auburn spikes while she lies in the sun, nursing her wounded leg. Her crest rises, and her tail quivers.

You're late, she thinks. *The fight's over.*

We were occupied, he replies. *Don't be mad.*

And of course, she isn't.

In turn, when he sees Lightning, Rock forgets his grudge, forgiving her for drugging his food, and squeezing her in a rib-bending embrace, lifting her from the ground.

Crag will be very glad to see you, he thinks. *Still toting that cutter, I see.*

Legitimate this time, thinks Lightning, and she shows him her scarred forearm as proof.

And howdy hoo! Rock thinks as he steps back and drops to four legs, taking a long look at Joy.

Howdy hoo, amoti Rock, she replies, and she bows.

Amoti? Well! I like the sound of that. C'mon. Show me where Bruiser is. I've got stories to tell.

He does indeed. And though there is much to be done in and around the Skull, he never lacks an audience as he sits near Submission and shares all that he and Crag experienced over the past moons. He tells of Cyclonia and their escape with Lieutenant K, their journey across the plains, and the rogue kezel.

Won't believe it, he thinks. *But that rotter was gone as gone when we came back for him. No trail and no smell, what with the storm and all. Slippery sneer, that one.*

And dangerous, thinks Brook. *He'll need catching.*

He'll get it, thinks Submission wearily. *Go on.*

Rock does, telling them about the titanic derka, the crashed shuttle, and the remarkable events atop Rite Butte. He shakes his head.

I missed it, but Crag saw it all. He was standing guard while I went to get some snow for the Moondweller's injuries. Old Stoney snuck out when his back was turned. She saved the day, and no mistake. Woulda been the end of Thunder for sure. Biggest greenie Crag ever saw...

He pauses.

Not that I'm saying it excuses what she did. But she made a change there at the end. That's gotta count for something, doesn't it?

That's for others to say, thinks Vale.

Of Shimmer and the scion, Rock can share little, for they had vanished with the passing of the storm.

But they left our throwers, he thinks. *Wrapped up neat as can be. And there were signs of fighting. Bunch of blood and some blue corpses, half-buried in the snow. Not*

A.P. Malloy

a gold or bronze, but one gray, with a missing antenna, head cut clean off! Not that I'm complaining. And those giant tracks moving due south. Hope that's the last of 'em...

His snout wrinkles.

Anyway, then Moondwellers showed up in one of those flying things. Picked up their people and away they went. A lot of mumbling and babbling! Who knows what they were saying? But a couple of them bowed to us—well, mostly to Thunder—so that seemed promising. And not a whisper from the Redteeth the whole time. We got back to the home caves easy freezy and gave them all a nice surprise. Crag and Yellow and their wabis! Hoo! You never saw the big lug so happy. But the place is looking rough isn't it? It's going to take a long time to regrow those accrete. And a real shame about Ancian and the rest. It's been a tough go these last couple Reds...

+ + +

The time comes when Big Brother moon swings around from the east, herded by his api and ami, and the three together fill the sky with a spectral glow. But the Oli-su is nowhere to be found, and Lightning wonders if they have seen the last of her violet face. The moons, however, do not wait around to answer questions, and she is not sorry to see them go. For Submission has re-gained his strength and is ready to return to the Sugarfoot range as soon as the trails are cleared.

Home, Lightning thinks to Joy, and never has the word seemed so sweet.

The Redteeth are allowed to climb out of the pits one at a time, blinking, scowling, and wobbly from hunger. They are surrounded by the homeward bound Sugarfeet and enough Bristles to ensure good behavior. Brook is among these; so is Pond.

Don't think we'll forget this! thinks a Redtooth.

I won't, Submission replies. *And you shouldn't.*

Vale leads the remaining Bristles in a chorus of howls, and it seems the entire range has gathered to clash their teeth and flare their spikes as their allies and enemies march into the accrete and out of sight, followed by those Bristles chosen to bear the fallen.

The defeated Redteeth are driven over the Spine, and then along its western side, angling southwest to where the Bloodwater splits to become the Sour to the north, and the Sweet to the south. At this point, they ford the Sweet and enter that part of the range ruined by scion. Then past the mouth of the Sugarfoot caves, where the bearers of the dead lay their burdens.

Peering out at the procession, the jabis Pockets, Cranny, Edge, and Splay hurl insults at the defeated Redteeth, but not for long.

Stop that! thinks Snapper.

Show some dignity! thinks Trapper.

Humility in victory, thinks Old Buttons.

And the jabis still their minds and follow Thunder's example as he, with one eye bandaged, moves to join the Sugarfoot escort. Up and down the rolling trail they drive their enemies, but there are no more insults, and when one of the Redteeth stumbles, Rock is quick to help him to his feet. Then off to the southern bridge, where the Redteeth are driven across. They don't look back, but had they, they would have seen the fallen accrete dragged back to the Sugarfoot side, where it stays—for now.

I'll be expecting regular reports, thinks Brook when they have returned to the Sugarfoot caves.

You'll get them, thinks Submission.

In person, Bruiser.

I wouldn't have it any other way.

Bridger steps forward, damaged but proud, her api, the white-spiked Trapper on one side, her wotis Digger and Cranny on the other, and Digger's fancy Tail behind, ridden by the wabis Knoll and Tor.

I'll only say this once, thinks Bridger to Brook. *But I am heartbroken about what Stone did. Feather might still be alive. And to think my own woli was to blame. But I swear: my family and I are at your service whenever there is a need. We will pay that debt.*

A.P. Malloy

You humble me, thinks Brook, for she knows Bridger's losses, including her fancy Pounce and her woti Blue, fallen trying to reach the Skull. *There is no debt, and the service, while I live, is mutual.*

And Brook gathers Pond and the other Bristles, rubs noses with Submission, and leads her clanmates back east, toward the River Sweet.

+ + +

The Sugarfoot kezel, a clan that boasted nearly fifty members only two Reds ago, has been reduced by a third, and not one is unscarred by injury or grief. No healing can take place until the dead are properly honored and lain to rest, and the effort saps mind and body alike. But in this, Cliff is a great help, along with Piedmont and Fluvial, at last set free from their pit. They work together bearing bodies to the High Step, and Piedmont has the wits to keep his thoughts tethered.

Bee-yoo-tee-full place, is all he thinks when they reach the highest of the accrete-covered terraces. *As good a place to honor these here as could be. Bee-yoo-tee-full.*

Lightning at first worries about the reception she will receive, and she keeps Joy close, staying near Submission and her oti-kans as they dig graves. But the clan, it seems, has moved to a place beyond blame. Death, the great equalizer, has made every member precious, regardless their age or history.

I'm glad you're back, thinks Boots.

Thank you, thinks Lightning. *I'm glad to be back.*

You too, thinks Serenity to Joy.

At which Joy buzzes and bows low.

No one happier than me, thinks Crag, and he leans down to touch Lightning's nose, something he has never done before. *Happier or prouder!*

When the clan has gathered atop the High Step, the departed have been lain to rest, and the mournful howling has at last faded into the distance, the assembly falls silent. Even unruly wabis sit quiet while Trapper and

Old Buttons take turns reciting the litany.

Melt, thinks Trapper, *fancy to Curly, api to Hurly and Burly, and my beloved wabi-gap.*

Fang and Fall, thinks Old Buttons, *api and ami to Curly, Boots, and Edge.*

Measure and Crunch, thinks Trapper, *api and ami to Bliss, Snapper, and Tail.*

Hail, thinks Old Buttons, *fancy to Snapper.* And to Lightning's surprise—but not Joy's—Thunder stands close to the pregnant, grieving ibiwa, his head bowed.

Blue, fancy to Boots, api to Cloud.

Pounce, fancy to Bridger, api to Digger and Cranny.

And the list goes on. There is little Scale, Stone and all her family, and of course, Ancian. And when all have been named, the clan stands silent, wind whispering through the accrete, cremlins watching from above.

Don't lose hope, thinks Submission, rising to two legs. *The price paid here...so high. But not a single spike is wasted—if we dedicate ourselves to their memory. We owe it to them to make sure their sacrifice was not in vain.* And he stands close to Lightning, but he looks to the east.

+ + +

In the moons to follow, there is little time for grief.

Nothing soothes the heart like meaningful work, thinks Old Buttons, and there is plenty of that, including keeping a watchful eye on the Redteeth. Submission puts Crag in charge of security along the southern half of the wedge, from the Sour to Rite Butte, but as he is now an api in his own right, he delegates some of this responsibility to Thunder, Cranny, and Pockets. Rock is given the northern half, all the way to the island crossing, which, for the time, remains intact. For reasons she can't explain, Lightning joins him in this effort, sometimes climbing to the top of the moon cave or scouting up and down the east bank, sometimes gazing out across the island crossing, memories stirring.

Ancian was a Redtooth, she thinks to Joy. *Have I*

told you that? Which makes me one fourth.

And makes your ami-kan one half?

Yes! Good thinking.

Do you know who he was?

And Lightning knows she refers to the bibija whose white spikes still haunt her dreams.

No. I suppose there was a relation there some-where—Ancian only knows!—but to me he was...

An enemy?

No. But a stranger. A threat.

You wonder if he had a fancy, maybe some wabis.

Lightning does. And she recalls her vision in the future, through the glowing door. All the Sugarfoot clan has plenty of Old Buttons' 'meaningful work' to do, but so does she, and some of it, she is beginning to see, seems destined to take place on the other side of the wedge.

Building bridges, she thinks to herself, but has no time to explain, for here comes Cliff. The Clawpaw has requested to be part of the northern security detail as well—for reasons he could explain perfectly well but does not—and he has come to take his turn.

Looks like Piedmont and Fluvial are sticking around, he thinks. *Bruiser's got 'em out planting scales. Did you know if you plant a blue next to a yellow it'll grow to be a green? That's what Trapper says.*

Yeah, thinks Lightning. *In a hundred Red moons. We'll be planted ourselves, up on the High Step, before things are back to the way they were.*

Joy's buzzing is melancholy, but Cliff is in a good mood that can't be shaken.

Better than Scratch Valley. I'm never going back.

Yeah? How does Submission feel about that?

It was his idea!

Of course, it was. Well. Don't mess up sentry duty.

He won't, thinks Joy. But then she adds, just to be sure: *Splay is close. And Bridger's gathering fungus with Bone near the sulphur. Howl if you need them.*

I won't, thinks Cliff, puffing up his spikes.

Aranae in Red

+ + +

Accrete do indeed grow slowly. Neither Trapper nor Old Buttons—nor even their gapis and gamis—had been alive when the first living stalagmites had gained a hold on the Sugarfoot range. What had taken the scion hours to lay waste had taken generations to grow, and none could see a future on that part of the range that would be anything but bleak and barren.

Wabis, on the other hand, change from one moon to the next, spikier, hungrier, and more difficult to corral. But all of them settle in rapt fascination when Snapper gives birth and the newest clan members enter the world.

So slimy! thinks Cloud.

So small! thinks Wander.

Where are their spikes? asks Hurly.

What's wrong with their eyes? asks Burly.

Spikes take time to grow, Old Buttons replies. *And there's nothing wrong with their eyes. They're not used to the light. It's like the keel, before they crossed the Wall. Have you heard that story before?*

Yes! thinks Needle.

No! thinks Blade.

I don't remember, thinks Knoll.

Will you tell us? asks Tor, and of course Old Buttons is glad to, for it beats planting scales, and she is too stiff to dig for crystals.

Snapper names the twins Hope and Promise, and she is grateful for the attention they are given by all the clan, but especially by Thunder, who dotes on them from the first. They never feel the lack of an api, so diligent is he. Snapper never asks why, and Thunder never explains, and Joy, honored by the trust she has been shown, keeps Thunder's secret all the days of her life.

In the regrowing of the clan, Rock and Bliss do their part as well, and it is not long before they are able to share good news.

Gonna be a gapi-kan, thinks Rock to Submission.

Again, thinks Crag. *And look! Visitors!*

A.P. Malloy

For here come Skinner and Crest, traveling down the Spine and along the Sweet. Their official business—reporting for their chief—is conducted so quickly (*Everything's good, Whitetails are behaving, Brook says hello.*) that Lightning wonders why they bothered making the trip at all. But her answer comes soon enough when she sees them rubbing noses with Curly and Boots.

Work is good for the heart, thinks Joy, and she holds her sling close as she watches. *But love is best.*

+ + +

During this time, the humans visit only once.

This is how it goes:

Cliff, standing watch at the northern crossing, has just been relieved by Splay and is marching home along the wedge's eastern bank.

Home, he thinks. *There's a nice thought,* and he marvels that the word should be applied to the Sugarfoot caves and not a hollowed-out accrete.

He has just drawn within howling distance of the moon cave when a faint whining grows to a mighty roar, and a twinkling shape appears on the northern horizon, soaring beneath the clouds. The flying thing, the likes of which he has never seen, but which reminds him of Albion, passes overhead and flies on, trailing smoke.

Trouble already, he thinks of the Moondwellers. *Just like Lightning said would happen. Didn't take 'em long!* And with visions of fireballs and devastation in his mind, he hurries as fast as three legs can carry him, howling a warning every step-STEP-step of the way.

But when he arrives at the caves, panting and trudging through snow, the flying thing has landed safely in a clearing once occupied by regal accrete, and it is surrounded by kezel, none of whom are alarmed.

Relax, thinks Lightning. *Meet some new friends.*

And she introduces him to the Moondwellers who have stepped out of the flying thing.

There is one named Major, and he doesn't walk as

the others do. His right leg is encased in a hard shell of white, and he uses something like a single fork of accrete under each arm to support himself as he hops along on his other leg. Cliff likes him at first sight.

There is another named Maya, whose arm is wrapped in a sling and held close to her burgeoning torso. Following her is a full-grown biped holding the hand of one who looks like a red-headed jabi version of the others, and these are named Lieutenant K and Little B. They are escorted by a workbot, creaky and oddly dressed, who they call Li Jing, though Cliff can see no reason to name it, as it is obviously not alive. How could it be?

After these come two others, a male named Watt, bearing various parcels, and another named Kim—who carries what surely must be a thrower on his hip.

We are so glad to see you all again, thinks the one named Maya, and she hugs Joy. The latter returns the embrace, but she has eyes only for the red-haired one named Little B, and the two stare at one another for long moments, continuing to do so even as the other kezel prepare to feast and commune with these strange but esteemed guests.

+ + +

The home caves are not yet properly lit, but they have been cleaned top to bottom, and a vigorous scale fire pops and blazes in the feast cave. Only select clan members join their guests warming themselves around the fire. Submission has invited the Brigadier Bone, Trapper, and Old Buttons, the two grizzled beasts awestruck through much of the affair. Joy is there, for no one can understand the humans without she, Maya, and Watt working together. Lightning is present on Joys insistence, and Thunder on Maya's.

We would have been toast without you, she thinks.

Oh, he scratches his ear. *It was nothing,* hoping it is a proper response, for he doesn't know what toast is.

The major, thinks Maya, *wants you all to know he*

A.P. Malloy

has made it clear to everyone on the expedition: no one sets foot on this continent without an invitation.

She opens one of the parcels and takes out a blocky metal contraption she places on the ground.

If you ever need us, push this button and speak into here. The kezel nod and snap their teeth politely, but Joy raises the obvious question.

Nobody speaks your language.

Maya smiles.

Then we'll need to work on that, won't we?

And Little B, who has rarely taken his eyes off Joy, adds in a timid voice:

"Ettilly kooba la ruindun," and Lieutenant K nods.

He says, 'If you can think it, you can speak it.'

But there is obviously more on the boy's mind than that, and as the jabi Cranny enters the cave to deliver an offering of berries, fungus, and cremlin, and as the humans open another parcel and share blocks of cheese and salted fish, Joy sees him staring at her sling.

She removes the object and hands it to him.

He takes it reverently.

It's not the same, he thinks.

No. Before, it was a Book. Now, it's just a book.

He opens the cover and leafs through the pages.

A story, he says. *Say! Look at this. It's the story of you. Of all of us. And it's still writing. How interesting...*

Miraculous, I would say, thinks Maya.

Whatever that means, thinks Lightning. *But it's just a bunch of squiggly marks to us.*

Then that's another thing we'll need to work on.

Hosts and guests politely sample each other's offerings. Lightning doesn't hate cheese, but won't touch the salted fish, and while the berries and fungus are both given high marks, the humans pass on uncooked cremlin. As they nibble, they move awkwardly through conversation, with Joy working hard as the hub. For while Little B can understand kezel, humans, and Joy, only she allows understanding between them.

You have some of my DNA, Little B thinks to her.

Oh. Do I? Is it...do you want it back?

What? No. That's not how it works. It's yours now.

The lieutenant then regales them with a video projected from his eyes, similar to the one Ensign Morales had shared at the Hold, the lit, blue face of Aranae, her moons in their delicate dance, and the violet Oli-su, Little Sister, the Wabi-la moon. Submission and the others watch spellbound. There is a bright flash, and Dansim is sent spinning into space, never to return—and who knows what adventures she has?

Trapper sniffs at the images as if to smell his way to understanding, and Old Buttons squints her eyes.

Aranae is round? Like a snowball? And the moons too? And Weaver, the sun? Since when?

Don't ask me, thinks the Brigadier Bone.

Since the beginning, Maya replies. *Tell them the rest, Nikolai, won't you please?*

And the lieutenant dutifully recounts the fate of his companions near Dansim. Lightning can read his thoughts, but he has the foreign mind unique to his kind, and his feelings—if he has any—are a mystery. Still, the news he shares seems to warrant some sympathetic response. Joy beats her to it.

I'm very sorry, she thinks. *It makes me sad. Without the captain, I would have been toast.*

She looks at Maya.

Am I using that right?

But Maya is distracted. She toys with the silver vial around her neck as the image of Pujari Kashi appears in her mind, and she recalls her childhood fears of Shiva and the results of her third eye opening. But it had been her father's other offspring that had been the destroyer and renewer; she had simply been along for the ride.

Submission curls his lip.

I also am sorry to hear this, he thinks. *There've been too many lost. And plenty of blame at the feet of the one I'm told is called Sister Janet. I hope she's paid!*

It takes Maya a moment to translate this, but when she does, it is the major who responds.

A.P. Malloy

"You are not wrong," he says via translation. "Her methods were debatable, that much is clear. But her motivation, I think, was genuine. You must understand; we knew a version of her at an earlier time in her life, and she was dear to us."

Was? thinks Thunder, and Lightning watches the one named Watt as he sits with his eyes closed. His emotions, at least, are no mystery.

Nikolai, thinks Maya. *Would you share the story?*

And the lieutenant tells them of Captain Monroe's quest to find *Destiny,* and of the villainous characters who had kidnapped their friend Sleeo, using him to track the captain and his crew. He tells how Janet had volunteered to do what no one else could, and how, before she had given her life to destroy the enemy, she had saved Sleeo (*'downloaded'* is the word Lieutenant K uses), and sent him, via data stream, to the safety of the new *Destiny.* Cybernetics, downloading, and data streams mean nothing to the kezel, but they appreciate sacrifice and courage. They also appreciate justice, and when Lieutenant K adds Sister Janet's revelation of Magister Healey's attempted mission sabotage, they approve when learning he has been sequestered in the brig.

The lieutenant then projects another image, a pale, white-haired man in a wheeled chair.

This is Sleeo Fort. He made me. He is alive—in a virtual sense, until we can get him a proper body—because of what Sister Janet did.

Maya holds Watt's hand, and he sits with his head bowed, chewing his beard.

So, you see, thinks Maya. *We are trying to forgive the Sister Janet that you know, because this is the good she was capable of—is capable of still.*

And where is she now? asks Lightning.

Aboard Destiny. *Watt has been working with her.*

Working to do what?

But it is Watt who replies, looking up at last.

To heal, he thinks, and he looks around the firelit circle at the scarred, bandaged, and broken. *We all are.*

Aranae in Red

+ + +

After the food has been eaten, the party breaks into smaller groups, each going a different way.

Not me, thinks Trapper. *I'm exhausted.*

But the Brigadier Bone escorts his ami-kan—Old Buttons—Deputy Kim, and Lieutenant K to the cave where throwers and cutters are secured. The lighting is poor, and neither side can understand the other, but the Deputy and Lieutenant are men of action, and their delighted exclamations at the antique weapons translate easily across cultures.

Submission and the major have Big Business to tend, and they need someone to facilitate the exchange of ideas. So, Li Jing and Little B go with them, helping the major as he crutches his way out of the feast cave and up into the sunlight. Submission is about to invite Thunder, but the major gets there first.

"Everything I do from now to the end of my days," he says via Little B, "is possible because of you."

You would probably have done the same, Thunder replies, and he means it.

Lightning and Joy are part of the third group, with Maya and Watt, and they go outside too, but they take the back exit, past the remains of the biting cyrilis.

I'm sorry you can't see our home at its best, thinks Lightning. *We're not the only ones who need healing.*

Maybe this will help, thinks Maya, and she motions for Watt to open the last of the parcels. He holds it for Lightning and Joy to see.

Ooh, thinks Joy, and she touches one of the small, rainbow cubes tucked inside. *Pretty.*

We discovered these going through the colonists' data base, thinks Maya. *They have many amazing things in storage. There's more where these came from.*

Data base, data stream, thinks Lightning. *No offense, but whatever data is, if it came from the old Moondwellers, I have my doubts.*

As you should, thinks Maya. *But I think you'll like*

this. It's how they expedited the accretion. Grind up one of these and rub the powder on any scales you plant. Mind the sun, though; it doesn't like UV radiation. You might be surprised at the results.

Lightning takes the parcel, offering thanks, and she politely ignores the words she doesn't understand.

The groups eventually reunite, and they are for a time overrun by wabis, for no amount of oversight can harness their raging curiosity. Little B shies away, eventually climbing on top of the lieutenant's shoulders, but Maya beams, immersing in spikes and slobbery kisses as well as pregnancy and injury allows.

When at last the time comes for their guests to depart, the major reaffirms his promise.

"There's a lot of info and materials we're going to need from the various sites, and neither the current refinery nor that dam ought to go unmaintained. But nothing happens until you say so."

Keep that promise, thinks Submission once he has sensed the translation, *and you'll be welcome.*

You should come back for the party, thinks Joy. *Lightning and Thunder will be ibiwas on the next Red.*

Not sure there will be a party, thinks Lightning.

Of course, there will. Silly! You should come too, thinks Joy to Little B. *You can teach me to read.*

And Maya kisses Joy's forehead.

Maybe we will, she says.

Then off they go in their flying ship, and all the Sugarfeet gather to watch, even Trapper, whose nap is interrupted by Piedmont's ongoing commentary.

Never seed a such in all my moons! You, Old Timer? Ever? Bet not! And I seed a plenty o' crazy things, sur-ee, you can cache that and eat it later. But a flyin' contraption all filled up proper with Moondwellers like a regglar gutted plumpie? Never!

+ + +   + + +

On a day when their duties are light and their time

is their own, Lightning and Cliff wander the range, rubbing rainbow powder on scales and planting them here and there. The work isn't hard, but it is slow, and they don't get far from the caves.

Eventually, they meet Thunder near the awling ledge, playing with the wabis Hope and Promise—though he has nick-named them Biter and Fighter. They call him Apoti, which is not strictly accurate, but no one corrects them. For a while, Cliff takes over, allowing Lightning and Thunder a chance to be alone.

Never expected things to play out like this, thinks Lightning. *Those future kezel didn't know it all.*

Or they knew but didn't share, thinks Thunder.

Maybe. But listen. I didn't bring it up at the time, but when we were there...all I could think was how they talked about the other you as if...you know...

As if he had died.

Yes! 'Our Thunder did,' and 'our Thunder was.' Never does or is. It started to worry me.

Me too. But I've been thinking about that. I think I understand why they did it.

You mean you think they were lying?

Not lying so much as allowing me to come to a certain conclusion. I think they wanted me to believe it would mean the end of me. I think they knew that's the only way it would have value. I didn't know it at the time, but some noble sacrifice was pretty much the only thing that could have cleaned the stain...

You mean the reason you were walking around in a storm cloud the whole time?

Yes. Don't get me wrong: I didn't want to die. I just didn't want to hate myself anymore. And when I was up on that bluff, after all that talk in the future, I knew— knew!—it was the end for me. And I never felt better. I knew I was going to pay the price.

I'm glad it wasn't the end.

Yeah. Me too.

Ever going to tell me what the price was for?

No.

A.P. Malloy

How about your fancy?

Thunder is about to ask who she refers to, when the answer appears in the form of Snapper, looking fit and clean in her new vest. Thunder squirms at the sight, but his tail also quivers, and his ears relax.

Maybe, he thinks. *Some day.*

Surprising them both, two large bombas appear in the sky, their feathers rippling as they circle in to land.

A great day for flying! thinks Joy, and she climbs down from Eron's back and squeezes Lightning in a hug big enough for two kezel. *Are you ready?*

Ready for what?

Making the list! Who comes to the party? And what supplies do we need? And what are everyone's jobs?

That sounds like a lot of work.

Yes! The fun kind...

+ + +

Mother Green makes a solo flight across the sky, sleet and hail in her shimmering train.

Six sleeps later, it is Father Blue's turn. He joins his fancy, and snow falls hard as they eclipse the sun.

When, nine sleeps later, Brother Orange joins the family, he laughs thunder and juggles lightning, leaping over the sun, boastful as always, and the three of them together shake the foothills.

But Sister Violet misses her turn, and kezel on every range at last accept that the Wabi-la is gone and will not be coming back.

More sleeps pass, more waking times, bringing with them various iterations of this lunar parade, every storm with its own personality, each respite different from the last, and over time, the Sugarfoot clan slowly regains its hold on healthy bodies and peaceful minds.

Then there comes a time when Ami, Api, and Oti rise from their slumber on the east end of the world as if wakened by the same herald. Not long after, Gapi-kan the Contraine rises above the opposite horizon, bloated, fiery, and threatening to bumble into the others and end the world. But as always, when the reunion is complete, the family goes its stormy way with no worse damage than yet another hellish blizzard.

And then it is time for the party.

+ + +

KERRACK! exclaims the thrower, and the Brigadier Bone bares his teeth, pleased at the sound—but even happier at the smell of the wisping smoke.

Feast time! he exclaims, and he howls mightily.

Who is in attendance? Who isn't!

Among the able-bodied kezel, every Sugarfoot and Bristle not occupied with sentry duty or wabi care joins the celebration. From over the Spine, here comes Brook and Pond, but close behind are Skinner and Crest, who have made the journey many times in the past moons. On their backs they carry cremlins, virbles, and sneer, and in their pockets are precious crystals for heating and light. And they are not the only Bristles, for here also are Bluster and Smoke, Berm and Bite, Pitch, Stitch, and Trim, and they, too, bear contributions and gifts—but no babelrack, and no bomba, for this is the new rule of the land, and no one dares break it.

Vale sends his regrets, thinks Brook to Submission. *Legs are feeling pretty gimpy. But he wants you to know the Whitetails are behaving.*

A great surprise is had when Crag jogs in from his wedge watch in the south, escorting two naked Renders, Tie and Bow, who have made the journey on their chief's orders to see if rumors are true. They gaze at the assembly in astonishment, but this is just the beginning.

Look who I brought! thinks Joy, and she splashes across the Sour, leading Oracio, Orton, and Ugo, the only elder bombas willing to use the transporter. They remain on the heights overlooking the caves, anxious and muttering until their escort arrives, a squadron of fit bombas, landing in a protective circle. Even then, they watch the proceedings with utmost suspicion.

Thank you for coming, thinks Lightning, climbing up to greet them, and she introduces Cliff, who shares with them a pile of their favorite scales and berries, gathered from distant parts of the range.

When the brood returned from Congress, thinks Oracio, *they agreed that your promise needed some testing. I will not deny we are...nervous.*

When Submission climbs the heights, many of the bombas raise their spurs, but he bows so low and long, and his introduction is so courteous and sincere, they soon relax. He rises and looks down at the gathering.

Let everyone know! he thinks in his boldest tone. *These and all bombas are Sugarfoot friends. Harm to them is harm to me. On this range, they are free and safe!*

And the kezel below, already in good spirits, howl and clash their teeth, and many of them bow.

A thing I never thought I'd live to see, thinks Eron.

Good berries, though, thinks Arris.

And fresh scales, thinks Orris.

Here, thinks Oracio, and he motions to Ubert, Onri, and Azel. They step forward and produce for Submission large clawfuls of awl glands, and from that point forward the party becomes jolly indeed, and all the kezel agree that bombas make fine guests.

When the humans arrive in their shuttle, a great clearing is made for them to land, for even those kezel who have seen the ship before have not lost their awe, and those who have not stand with mouths wide and ears pinned. The sight of Moondwellers stupefies the Renders, and they know in an instant every difficult stride from their distant range has been justified.

Out walks the major, no longer on crutches and with a female name Charlotte holding his arm.

And here comes Maya, hugely pregnant and supported on either side by Watt and Deputy Kim.

How precious, she thinks, and she points at the colorful stumps that have formed, well ahead of pace, all throughout what had once been a charred wasteland.

Aranae in Red

Little B, flanked by Li Jing and the lieutenant, stares wide-eyed, but he is no longer afraid of the wabis who come barreling forward to greet them.

And what do they eat?

The menu is as delicious as it is varied.

Of course, there is the kezel bounty, the likes of which hasn't been seen in living memory even without babelrack and bomba. The stars of the feast: two full-grown talihew, courtesy of Rock, Crag, and the Brigadier Bone. There is also the awl Cliff and Piedmont had snared. Best of all—from Joy's perspective—is the human shuttle, loaded with every item known to have kezel approval—and some which are discovered to have bomba approval as well. Joy doesn't search long before finding cake and ice cream, but there are also bubbly drinks, savory dishes, cheeses and crackers, and more chocolate than anyone could eat.

Be careful, Master Bodhi, thinks Li Jing. *You don't want to get a stomachache.*

Li Jing! It's a party! Little B looks at Joy. *Isn't Li Jing shiny? They fixed her up real good on* Destiny.

Joy agrees that it is so, but her eyes are most often on Little B, and they rarely leave one another's side.

And what do they do?

So many things, in fact, that some of the guests fall asleep long before the fun has ended. Races and wrestling matches take place early, and the human and bomba onlookers make a fine audience, cheering and squawking, and not a little awestruck at the displays of kezel ferocity and strength.

"Good friends," the major says. "Bad enemies."

And when Maya translates, the bombas agree.

This is not news to us, thinks Oracio.

Wabis who don't know any better approach their winged guests without bowing—or any other show of courtesy—begging for rides. Their appeals are so endearing (and Joy's demonstration so irresistible) that soon a carousel of bombas takes to the sky, each carrying a wabi on its back, ears pinned and breathless.

A.P. Malloy

Deputy Kim and the Brigadier take turns demonstrating thrower use, and the major joins, for they had been his in another timeline, and what use is military training if a fellow can't fire a gun now and then?

Ever heard such a noise? thinks Piedmont. *Huh, Clawpaw? Ever? Or seed such a thing as those old throwers? Bits and pieces! What wondery tools!*

Deputy Kim is very good at shooting, and the major is excellent. But when Lieutenant K takes his turn, he puts on the finest show, never missing a target, even when they are thrown aloft. The kezel howl in honor.

Sheesh, he thinks. *Thanks, everyone.*

And when the noise is over, the humans and their synthetic companions surprise everyone with a song, serenading Lightning and Thunder, newly arrived to the world of ibiwas. It is a threshold not every kezel reaches. Little B is shy, and Joy is unpracticed, but he mumbles the words, and she hums the tune, and they both gently hold the sling that rides over her shoulder.

Great howling and squawking and clacking of beaks follows the end of the song.

Story time! thinks Submission.

And that is how the party ends, with those who are still awake gathered around Trapper and Old Buttons, listening to tales of red moons past, translated by Maya and Watt, until few eyes remain open.

Eventually, guests rouse themselves and take their leave, away to their various homes, the winged bombas first, then the humans, their shuttle roaring off to the sky. Those kezel inclined to stay, (Brook, Skinner, Crest, and the bemused Renders), are given lodging in the home caves. But Lightning, Thunder, Cliff, and Joy escort the elder bombas to the moon cave transporter, for, as Ensign Morales promised, Sister Janet's security measures have been disabled.

We will consider the kezels' rixli dilemma, Oracio promises. *I am sure there is a solution to be found.*

Thank you, thinks Joy. *And now that the transporter goes both ways, we'll visit often.*

Aranae in Red

And this makes saying goodbye easy. Then she and the others fall asleep in the comforting shadows next to the water curtain, and their dreams are of singing.

+ + + + + +

But not every day can be a party. Some days are just days, with average goings on, and that is exactly the way Lightning likes it. There are trails to be cleared, talihew to be hunted, her vest to be dyed, and accrete to be cultivated. Someone has to dig for crystals, and biting cyriles won't plant themselves. And of course, the borders must be patrolled, and wabis taught the Way. Lightning wonders occasionally about Shimmer, but Joy is not worried. Lieutenant K had returned many pilars to the new queen, reporting her to be greatly pleased.

We'll see her again, thinks Joy. *Some day.*

In the meantime, moon-to-moon business is enough for Lightning, who is tired of adventures. She spends her waking times grateful for the normal and routine and is never once tempted to rob a cache.

One particular day, bright and clear, the moon cave island is where these average goings on take place. Joining her beneath the lavender fan is Maya, with baby Grace on her lap, the former continuing to teach Joy how to read, the latter watching and mimicking. Joy, in turn, teaches Lightning—or at least, she tries.

I'm sorry, thinks Lightning. *But Ancian was right; I'm pretty terrible at this.*

I think what you're doing is amazing, thinks Maya.

Amazee, thinks Grace, and she shouts the word, delighted by the sound of her own voice.

A derka passes high overhead.

According to Janet's research, thinks Maya, *we won't know if Thunder's seed derka worked for another three to five red moons.* They huddle beneath the accrete and watch as the derka sails out of sight. *So for now, the rule is stay camouflaged or stay sheltered!*

But Joy has no patience for this topic. She opens

the book, turning to a random passage, eager to demonstrate her new skills. She takes a breath and begins to read, her voice buzzy but clear.

"The android wr...wr...wrinkles her brow. 'I've never heard of the Ga...lac...tic Guild.' She looks at the l...lieu...ten...ant and the ensign, and her ex...pres...sion is pinched. 'You're wearing stolen gear.'"

Joy frowns.

What does 'pinched' mean?

Maya makes a sour face, her lips puckered.

Joy copies the expression, exaggerates it, and the baby laughs. But here comes Little B out of the (no longer secret) tunnel, followed by Cliff, and Joy composes herself, brushing dirt off her overalls as Little B sits near Lightning, running his hand down her spikes.

It's your turn, thinks Joy, and she gives him the book. *Then Lightning again. Then lunch.*

Where should I start?

Start where you left off, thinks Maya. *You were getting close to the end.*

Little B's smile is shy, but he turns to one of the last chapters and begins.

He takes his time as he reads to them, for Mother Green has danced herself offstage, followed by her fancy, and the weather is fine. He reads about Shimmer and Stone, the captain and ensign, and Janet MacLean, the mention of whom makes Maya eyes gleam. Little B's voice is high and clear, and he rarely stumbles, only asking for help with 'Khristorovdestvensky,'—and once again when Grace claims the book and bites its cover.

And still he reads on, telling of Thunder, Maya, and the major, and how disaster on opposite ends of the solar system had been averted by a similar sacrifice. And Maya holds Joy's hand, and Joy clutches Lightning's spikes, and Cliff closes his eyes, his imagination aflame.

And when at last there are no more words, they take a deep breath, and Grace yells, "Hungy! Wunch!"

But before they go, Little B turns back to the very first page and gives Lightning another try. She scrunches her snout and concentrates on the fine, black marks, try-ing to dissociate them from the smell of the book itself, trying to see them as signifiers, with a meaning beyond their concrete existence. She recalls the Moondweller doc-ument, with the faded blob Ancian had claimed was a derka, when her nose had told her it was clearly nothing but toxic ink on indigestible parchment. And she recalls the epiphany when Crystal had helped her recognize the meaning behind the blob, inspired her—just for a mo-ment—to ignore her nose and trust her eyes.

And snap! Just like that, she is at last able to de-code the first three words, so obvious and natural they fall easily from her mind like ripe fruit:

In the beginning...

A.P. Malloy